BEHIND
THE BROKEN IMAGE

BEHIND
BROKEN THE
IMAGE

DEBRA M. COOPER

REMUDA
Ranch

Behind the Broken Image
Copyright ©2006 Remuda Ranch
All rights reserved

Front Cover Art by David "3D" Ferreira
Cover Design by Alpha Advertising
Interior Design by Pine Hill Graphics

Published by Remuda Ranch
Packaged by ACW Press
PO Box 110390
Nashville, TN 37222
www.acwpress.com
The views expressed or implied in this work do not necessarily reflect those of ACW
Press. Ultimate design, content, and editorial accuracy of this work is the responsi-
bility of the author(s).

Publisher's Cataloging-in-Publication Data
(Provided by Cassidy Cataloguing Services, Inc.)

Cooper, Debra M.

    Behind the broken image / Debra M. Cooper. — 1st ed. — Nashville, TN :
ACW Press, 2006.

    p. ; cm.
    (Series on eating disorders)

    ISBN-13: 978-1-932124-75-0
    ISBN-10: 1-932124-75-6

    1. Eating disorders in adolescence—Fiction. 2. Eating disorders
in adolescence—Treatment—Fiction. 3. Family—Fiction.
4. Adolescent psychology—Fiction. I. Title.

PS3603.O774 S43 2006
813.6—dc22   0606

Printed in the United States of America.

Dedication

This novel is dedicated to the millions whose lives have been touched by anorexia and bulimia. To those who struggle daily with these devastating disorders; to the friends and family members who feel helpless and heart-broken; to the caring, compassionate professionals involved in treatment. To all of you ... where there is life, there is hope; where there is hope, there is healing; where there is healing, there is life abundant.

Acknowledgments

I want to thank the staff of Remuda Ranch for their excellent input regarding intensive inpatient treatment. Special thanks for sharing their time and talent go to Ted Burgason, MA, LPC; Amy Gerberry MA, LPC; and especially, Dr. Amy Lerner Wasserbauer, Ph.D.. Only through these professionals was it possible to transform each character in this book from a vague concept, to a real person with very real issues and needs. As always, I thank Ward Keller, founder and CEO of Remuda Ranch, for giving me the opportunity to write this book.

Part One

Chapter One

The room was dark, except for a trickle of weak amber light leaking in beneath the closed door. It emanated from a ceiling fixture on the second floor of the modest Santa Rosa home. Abby Cardoza lay cocooned in her bed, feeling safe and secure with piles of thick wool blankets draped over the pastel bedspread. Flat on her back, she stared idly at the ceiling. She conjured a mental image of the room surrounding her: the colorful and fuzzy stuffed animals lined up like vigilant soldiers on the top of her dresser; the pyramid of library books stacked neatly on her desk; the closet door shut, the desk chair pushed into its place, the empty trash can tucked against the unadorned white wall. Thinking about the orderly condition of her bedroom always gave her comfort.

Though fatigue tugged at her tired mind, she waited patiently to take part in the nightly routine. Soon, a scrabbling sound came from beneath the bed. Abby smiled, knowing it was Peeper, the family cat. She had named him Peeper because of the uncharacteristic baby bird noises he had made as a kitten. He leaped up alongside Abby's feet, causing the mattress to quake. At eighteen pounds, the cat seldom went unnoticed. Whether lumbering across the family-room floor with his furry gray belly skimming the cream-colored carpet, or pacing before his empty food dish and yowling plaintively for more cat chow, Peeper possessed an undeniable presence. Currently, the cat was a blurry, if bulky, outline poised at the foot of the bed. Abby lay still, anticipating the feline's course of action. For some unknown reason, he followed the same scenerio every night.

Peeper embarked on his journey, placing one paw on Abby's left leg, followed by a second on her right. He pressed down tentatively like an ice fisherman testing the frozen surface of a pond before venturing out. Reassured, the cat boldly proceeded. He teetered somewhat on her bony shins, but remained resolute. Slowly, surely, he moved along the top of her body. She winced only slightly when his considerable weight rested on her concave abdomen, but soon enough, he went on. Eventually, he reached his goal. Paws consolidated in close proximity, he hunkered down and stared into Abby's face. With noses nearly touching, his long silky whiskers tickled her sunken cheeks.

"Hi Peep," she whispered to the cat. He leaned a fraction of an inch closer as if needing to visually verify that it was, in fact, Abby. Their noses touched. Seemingly satisfied, he hunkered all the way down, all four paws and one fat belly resting on the thirteen-year-old's chest. Eighteen pounds of cat on one small sternum and a span of delicate ribs. He tucked his front paws together, muffler style. Already she could feel the welcome warmth of his body seeping through the blankets and her pink flannel nightgown. A resounding purr filled the silent room. Abby felt the vibration throughout her entire torso. Though she could not see the cat's eyes, Abby knew they were slit in contentment. She wondered what the cat would do when she was gone, but dismissed the question, preferring not to think about it.

After a while, Peeper stood and relocated to his standard spot at the end of the bed. He paused to lick a paw, scratch an ear, then flopped down on the blanket. The nighttime ritual now complete, Abby turned on her left side and curled into a tight ball, unwittingly mirroring the cat's posture. Though the two assumed identical positions, their individual motivations differed decidedly. The cat sought comfort; the girl sought warmth. Despite the blankets, Abby shivered. Coveting his body heat, she wished in vain that she could entice Peep to join her beneath the covers. But she had tried this once before and knew better than to ever try it again. It had been a complete disaster with claws extended and fur flying. Cats. Who could figure them out? Not Abby, and she was definitely too cold to try.

Pressing her thin thighs against her crossed forearms, which in turn were flattened against her chest, she resembled a human accordion. Her toes felt numb with cold. She tucked her chin and blew hot air into her clenched fists. If she didn't warm up, she would be forced to endure yet another sleepless night. However, even if she somehow managed to banish the cold, the pain would remain. These days, simply lying in the bed hurt. She felt as though her thinly sheathed bones rested on a rock-hard slab of concrete instead of a cushioned mattress. Every point where contact was made—shoulders, hips, knees, even ankles—radiated with dull pain. But in some distant, deep part of Abby's mind, she knew without reservation that the discomfort created by cold or the pain associated with an extremely thin body, was something she absolutely deserved…because she was bad.

Abby heard an unexpected sound somewhere in the room. Through sheer willpower, she forced herself to stop shivering, even stop breathing. She listened intently, every nerve on red alert. She heard it again. It was the doorknob. It was turning. Her bedroom door was being opened. She fought the knee-jerk fear, knowing she was safe.

"Abby, you awake?" Her little sister was silhouetted in the doorway.

"Sara?"

"Can I come in?"

"Of course."

Sara nudged the door shut behind her, then padded on little feet across the room to where Abby lay. Sara bumped against the bed, then said in a small surprised voice, "Hey Peep, how you doing?" The greeting was followed by the sound of a loud smooch, undoubtedly planted right between the cat's eyes, a favorite spot for kisses. The cat's deep purr chugged back into life, now with even greater zeal. "Can I get in with you?" Sara asked her sister.

"Shouldn't you be asleep in your own bed by now?"

"Yeah, but...please?"

"Sure, crawl in."

"You have a million blankets," Sara said as she slid in and snuggled up to Abby.

"And you have Teddy," Abby remarked, referring to the stuffed brown bear with the utterly unoriginal name that had accompanied Sara into the bed. "I thought you weren't going to sleep with him anymore."

"Just tonight. He said he was lonely. He needed me bad."

"Did you need him, too?" Abby wrapped her arms around Sara and Teddy and drew them in even closer. Sara, toasty as a miniature oven, radiated much-needed heat.

"Maybe a little. Ab, why are you going away?"

Abby cast about for an acceptable answer. Recently, focusing clearly on one subject had become difficult. Her thoughts would leap and jump like popcorn kernels in a hot pan. She just couldn't concentrate on anything like she used to. At last she found an answer. "Because Mommy and Daddy want me to go. I've been a little bit sick and they want me to get better." Desperate to cut this discussion short, she tried to guide her sister down a different conversational path. "Did you see Mommy and Daddy before coming upstairs?"

"Yeah, she was praying with her beads and he was watching TV…but not really watching, just sort of staring at the screen like he does."

Abby had no difficulty at all picturing her parents, each coping in their own way with her problem. Their strategies were as different as her parents themselves: Mary Cardoza relied on religion, while Jim depended on the mind-numbing diversion of television. Lying in bed, cuddling with her sister, Abby was suffused with guilt as she considered all the pain she had caused her family. Sara shifted her position in Abby's embrace and rearranged Teddy to fit more comfortably in the crook of her arm. "But what's wrong with you; why are you so skinny and sick?"

Abby's conversational redirection hadn't worked. What could she possibly say that would make sense to a four-year-old? Before an answer could be formulated, Sara blurted out what was really on her mind, every word punctuated by unconcealed anguish. "Abby, I'm scared. You're going to go away and never come back. You're going to die and I'll never see you again. That's what happened with Beth's grandma. She was sick. She went away and died."

Sorrow swept through Abby's heart. If it could have actually broken, fractured into a thousand pieces inside her body, it would have. The guilt intensified. How many nights had Abby lain in this very bed and prayed to God to let her die, believing she did not deserve to live? Now all those prayers came back to haunt her. Did she still want to die? Abby really didn't know the answer. But one thing she knew without a doubt was that she loved her precious baby sister more than anything or anyone in the whole world. She never wanted to hurt Sara; she never wanted to hurt anyone. Abby clutched Sara tighter, kissed the back of her head and nuzzled her silky lavender-scented hair with one cheek. "Remember when you were little and we used to make promises to each other?"

Sara's tiny head nodded emphatically beneath Abby's cheek. "Uh-huh, I remember."

"Remember how they were always special because we only made them if they would never, ever be broken?"

"Uh-huh."

"Well then, I am making you a promise right now. I will not die. I will get better and come home to you." Then a new thought popped into her mind, something she knew Sara would like. "No, better yet, I'll make it home to all three of you—you, Teddy and Peeper. Okay?"

"Promise, promise, promise?"

"Yes."

Sara sighed in satisfaction. Abby could feel her little body relax, grow heavy in her arms. The two remained silent, peaceful for a while. Then, in a voice only inches from sleep, Sara issued one final question. "How do Teddy and Peep know you're going away? Did you tell them already?"

Abby smiled at the sweet, simple way her sister's young mind worked. "I'll tell them tomorrow."

"Make sure and tell them about the promise, too, so they won't worry while you're away."

Abby gave her an extra-tight squeeze. "Okay, I will."

Sara drifted off to sleep, secure in her sister's arms. Her healthy body heat eventually warmed Abby, causing her to grow drowsy. Yet before she slipped into unconsciousness alongside Sara, one very clear thought reverberated repeatedly in Abby's mind: "Please, dear God, please let me keep my promise to Sara."

⸻ ❧❧❧ ⸻

Scott Kent slouched in a chair alongside the hospital bed. Gazing at his sleeping wife, he realized he felt nothing, absolutely nothing at all. It was as though an emotional vein had been opened somewhere inside of him and every possible feeling had simply drained away. All that remained was a nebulous sense of loneliness and isolation tinged with a hint of despair. He looked at her dispassionately as if contemplating a still-life portrait of a slumbering patient instead of the woman he'd married. Even in this sterile environment with its unforgiving institutional lighting, she was beautiful. Her golden-blond hair fanned out on the pillow and her face in repose appeared somehow freed of the strain it always bore. Yet, looking closer, he couldn't miss the overt manifestations of her illness: the purplish shadows beneath her eyes, the cracked surface of her lips and the dry, parchment-like quality of her skin. His wife, so beautiful on the outside, so darkly troubled on the inside.

Oblivious of his own action, he reached out a hand as tentative as a schoolboy and picked up a single tendril of hair. He sifted the strand between his fingers, marveling anew at its silky texture. This was perhaps the only part of her that had not yet been damaged. It was probably only a matter of time before her hair, too, would show a negative effect. Unbidden, his severely over-taxed mind flashed back to a moment when they were first married, snuggling together in their cozy bed, her cheek resting against his bare skin, her long hair cascading across his chest. They would cuddle for hours, talking, making plans as he stroked her hair and frequently planted kisses on the top of her head. He smiled at the recollection. Suddenly, reality bounded back. Scott released the lock of hair as though it had singed his skin. He slammed his mind shut on the poignant memory.

Scott dropped his face into his cupped hands, massaging his forehead with his fingertips. Eyes closed, he grew more acutely aware of the room's medicinal odor. Outside in the empty corridor, the hospital PA bleated often, summoning this physician or that surgical team.

In the midst of his reverie the door burst open, fracturing the stillness of the room. Grayson Stockton strode in, held the door deferentially for his wife, then went directly to the bedside. Pamela Logan Stockton remained in the doorway, her imposing presence immediately dominating every inch of the small space. The familiar fragrance of her expensive perfume wafted in like an unseen cloud. She took in the scene with one swift glance that missed nothing: the semi-reclined hospital bed, the IV line snaking down into her daughter's right forearm, the other arm tucked discreetly beneath the crisp white sheet, her son-in-law slumped in a nearby chair. "Good God, Scott, what's going on here?" Clearly, in the short time it had taken them to drive to Carolinas Medical Center, Pamela had managed to get suitably worked up.

Now called upon to explain the situation, Scott searched for the appropriate words, but found none. "She…"

"She what?" Pamela demanded, her voice like steel. "Is she sick again? What's it been, three times she's been hospitalized this year? What is it now—dehydration or is it that electrolyte business again?" She took a step toward Scott, arms folded across her chest, lips compressed into a hard, thin line. He knew the look. It was meant to convey extreme vexation and disappointment. Though it generally proved effective with her daughter, he was nonplussed. Before he could even begin to answer the myriad questions being put to him, she went on, "Look at this," she flung out one slender, beautifully manicured hand, gesturing to the still figure in the hospital bed. "This is ridiculous. She's your wife, why can't you take care of her? Is it really too much to ask? You…"

"Now Pam, give him a chance," Grayson interjected in his softly accented Southern voice, reaching over and touching his wife on her shoulder.

Only moments earlier Scott thought he was bereft of all emotion. He was wrong. Anger suddenly catapulted through him at the undeserved blame assigned to him. He shot to his feet and faced his mother-in-law. "Pamela, shut up. You have absolutely no idea what's going on here, you never have." Stunned, she recoiled as though she'd been slapped. "Yes, your daughter is sick, far sicker than you know, but it doesn't have anything to do with me. I wish it did, then maybe I could fix it. It's something inside of her, eating away at her, killing her. I don't know what it is. Tonight I came home early from work. She wasn't expecting me. I found her in our bathroom…" His voice cracked and words failed him. He cleared his throat and tried again. "She was all alone, sitting on the counter, she had a razor blade. She was cutting herself."

Scott's anger, though quick to ignite, fizzled out with equal rapidity. He staggered back, groped for the edge of the bed, clutched the steel railing to steady himself, then collapsed into the chair. His explanation continued in a dull monotone. "She was slicing the inside of her arm and just watching, staring as the blood streamed out and pooled in the sink. The cuts were deep. I've never seen anything like it in my life. Never. There was no expression on her face. None at all. She was blank. It was as if she wasn't even in that bathroom anymore, but had gone somewhere else altogether, a place I couldn't reach her, maybe no one could. I didn't know what to do. I called the paramedics and they got her here. The doctors sedated her."

"Did you tell the hospital staff she was my daughter?"

"Of course," he replied, without mentioning that the prestigious Logan name was probably the only reason why the authorities weren't called to report a suicide attempt. Thank God Pamela's family continued to hold enormous clout in Charlotte, North Carolina.

"Cutting herself?" Grayson reiterated, shocked.

Scott nodded. "It's not the first time either."

Grayson held his daughter's limp hand, running his thumb back and forth across her fingers. "She's done this before?"

"A while ago, I began noticing these lacerations on different parts of her body. When I asked her about them, she always seemed to have some sort of explanation. Like, she'd say she'd cut herself while shaving her legs or while working in the kitchen with a knife. I didn't think she'd lie to me. I had no reason to think she'd actually harm herself, not like this. Only now, after what I saw tonight, can I look back and realize how long it's been since I've seen her other than fully dressed, even at night. Just lately, she's taken to wearing long robes and nightgowns. How was I to know it was because…"

Sounding perplexed, Pamela spoke again. "But why? Why would she do that? She has a perfect life, she always has."

He shrugged, shook his head in shared bafflement. "Who knows why she would hurt herself? Maybe she does, but I'm not even sure of that."

"You and I haven't spoken of this in a while," Pamela ventured. "Is she still doing…the other thing?"

"The vomiting? Probably. I have no reason to think otherwise. Occasionally I find signs that she's been doing it, but she hides it pretty well. She spends virtually all of her time alone. She never goes out anymore. Who knows what she's doing? Obviously, the psychologist, all the counseling, the antidepressants haven't helped whatsoever."

Pamela, as if suddenly snapped with a rubber band, gave a little start, finally evoking something resembling genuine concern. "Scott, where's Logan?"

"Don't worry, I called Jennifer. She's with the baby at home. She'll stay there all night."

The room fell silent, each occupant consumed with their own thoughts. From his seat beside the bed, Scott regarded his mother-in-law. As always, she was meticulously turned out. She never deviated, never strayed from perfection. Even at this late hour her makeup appeared fresh, every hair was in place. Her apricot silk pantsuit could have just come off a designer rack at Montaldo's. How did she do it? More important, why did she do it? Pamela was, quite simply, a study in contrast. On the outside, delicate, beautiful, sophisticated; on the inside, solid ice.

Gray plunged a hand through his thick dark hair, now silvering a bit around the temples. "So what needs to be done here?"

Composure restored, Pamela expelled a breath. "Gray, it's time to make that call to your colleague in Arizona. He said he could get her into the treatment center whenever we were ready. I think it's time to send her to that ranch."

"But what about that problem you had with the facility? Remember, we discussed it."

"Yes, and I still think all that religious nonsense we read in the literature is absurd, to say the least. But about now, honestly, I'd send our daughter to hell if I thought that could fix her."

"Fine. I'll call tonight. We can probably have her on a plane tomorrow." Grayson paused and gave his wife an inquiring glance, knowing there was more on her mind. "Is there something else?"

She lightly tapped an index finger against her pursed lips in contemplation. "I was just thinking…there's really no need to say where she's going. No one has to know she's going into treatment. We'll tell people she went out West for…" A faint furrow creased her unlined brow as she considered. The frown was replaced with a look of satisfaction as the solution occurred to her. "That's it, a small vacation, a sort of reunion with a group of her fellow debutantes. We could say they went to a resort. I seem to remember they have horses at that facility. Yes, that makes sense; it will work."

Scott listened to the two of them as they decided the future. In normal circumstances, he would have taken issue to their complete disregard for him in his role as husband, but he had left normal behind so very long ago. What was normal, anyway? Not what he had been living lately. And the truth was, Scott was just plain exhausted, worn out. He had been working too hard for too long to keep it together. He had nothing left to give. He was acknowledging defeat. Let Pamela, and to a lesser degree, Grayson, plan to their heart's content. If they had bothered to ask, he would have expressed complete agreement with the decision. It was time for her to go somewhere and get the help she needed; time for him to concentrate more fully on his work and his son. As the confab continued across the room and the voices melted into a steady drone, Scott allowed his head to drop onto the back of the chair. His shoulders slumped in weariness and he closed his tired eyes.

From her position in the bed, Alexa Stockton Kent drifted along in a medication-induced haze, listening to her parents conspire. Several minutes ago a loud noise had jarred her from the sedation. A door hitting the wall? Perhaps. All she really knew was how utterly sublime it felt to be tucked into this comfortable bed, sailing along aimlessly, without a care in the world. Alexa gave it some thought, her medication-muddled mind seeking to categorize the sensation. It was as though she was an enormous helium balloon traveling high above the ground, encouraged by a whimsical breeze to bounce this way and that.

Bounce, bounce, bounce. Or perhaps it was more like being an autumn leaf drifting lazily on the cool surface of a meandering brook. She liked that concept too. She wondered if this was what death was like. Simply floating without worry or care until you ceased to exist.

With eyes closed, it had been difficult to stay awake. The seductive fingers of the medication kept pulling her down toward the blissful void of sleep. Yet she had remained as attentive as possible; after all, it was her life. But now the conversational details were evaporating like wisps of steam dissipating above a boiling teakettle. Only one thing remained absolutely clear: they were sending her away. No surprise. Alexa was sick—maybe even...*crazy.* Everyone, who was anyone, knew mental illness just wasn't done in polite Southern society. She had to go—now.

But for the time being, she drifted along weightlessly, content. Her thoughts grew muzzy. She pictured her parents as they spoke; he, striving to appear engaged, agreeing to anything that might placate his wife; she, working equally hard to resolve this situation, in order that she might return home and concentrate on vastly more important things such as next week's fashion show fund-raiser or a future luncheon. Alexa noticed her parents always spoke of her in the abstract, referring to their own daughter as *she* and *her,* never Alexa. It was as if they didn't even know her at all, as if the three had never formally met.

She had a partial recollection of her father briefly holding her hand. It had felt so good, so warm and comforting. Poor daddy, he had to live with *her.*

Alexa's thoughts tiptoed slowly on to Scott, but didn't stay long. Her heart went out to him. She felt real empathy for her husband, in a detached, remote sort of way. But she couldn't help him; she couldn't help herself; she couldn't help anyone.

Suddenly, from out of nowhere, her mind was pierced with vivid images from earlier that evening. They relentlessly flashed across her mind's eye like freeze frames, one after another, each sharper than the last. She saw with nightmarish clarity the razor blade gleaming in the fluorescent bathroom light; the red blood spattering the pristine white tile basin; Scott's face framed in the doorway, first shocked, then horrified, and finally, distorted by naked, atavistic fear. From there the images began to blur as though viewed through a rain-streaked glass. Her husband, grabbing the blade, then trying to snap her out of her trance-like state by screaming her name and shaking her violently. Her limp arms flopping this way and that like those of a rag doll. Blood flying everywhere—tattooing the mirror, floor, Scott's face and clothes—every available surface. It was bad, really bad. Eventually the tirade ceased. He let her go and as she crumpled to the bathroom floor he went for the phone. Alexa balled up into the fetal position and went away, far away where no one could reach her.

The images finally faded. Allowing the drugs to reassert their power over her, she succumbed gratefully. Within moments, Alexa joined her husband in welcomed, wonderful sleep where she and her shameful secret were safe.

⸺◈◈◈⸺

Robin Hamilton stood alone in the back yard, the fenced area bathed in silvery moonlight. Though this particular space had precious little to recommend it—a patch of withered, sun-scorched grass, the obligatory Southwest swimming pool, a rusting swing set abandoned in a remote corner—it offered what she needed most: solitude, a venue to escape her mother. What's more, it was hot out here, at least ninety-five degrees. She reveled in the Tucson heat, wishing she could somehow bottle it, then take it back with her into the frigid air-conditioned house.

Behind her, the sliding glass door cracked open. "Robin, phone for you."

The teenage girl stiffened at the sound of the maternal voice. She turned and headed toward the house, dry grass crunching beneath her bare feet. Stepping inside, Robin's senses suffered an immediate assault. The unexposed skin of her arms and legs prickled with goose bumps from the icy chill; but far more devastating was the pungent aroma of freshly made popcorn. The fragrance hit her with the force of a gunshot blast. Her empty stomach spasmed and she nearly swooned from sheer longing. Recovering, Robin willed herself to stop breathing. She glared at her mother and marched right past her as if she was merely the hired help, unworthy of acknowledgement. She headed for the hallway, passing through the family room where her little brother sat watching TV with his bare feet propped on an overstuffed ottoman. Robin watched as Josh, eyes glued to the screen, scooped up a generous handful of butter-drenched popcorn from the huge wooden bowl and crammed it into his mouth. As he crunched, two or three fugitive kernels fell to his lap. Robin had to tear her gaze away. The deep depression in the other couch cushion testified that her mother had been sharing the snack with him. They were obviously enjoying the television show together. Robin was disgusted, grossed out. The two of them were always together, talking, laughing. Josh was such a little geek. He really needed to get a life.

Still holding her breath, Robin went to her room, slammed the door defiantly and locked it. She snagged the cordless phone from the dresser and punched the on button. "Hello."

"Hey girl, thought you were going to call?" It was Amber Atkins, Robin's best friend since second grade.

"Yeah, I know. Sorry, I couldn't."

"What's up?"

Robin flung herself onto her queen-sized bed, propped her chin in the heel of one hand. "It's my parents again. It really hit the fan tonight. They're all freaked out about my doctor appointment today. He said he wanted to put me in the hospital, again. Like I'm going to die or something. Is that lame or what? They say they've had it with me. They're going to send me to that camp, or farm, or whatever they call it. More like having me committed."

"When?"

Robin flopped over on her back, slung one leg over the other and began jiggling her foot. "Like now. Tomorrow."

"No way."

"Way."

"But they can't. What about school? It starts in a week. It's senior year, our last year together. And Rob, what about the team? We're toast without you."

Robin briefly considered telling Amber that the doctor had ordered her off the swim team, but decided against it. She sat up and crossed her legs. Now the bright light was irritating her. She leaned over and fiddled with the switch, dimming the bedside lamp. "I know, don't think I didn't tell them all that. Didn't faze them. They said I should have thought of that before, back when they were first getting on me about my so-called eating disorder."

"That totally sucks. What are you going to do?"

"What can I do? Until I'm eighteen, they like own me." She snatched an emery board from the table and started filing her nails, clamping the phone between her head and shoulder.

"Rob, can't you just do what they ask? I mean, like for now?"

"Great, so now you're on their side."

"No I'm not. I just don't want you to go away. It's just…"

Alert to a new ominous tone in her friend's voice, Robin slammed the file back onto the table, then sat still as stone. She gripped the phone so hard her knuckles bleached white. "It's just what, Amber?"

"Well, I do sort of agree with them; I kind of wish you'd stop all this dieting. It's gone too far. You know, ever since you started losing all this weight and stuff, you've changed, you're like different, you..."

Robin cut Amber off mid-sentence. "Aren't I a better swimmer? So what, that's suddenly like a bad thing?" Now she was glad she hadn't told Amber what the doctor had said.

"That's not what I mean at all. Sure, you're faster and that's great for the team, but you've changed in other ways, too. Ways that aren't good. I worry about you. You're not like *you* anymore. When was the last time we went to a movie together or just hung out. We used to laugh together all the time; but Robin, you don't even laugh anymore. And it's not just me, other girls have noticed."

"Don't give me that. You know they're totally jealous of the way I look. They wish they were thin, too. They're just a bunch of fat pigs." She snorted derisively, then continued in a sing-song voice, "But no, they just can't give up their precious Twinkies."

"Yeah sure, it was like that in the beginning, a ton of girls were jealous because you were looking way awesome. But it's not like that now. Really, we've talked about it. No one thinks you even look good anymore, you're just too skinny. Really Rob, even I think so, and I'm your best friend."

"Best friend?" She narrowed her eyes. She grabbed a handful of her hair and pulled hard. A casual observer would have winced at this behavior, but it made Robin feel calmer, more focused and in control. "Oh right. You sure don't sound like one; you're just like all the others."

"That's not true. I..."

"Look, I gotta go. I have things to do."

"But Robin, please wait. When will I see you? When will you be back?"

"Who knows?" Never pausing for one moment to examine why she wanted to hurt Amber so much, Robin lashed out, "Maybe you'd better find a new best friend, someone else like me you can dis behind her back." She punched the off button and threw the phone onto the bed. She jumped to her feet and began stomping around her room.

Robin was mad—out-of-control, spitting mad. The anger, merely simmering earlier that evening, had escalated into a pure black rage. She paced with a manic intensity back and forth, back and forth, on the carpeted floor. She was furious at her parents, Amber, the whole world. She hated everyone, everything. Her fingers, hooked into claws, raked savagely at her exposed neck. Dark red streaks instantly welted on the sun-bronzed flesh. Then she grabbed a hunk of her hair and yanked viciously. She smiled, hearing the follicles rip from her scalp. She flung the sacrificial strands to the floor, then kicked at them violently with her bare feet. Dizziness eclipsed her passion and she had to stop. She stood still, her heart beating frantically in her chest. She panted through her open mouth like a wild animal. Beads of sweat popped out on her forehead. Stooping, Robin snatched a few hairs from the floor and ripped them to pieces in a renewed frenzy. It wasn't enough. No matter what she did, her agitation only escalated. She felt like a giant itch in need of serious scratching. Her eyes strafed the room, searching for some form of release.

As her gaze lit upon the bed, Robin suddenly remembered her treasure. She had been saving it for another time when she would be all alone in the house, but why not now? After all, they were going to take her to that asylum tomorrow. Eagerly, she fell to her knees and crawled toward the head of her bed, a nearly hysterical giggle pealing from her lips. She dropped to her stomach and slithered like a snake, her jutting hip bones protected only by thin denim shorts, digging into the floor. She insinuated the upper half of her torso beneath the bed. She stretched her right arm out as far as it could possibly go. Her groping fingers encountered only a few empty laxative boxes she had hidden under the bed and failed to discard. She pushed them aside and swept her hand from side to side, searching. Nothing. Panic streaked through her. She knew it was there—it had to be. She gritted her teeth, extended even farther. Her muscles screamed under the strain, her shoulder felt as if it might dislocate. As her exploring fingers touched something, Robin shuddered in relief. Clamping her index and middle fingers together, she managed to snag the very edge of the cherished item. Holding her breath, she eased it toward her gradually, inch by inch, until she had a firm grasp on it. It came into view. She felt as a miser would when encountering bulging bags of gold coins. Though no gold was contained in this plastic grocery bag, the contents were equally precious to Robin. Two shiny, one-pound packages of M&Ms. Elated, her mouth watered in anticipation.

Secure in the knowledge the bedroom door was firmly locked, Robin tore into the first bag. Desperate to get the chocolate candy into her mouth, she paused for one brief moment, knowing everything must be done just so. First, she poured the bag's entire contents onto the floor, then scooped up whole handfuls, relishing the feel of the cool candies on both palms. The brightly colored M&Ms gleamed in the light: blue, red, green. Mesmerized, she allowed them to sift through her splayed fingers. The tantalizing scent of the chocolate, the slick sensation as the dime-sized discs trickled through her fingers, the tinkling sound as they pinged back onto the pile—it was sheer ecstasy. The desire she felt was almost sexual in its intensity.

Robin shoved a handful of M&Ms into her open mouth and swallowed, hardly taking time to chew. The first handful was quickly followed by another, then another. Robin used both hands, greedily jamming the candy into her mouth until the first pile had vanished and the strays were plucked from the rose-hued carpet and consumed. Without delay, she ripped into the second package. The frenzy continued unabated, until every last tidbit was gone. Finally sated, the girl sat perfectly still, eyes closed, breathing evenly, calm now. She sighed blissfully, content as a cat curled up in a late-afternoon sunbeam. For once, she wasn't cold. Drowsy, Robin could have easily lain down right there on the floor and slept for days. But of course sleep would have to wait. The last, and most important, step of the ritual must be completed. A sly smile crept across her face as she neatly folded, then returned the empty candy packages to the bag.

Robin savored the rarely felt peace for just a few more precious minutes, then got to her feet. She went across the room to the locked door where she listened intently for sounds of anyone outside in the hall. Satisfied, she flipped on her CD player just loud enough to drown out any noise. She stepped over to the window and silently eased it open. She had removed the screen months ago specifically for this purpose. Leaning out, she surveyed the side yard. As expected, it was empty. Clutching the plastic grocery bag tightly in both hands, she bent over and threw up into it, right on top of the M&M logos. Within moments, a renewed sense of euphoria rippled through her like a gentle, tranquil stream. All the anger had left her, it now resided in the bag with the chocolate. In the beginning, making herself vomit had proven difficult, but now it was easy. Especially with something as smooth as chocolate with only the occasional sharp candy-coated edge to scrape her throat. Robin didn't look down, not wanting to see the blood that was surely there. Lately that had happened a lot, but she wasn't going to think about that now, not when she felt so good. She tied a secure knot in the bag, then eased it onto the ground. She was done with the food, done with the rage. Robin felt just fine.

Back inside her room, she shoved a piece of sugarless spearmint gum into her mouth and chewed vigorously. She located a couple of old school papers, wadded them up and tossed them into her already half-filled trash can. Then, confident, relaxed, Robin picked up the plastic can, strolled out of her room and down the hall toward the back door, humming a nameless tune. Her mood was so ebullient, the lingering scent of popcorn didn't bother her in the least. She didn't even pause to snipe at her idiot brother as she passed by the open door of his room.

From somewhere inside the family room, her mother called out to her. "What are you doing?"

Robin blanched at the note of suspicion that underscored the seemingly benign question. Her mother was driving her crazy. Not only did she observe her like an insect under a microscope at every meal, but Robin wasn't even allowed to close the door while going to the bathroom anymore. It was ridiculous. Her mother wanted to control her entire life. "Just taking out my garbage," she called back through clenched teeth.

"Will you please come here?"

Robin walked into the room. Her mother sat alone, reading a textbook, probably preparing a lecture. She was wearing that tattered sky-blue terrycloth robe that Robin detested and those old house slippers that always made the most annoying scuffing sound on the Mexican-tile floor. Lute Olson, the family golden retriever, snoozed peacefully near the couch, chin resting on forepaws. At her approach, he lifted his head, gave Robin a dopey dog grin and thumped his bushy tail in greeting. "What?"

Her mother waved a hand toward the plastic container. "Just let me look in there before you take it out."

Robin emitted a labored sigh and rolled her eyes. "Chill, Mom, it's just trash."

"You know what I told you. I need to see it."

"Whatever." She went over to the couch. Her mother peered into the can, pushed the papers this way and that, found nothing. "Satisfied?"

"Yes." Confusion and contrition fought for supremacy in her mother's expression. Contrition won. "I'm sorry, it's just that…"

"I know," Robin broke in. "You don't trust me." She whirled around and headed for the back door. She snapped her fingers, beckoning the dog. "Come on, boy, you don't want to stay in here, either." Lute, eagerly anticipating an adventure, or perhaps a snack, leaped to his feet. He trotted alongside her, panting happily, collar jingling.

Robin went directly to the side yard and retrieved the still-warm plastic bag from beneath her window. Lute's floppy ears shot forward as he eyed the object suspiciously and gave a low growl. Clearly relishing the idea of a foreign intruder in his back yard, the dog emitted a small woof, then hunkered a bit, the fur on his back bristling between the shoulder blades. He hopped back a few paces as Robin approached, brandishing the bag. "Don't be so dramatic," she told him as she strode by. Reconsidering the degree of threat posed by the bag, the dog pranced along behind her. Together, they went over to the giant trash bin and disposed of it along with the rest of her garbage. In the distance, she noticed lights emanating from the university; probably the Wildcats having nighttime football practice, or some stupid event for incoming freshmen. She dimly remembered her father attending something on campus tonight but didn't know, didn't care. He was never home anymore, anyway. She summoned Lute and the two went back inside, he to inspect his food dish, she to lock herself back in her room. Robin Hamilton climbed into bed...and slept.

Chapter Two

The sun peeked over the eastern horizon, stretching forth long fingers of shimmering light and ushering in a new day. As it moved from east to west, it brought three cities and, in turn, three households to life.

In Charlotte, North Carolina, the sun's rays barely penetrated the thick cloud cover. These smothering gray clouds were illustrative of the dismal mood hovering over the Kent home in Eastover. Depressed, Scott woke up early, dressed, then checked in on his son. Logan, snuggled in a pair of bright yellow and green Donald Duck pajamas, was in his usual sleeping position: little legs pulled up beneath his tummy, arms pressed closely to his side, bottom propped up in the air. He looked like a little yellow bug. Scott stood for long minutes in the nursery, hands gripping the blue plastic crib rails, gazing down at his child. His love for this boy was so overwhelming it nearly took his breath away. Contemplation of his son led Scott inextricably to the nagging questions for which he had no answers: How could Alexa do this? How could she jeopardize her own life? Weren't he and Logan worth living for?

Scott reached into the crib and gave the baby's warm diaper-clad bottom a gentle pat. "I love you little guy," he said in a hushed tone, then left the room. He crept quietly down the hall, past the guestroom where his sister slept, the baby monitor perched on the bedside table. As he drove through the oppressive mist, Scott wondered if Logan would actually miss Alexa while she was gone. Probably not. She had never been the most attentive of mothers, which was another thing Scott never quite understood about his wife.

Alexa was waiting for him in the Medical Center's lobby, ready to go. The fifteen-minute drive to Douglas International Airport was made in disconcerting silence, only the whisper of the air conditioner filling the void. The suitcase he had packed for Alexa's trip was wedged between them on the BMW's leather seat like a tangible symbol of all that divided them these days. Parked at the airport, he walked her to the gate, gave her a perfunctory kiss, then watched to make sure she got on the plane. The flight was nonstop; she would be met on the other end by representatives from the treatment facility.

In Tucson, Arizona, the day dawned hot, promising to bring new meaning to the word sweltering. The blazing sun, suspended in a cloudless blue sky, bore down relentlessly on the red-tile roof of the Hamilton home. Inside the white stucco house, the emotional temperature threatened to exceed the external heat by several critical degrees. Robin was scorching mad. Her temper flashed white-hot at every turn. She refused to eat breakfast, refused to pack her bag. She screamed at her parents and swore as though possessed. She berated first her mother, then her father, calling each the most vile names she could conjure. To avoid becoming a casualty of this particular family war, Josh retreated to his bedroom; Lute skulked in immediately behind him and hid in the boy's closet. The tirade continued unabated throughout the morning. Eventually, Robin ran out of steam and her anger was reduced to a simmering silent rage. Stanton Hamilton, pushed far past his own boiling point, finally ordered his daughter into the back seat of the family's SUV, then got behind the wheel. Robin's mother, Natalie, was already buckled into the passenger seat. With Robin sulking in the back seat, headphones clamped securely over her ears, the three-hour trip to the treatment facility was made in absolute, and very welcome, silence.

In Santa Rosa, California, this new August day was defined by rain. The sun was never even granted a cameo appearance. Flat-pewter rain clouds covered the sky like an impenetrable carpet. A steady rain pulsed down on the roof of the two-story Cardoza home in Rincon Valley. Inside, the shower continued in the form of tears. Everyone, except Abby's father, Jim, cried, almost without ceasing. Abby wept while explaining the near future to a stuffed teddy bear and an overweight cat; she cried while hugging her mother good-bye; she broke down completely at having to leave Sara behind. Abby and Jim climbed into the family's Honda, pulled out onto Canyon Drive and settled in for the one-and-a-half-hour trip to the Oakland airport. He would fly with her to Phoenix and deliver her to the center she would call home for a very long time to come.

Hours passed. The sun rose to its zenith, continued on its westwardly arch. And soon it was just past midday in Arizona. Ribbons of sunlight streamed into the office where Kyla Garretson sat at her desk. She scribbled the previous response on the patient inventory before moving on to the next question. "So Sara is Abby's only sibling?" Pen poised above the appropriate blank line, the therapist waited for the expected response. When none came, she prompted, "Jim?"

The man seated across from her on the plaid couch was as still as a glass figurine. Head bent, Abby's father stared transfixed at the afternoon light puddling on the floor near his feet. During the long interview, the sunbeam had crept slowly across the dark green carpet. In mere moments the advancing light would take his lace-up leather shoes hostage. Kyla placed the blue ballpoint pen on top of the papers and studied the man. Nondescript was a word that came to mind; Jim Cardoza was quintessentially average. Not tall, not short; large nor small; handsome nor ugly. His brown hair had receded far back on his scalp and he sported a small moustache, perhaps as indirect compensation for his balding head. All in all, he was just an everyday guy, without a single pretension. Yet, the deep lines of anguish carved into his face and the weary droop of his shoulders testified that he was miles and miles away from an everyday situation.

Jim, armed with a high school diploma, had done a stint in the military, then had relocated to Santa Rosa. An electrician by trade, he had built up a small business. He had done his duty, worked hard, provided for his family. In short, nothing in his fairly average life had even remotely prepared him for what he was up against now.

Leaning back in her desk chair, Kyla read the contours of his face as easily as a cartographer deciphered a familiar map. She felt she knew exactly what he was thinking. She cleared her throat to snap him out of his reverie. "Jim, she's okay, she really is." Her tone was gentle, understanding.

He looked up. So much pain was showcased in those dark brown eyes. She had seen that same galaxy of emotion—hurt, grief and dread—reflected in the eyes of so many parents. "Are you sure? Is this really the right thing? Her mother and me…"

She nodded and offered him a small sympathetic smile. "I know. Both of you love your daughter very much. You want to do the right thing. And you are. We are going to give Abby the help she needs."

"It's just the way she carried on when I left her. She wouldn't let go of me. It was like…" Again, his voice faltered, a small shudder ran through him. He dragged a hand down the front of his face, his fingers finally coming to rest on top of his slightly parted lips, his fingertips pressed against his moustache.

"Like you were leading her straight to the gallows. I know."

Kyla did know. Even when treatment was agreed upon, which was rarely the case, separation often proved difficult. Clinging and crying was fairly typical and full-fledged hysteria wasn't out of the question, either. Yet, most of the time, extreme histrionics or tantrums by the patient were contrived, just another manipulation of the parents, a last-ditch effort to get them to reconsider and take her home. Sometimes, it actually worked.

During her five years as a therapist at the ranch, Kyla had seen it all. She remembered an adolescent who simply refused to get out of the car. Ninety-eight degrees in the Arizona desert and she sat in that back seat as if her butt was literally welded to the cushion. One by one, various therapists took a crack at her, trying to stumble upon just the right argument that might hit home with her. Fifteen minutes was about the maximum amount of time anyone could stand the heat. Of course, the girl was fine. At a shockingly low body weight, mere skin draped over bones, she could take the heat. Yet, with dehydration lurking just around the corner, time was not on the therapist's side.

Everyone was desperate to coax her from the sweltering vehicle. To make matters even worse, she would take no fluids, no water, nothing, probably believing it was some sort of trick to medicate her. A full two hours went by before they managed to get her out of the car and into the air conditioned office. Once the parents left and they got her settled in, things went more smoothly. Kyla was certain that particular experience would go down in the annals as one of their more difficult admissions.

But Kyla had witnessed this separation between father and daughter; it had been excruciating for both. Clearly, Jim remained deeply troubled by it. He needed help, more reassurance. Kyla flicked a glance over at the inventory and decided she could probably glean the remaining information through simple conversation, then complete the paperwork later. "So Jim, talk to me about Abby, tell me what she was like growing up."

Jim's hand dropped from his chin onto his right thigh. It was as though his mouth had been given permission to speak. "Abby. Most ways, she's always been sort of an average kid. Quiet, never in trouble, an A-B student." He paused, his brow furrowed in concentration. "Let me think." Then he brightened. "When she was just a little thing, she was a lot like Sara."

"That's Abby's little sister?"

"Yeah, Sara, she's four. Mary's home with her now. That's why I came alone."

Kyla swung back and forth slowly, rhythmically, in her swivel chair. "Any other siblings?"

"No." Jim shook his head from side to side unwittingly mirroring Kyla's motion. "No, that's it. Mary and me, we wanted a bunch of kids, but it didn't work out. She had a lot of miscarriages. We felt lucky to get the two girls. Now, Mary's sister, Ruth, could pop them out like hotcakes off a griddle, but for some reason, Mary just couldn't. "

"So you say Abby was a lot like her little sister? Tell me about her."

Jim gave her a crooked grin, the first she had seen all day. "Sara is, well, how would you describe her? Sara is just Sara. Bright as a shiny new dime, a little chatterbox, wants to know everything, is into everything. Why, when she was a little baby, it was all we could do to keep her in one piece; always into every cabinet and drawer, nothing was safe, least of all, her. Once she learned to talk, well, it was just all over." He chuckled, remembering. "Now what is it they call her at Sunday school? That's it, a little scamp. Suits her just fine."

He paused in his explanation, got to his feet, drew a tattered leather wallet out of a back pocket and began flipping through it. He located what he was searching for and held the open wallet out to the therapist. "Here, this is Sara."

Kyla examined the photo and immediately found herself smiling. The little girl was standing outside, leaning against the trunk of a very tall tree, clutching an enormous gray cat in her tiny arms. The two of them looked as opposite as comedy-tragedy masks. Everything about Sara—her sparkling eyes, rosy cheeks, mischievous grin—captured a total exuberance and delight in life. In opposition, the cat's expression appeared pinched, defined by utter boredom and disdain. Kyla laughed out loud. "She is a scamp. And who is this with her?"

"That's Peeper. Not one of his happier moments."

"I should say not." She handed the picture back and he resumed his place on the couch. "And you say Abby was like that as well?"

Jim's smile faded. "Used to be, but I don't know, maybe somewhere around six or so, she started to change. It was gradual-like, so it's hard to say exactly when, but she got a lot more serious on us, quieter, just didn't talk as much, started spending more time in her room."

Never breaking eye contact, Jim patted first the pockets on his blue button-down cotton shirt, then the two on his trousers with the palms of both hands.

Kyla immediately recognized the familiar gesture. "How long has it been since you quit?"

"What?" He canted his head to one side, puzzled. Only then did he notice his hands. Abashed, he admitted, "Didn't even know I was doing that. When they say old habits die hard, they're not fooling."

"They also say it takes one to know one."

"You were a smoker, too?"

She gave an affirmative nod. "Uh-huh. Ten years now."

"Five for me. It's still tough. Hardly a day goes by I don't miss it, especially now. Mary made me quit when she was pregnant with Sara. She always hated it. Sometimes I bum one from a buddy of mine and just hold the filter between my fingers and maybe smell the tobacco. But I never light up."

The simple, easy talk had accomplished its purpose. She could almost see the tension ebbing from the man through a more relaxed posture, an easing of the facial muscles, especially around the mouth. Jim stretched out his legs and crossed his feet at the ankle, his shoes now fully bathed in the waning afternoon light. A comfortable silence descended between the two in her office. What Jim might be thinking about, she had no idea—perhaps his younger daughter or the former pleasure found in smoking cigarettes. Kyla, on the other hand, was fully focused on Abby's dramatic transformation from precocious scamp to the introverted, diffident girl she had met earlier. Any therapist would recognize this was relevant, but why did it happen? Now that was the million-dollar question. She picked up her braid and fluffed the reddish-gold tuft of hair at the end with her fingernails. It was a habit of hers when thinking hard. But she didn't have the luxury of time for contemplation. "Jim, you say Abby became quiet and withdrawn. Anything else? Any other new behaviors at that time?"

"No, don't think so. Wait, there was one other thing. I had almost forgotten. It was the craziest thing. About that time Abby started hiding food in her room. We'd find cookies tucked behind her shoes in the closet, sometimes crackers in her pajama drawer. Food, of all things. It made no sense. It wasn't like we were going to run out, those things were always stored in the kitchen. But for some reason, she would take things and hide them in her room like she was afraid they wouldn't be there for her when she wanted them."

"Ever discover why?"

"Never did. I honestly don't think she knew why she did it."

Kyla nodded, swiping the end of her braid along her jaw line back and forth in curt little strokes like a painter working in a confined space. "Okay, that works."

Jim blinked, startled. "It does? But how? Back then she was hoarding food and now we can't make her eat. That makes sense?"

"No, not to you and me, but at the time, it made sense to Abby. What else, any other unusual behavior?"

"Let me think…" Lacing his fingers together behind his neck, Jim threw his head back and gazed at the ceiling as if the answer might be found there. Outside the large window a slight breeze fluttered the vivid yellow blossoms of a Palo Verde tree, causing dappled shadows to dance across the exposed skin of his neck. "You know that hiding food thing didn't last forever, but one thing that never changed was the way she got about organizing her room. Real funny, picky about her stuff. Always had to be perfectly lined up, all of her things had to be exactly where she wanted them."

"A place for everything and everything in its place?"

"Yeah, like that, but real…"

"Excessive?"

"Yeah, right, like that. We never, not once, had to get on Abby about her room; it's always neat as a pin. Matter of fact, Mary hardly ever goes in there because if something gets moved, my golly, you'd think it was the end of the world. About the only time we ever see Abby get upset."

"Back to Abby and Sara, do they get along?"

"Get along? Abby and Sara are tight as ticks, best of friends, spend most of their time together."

"Would you say Abby is protective of her little sister?"

"Yes, absolutely. Abby has been Sara's self-appointed guardian since she was born. Always taking care of her, watching after her."

"And you say the eating disorder started around the age of eleven?"

"I guess. But it's hard to say. She hid it from us for a long time. She wore great big clothes. Then, when she started fainting at school and stuff, we had no idea it was one of those disorder things. We kept taking her to one doctor after another thinking there was really something wrong with her."

In Abby's defense, Kyla wanted to say that there really was something wrong with her, but this would serve no purpose. Abby's parents were not to blame for the lack of an adequate diagnosis. Yet, in Kyla's opinion, the doctors were at fault. My God, this girl had all the red flags of severe anorexia: malnutrition, extremely low body weight, amenorrhea. Short of actually coming right out and admitting it, which in her experience, the patient rarely did, the doctors should have recognized it.

Across the room, Jim appeared expectant, obviously anticipating another question. She yanked herself back from her mental tangent, back to the moment. "Can you equate anything in Abby's life with the onset of the disorder? Any trauma? A death in the family, a new school, a move?"

He considered the questions, reflecting on the past. "No, nothing. No one died, we've always lived in the same house. Each day is pretty much like the next."

"Dating?"

Jim looked shocked. "Boys?" Jim said the word as if she had asked him if Abby hung out with space aliens.

"Yes, boys. Abby is thirteen. Most girls…"

"You don't understand, Abby isn't most girls. She's a homebody, not many friends, doesn't go out really at all. It's like she's still just a little girl, not a teenager at all." Unexpectedly, Jim drew in a sharp breath, sat up straight, his face alert. The therapist could almost see the light bulb going off above his head. "Abby's grandfather had a stroke—think that's important?"

It took Kyla a minute to realize he had reverted to a former topic. "When?"

"About six, eight months ago." Hearing his own response, he realized the time-frame differential. Abby's onset had occurred far in advance of the stroke, by more than a year. He seemed to deflate right in front of her eyes. "Well, guess not."

"Were they close? You never know."

"No. Mary thinks Earl is just this side of the second coming, but Abby and him were never close."

Ever conscious of passing time and Jim's need to return to the Phoenix airport, she finished up. They stood and drifted toward the office door. She planned to escort him to his rental car, then return to the office to complete her paperwork. She noticed he stooped a bit, hunched his shoulders as he walked, making him appear shorter than he actually was. No wonder—he was carrying the weight of the world. They strolled down the wood-paneled hall, easy with one another, as if all problems had been left back in the office. Jim gestured toward her protruding abdomen and asked, "So, when is the baby due?"

Reflexively, she placed a hand on her denim-draped stomach and gave it a gentle pat. "Three months. It's our second. A boy."

Jim stood to one side, courteously allowing two women to pass in the narrow hall. Kyla acknowledged her colleague from the admissions office with a little wave and assumed the person with her was a patient. She sized up the blond woman with one swift glance, then watched Jim's reaction. He stood absolutely still as the young woman murmured a gracious thank you and continued down the hall. He gazed after her retreating form for several moments. Kyla couldn't blame Jim for gawking. Though appearance was never stressed or valued at the center, even Kyla was drawn in. This creature was breathtaking, though the therapist in her detected a hint of that

vapid, vacant look that often accompanied the highly med-
icated. Long after the woman had passed, the staccato tap,
tap of her high heels on the hard-wood floor continued to
echo and her floral perfume lingered in the air.

Kyla resumed walking and Jim fell in alongside her.
"That is honestly one of the most gorgeous women I have
ever seen in my entire life," he commented, voice dropping
to a discreet whisper. "She sounded like she was from the
South. Does she work here?"

"No, my guess is she's an incoming patient, just like
Abby."

"But she…"

"Doesn't look sick at all," she completed, having heard
similar comments a hundred times before. "They often
don't. But trust me, eating disorders are equal-opportunity
illnesses. As with so many other conditions such as depression or anxiety, you frequently can't tell who is afflicted
just by looking at them."

They turned a corner and headed to the front door,
passing by Tom Benedict's office, a close friend and colleague of Kyla's. From inside, Tom observed the two
through his office window, then shifted his attention back
to the couple seated on the lavender and green love seat.
Dr. Stanton Hamilton and Dr. Natalie Grant-Hamilton,
parents of his newest patient, Robin.

Stanton with his black horn-rimmed glasses, close-
cropped hair and stern facial features looked exactly like what

he was: a brilliant academician. His controlled, buttoned-down demeanor only served to reinforce this impression. His clothes, tan golf shirt and matching slacks, were meticulous and complemented his trim athletic build. Within moments of their initial handshake, Tom knew this was not a man anyone would ever call Stan, just as no one from Old Testament times probably ever referred to the deliverer of the Ten Commandments as Mo.

Natalie, also a professor, proved far less severe in her appearance: curly auburn hair held back by tortoiseshell combs; kind brown eyes; a plain, but not unattractive face that boasted not an ounce of makeup; a fairly plump figure. As with her husband, not even a suggestion of glitz was present in her no-nonsense attire. Yet, Tom thought this was probably due far more to apathy than reserve. She struck him as the type of person who would throw on whatever was available, provided it was clean, perhaps even the outfit draped over the bedroom chair the night before. This was not a woman you would ever find casually thumbing through the pages of *Vogue,* or heaven forbid, *Cosmo.*

The three had enjoyed an immediate rapport, though Stanton had proved far more remote and taciturn than his wife. During the past two hours, Tom had gone through the patient inventory, the completed paperwork on his desk. Now he sat in the wingback chair across from them, discussing their daughter's treatment, entertaining any additional questions or residual concerns they might still have. Both looked wretched, clearly exhausted by the difficult day. More than once during the long interview Stanton had removed his glasses to massage his forehead and bloodshot eyes. Natalie resembled an ice sculpture kept from the freezer for too long; she was beginning to melt down, both physically and emotionally. Tom had just gotten through explaining the schedule for teleconference calls.

Natalie took a sip of steaming coffee, then clutched the ceramic mug in both hands. She asked, "Do you think Robin will even talk to us? You saw how she was; God, it was awful."

"It was awful," Tom agreed. "But believe me, not unusual. Robin is mad and she wants you to know it."

"Could we have missed it?" Though still miserable, her tone was ironic.

"I don't think so."

Upon their arrival, Robin had treated her parents with undisguised enmity. When the time came to separate, she gave them a paint-peeling sneer, then stalked away. Natalie, who might have hoped for a small, if grudging, hug from her daughter, dropped her face into her open hands and wept. Even Stanton was visibly shaken, which Tom surmised was probably a very rare occurrence.

Tom sat forward. Pale yellow sunlight splashed across his back and warmed his shoulders. "Robin feels like a cornered animal, threatened from all sides. You and Stanton are trying to take away what has become the most important thing in her life, her eating disorder. No wonder she's lashing out. It would be as if I was trying to steal your air, all your reserves of oxygen. You'd fight like crazy to hold on to it, wouldn't you? That's what it's like for Robin; metaphorically speaking, she feels like you're trying to suffocate her."

Natalie shook her head emphatically. "You know I've read every journal and article I can get my hands on regarding this disorder, but I still don't get it. Oxygen keeps us alive. This disorder is killing her."

"I know it makes absolutely no sense to you and your husband, and honestly, it probably never will. But what matters is that right now it makes sense to Robin. The eating disorder is serving an extremely important purpose in her life. My job is to get her to figure out the function of the disorder—what its purpose is—then find new and healthy ways to get those needs met."

"It won't be easy. Robin hates therapy and therapists. She'll fight you every step of the way."

"I know. I've had dozens of patients just like your daughter. They are a real challenge. It may take a while, but progress usually does come.

"Will it work?"

Tom steepled his fingers, tapping the index fingers together as he formulated a reply. "All of us here are very good at what we do. If anyone can help her, we can. That's not just talk, that's the truth. You've seen our statistics." He cocked his head in the direction of the informational booklet Stanton was currently perusing. "And don't worry about whether or not she'll talk to you because she definitely will. That's one thing I can guarantee. Your daughter will not miss a single opportunity to tell you in great detail how bad it is here, how we are mistreating her, how she is being force-fed. You won't believe the stories she'll come up with in an effort to get you to take her home. I have a feeling Robin's a very smart young lady. She'll paint a picture that will make a Russian gulag look like a five-star resort."

Amusement flickered across Natalie's face. "And she will eat?"

He gave her a curt nod. "She won't like it, but she will eat. Our first goal is to get her weight up. But we must do it gradually. Refeeding is a lot more complex than merely forcing a girl to eat a cheeseburger. We have to be very careful, introducing food and fluids slowly. Robin has deprived her body for a long time; if we refeed too aggressively, it could compromise her heart. You already know her weight is at a dangerously low level." Tom stretched out a hand and snagged Robin's medical report from the desktop. He leafed through several pages and found what he was looking for. "Sixty-five percent of normal body weight; that's low. No surprise she's behaving so badly. Her ability to think clearly and rationally has been severely impaired by malnutrition."

"What about the vomiting, can you get that under control?" Natalie took a final swallow of coffee, then parked the empty mug on the glass-topped table next to her. "For the longest time, we didn't even know she was doing it. If it hadn't been for that dental appointment, we would never have known. Actually, we didn't know how much she was restricting, either. For months and months we were incredibly baffled as to why our dog kept gaining so much weight. We had no idea she was feeding him virtually all of her food. I hate to say this about my own daughter, but she is terribly sneaky."

"They all are. As a rule, girls with eating disorders are sneaky, deceptive and manipulative. It's part of the illness. As far as the purging is concerned, Robin will be monitored around the clock. If she purges, we'll know it."

"Another thing, not really about Robin, but…" All at once, a new look of extreme distress swept across Natalie's somber face. She bit her lower lip, nervously combed a few stray strands of wispy hair back behind one ear with her fingers. "I wanted to ask, I mean, since you do this all the time…"

Tom inclined his head, trying to encourage her with a look.

"Are other parents relieved, actually glad, to be leaving their daughters here? I mean, I feel so awful because I'm happy she isn't going back to Tucson with us." She paused, melted down a little more, appearing to shrink under the tremendous weight of all that guilt. "It has been months and months since we have had anything that even resembles peace in our home. To say nothing of the constant fear that she might actually die. Night after night I have lain in bed worrying about my daughter. In fact, several times a night I would go in and stand by her bedside just to see if she was still breathing. Sometimes she would lock her door and I was almost frantic with worry. I can't count the number of times I slept on the floor outside her room. Even I knew that was foolish; if she had died, it's not like I would have known. Somehow it just made me feel better being close to her." Remembering, Natalie's eyes filled with tears, her voice cracked. "Honestly, the strain has finally gotten to me. I don't know if I could take much more. I feel so relieved not to be going home to that." She looked like a woman huddled in a confessional who has just admitted the most grievous of sins.

"Oh Natalie," Tom responded, deep compassion punctuating every word. "The answer is yes, absolutely. Many parents can't wait to get out of here and place distance between themselves and their daughters. These are people, just like you, who love that child more than life itself. But probably just like you—they've had it. They've had it with the disorder, the lies, the rages. And just like you, they've had it with the fear of death hanging over their homes. Believe me, I've seen it again and again. They have taken about as much as they possibly can, and then they've taken a little more. Your feelings are not only valid, they are completely normal."

"I have been feeling so guilty, as if I am such a bad mother."

"Many parents do."

Stanton closed the handbook with an audible clap. He dropped it on the cushion between him and his wife, then turned toward the other man. A beam of late afternoon light bounced off the right lens of his glasses. Tom blinked, shifted his position to accommodate. "Going through the manual, I see there will be several religious activities Robin will be required to attend."

Bingo. Tom almost blurted the word out loud. He had anticipated this line of questioning for nearly three hours. A section of the inventory dealt with religious beliefs and affiliations. *None* had been Natalie and Stanton's response to all. "That's right. Robin must go to chapel every day and though participation is optional, attendance is mandatory. She also must take part in a Monday night Bible study. It's led by one of our therapists and focuses on spiritual growth."

Stanton frowned and rubbed his jaw in thought. "We are not a religious family, never have been. Can you explain why this is deemed so important?"

"Certainly." Tom settled back in the chair, flung one foot over the opposing knee, his favorite position. "Recovery, whether from alcohol, drug addition, or an eating disorder, is extremely difficult. Eating disorders are particularly difficult because people must eat; it is not an optional behavior. Research suggests that reliance on a higher power significantly bolsters the chances of complete recovery. Most patients know they cannot do it alone. Faith goes a long way in helping the patient to see that she has someone who can help her in her struggle."

"Chapel?" Natalie interjected. "What does that entail?"

"Lots of music, singing, prayer. The worship songs are lively, guitar and keyboard, they clap and sing. It's fun. There's usually a speaker, someone with a message regarding where the girls are in their recovery." Tom made a mental note to locate a worship CD and send it to them immediately as an illustration of what Robin would be exposed to in chapel.

Tom looked from one unconvinced face to another. It wasn't his job or his place to convert these two; he simply wanted them to understand why the spiritual component of their daughter's treatment was so critical. He dropped his foot to the floor, leaned forward, anchoring both forearms on his thighs, hands dangling between his knees. "Let me ask you something. Why did you bring Robin here for inpatient treatment? Why us? Surely, it wasn't our location alone."

They exchanged a look, wordlessly deciding who would respond. Stanton was elected. "No, proximity was merely an added bonus. After Robin was diagnosed, we got her into therapy with an excellent counselor, highly regarded in the field. They met together for weeks, then months. Not only did our daughter fail to improve, she actually lost ground. At that point, we started to research residential facilities. In terms of outcomes, this center was the best. That's all there was to it."

"You're right. Do you know why our success rate is so high?" Tom knew this question was a dead dog. It could lie there between them all day and no one was going to pick it up, so he continued, "It's because all of us working here not only are believers in Jesus Christ, but allow Him to work in the individual lives of our patients and ultimately heal them."

Tom looked again at the couple seated only inches away from him. Stanton, who had shifted his position as Tom spoke, now sat with arms folded across his chest, fists clenched at his sides. Nothing too subtle there; a master's degree in counseling wasn't required to interpret that particular body language. Fortunately, this continued recalcitrance was not replicated in Robin's mother. Her expression was quite different, one of...hope? Maybe...receptivity? Strategically, he held her gaze and addressed his final comments to her. "Robin will be exposed to Christian principles and beliefs. Will she come home wanting to handle snakes and bleed chickens?" He offered her a lopsided grin to emphasize his question was intended as a joke. "No, of course not. But if faith in God can help her to embrace and succeed in recovery, isn't it worth trying, even if it is something new?"

"Yes." Natalie's voice was adamant. Stanton remained silent, obviously still unconvinced, but unwilling to engage in additional discussion.

Close enough, Tom thought as he replaced Robin's papers on his desk. "Do either of you have any other questions?" They didn't. The subdued trio stood, left the office, then the building. Outside, a tranquil breeze scurried about. Dusk had settled in. The remaining light softly showcased the subtle textures and delicate hues intrinsic to the desert. As Robin's parents climbed back into their vehicle, the sun took permanent refuge behind the horizon. The day, which had seen three new patients admitted to the ranch, was done.

Though these patients were as different as three young women could be, they were linked by the common bond of an eating disorder. Each was embarking on a journey, taking the first step on a long road from discovery to recovery. Though starting alone, none would remain so; their families would ultimately come to the facility as important participants in this difficult journey. As with their loved ones, every family member would be changed forever—some for the better, others not.

As Alexa, Robin and Abby slid between the sheets of unfamiliar beds that night, each believed she would never get out, never make it to the other side. In fact, they would. In time, all three would pass through the intensive program and return to their respective lives and families.

However, in spite of the best therapy and medical attention, and even the patient's genuine, heartfelt desire to be well, one of these young women would not live to see the sun rise on her next birthday.

Part Two

Chapter three

The older man, the younger woman, relaxed on cushioned chairs and gazed out at the huge expanse of desert stretched before them. The black wrought-iron furniture was arranged on a narrow terrace just outside Dan Reznick's office in the center's main lodge. He felt this was an ideal setting for his first therapy session with Alexa Kent; not only because of the informal atmosphere but a late-afternoon rainstorm was threatening and this proved a perfect vantage point from which to watch it unfold. Already, the sky had darkened several shades and the temperature had dropped noticeably. With chairs angled toward one another, the two had spoken desultorily for several minutes about this and that, nothing of consequence. Just listening to Alexa speak was a pleasure due to the Southern lilt in her voice. Dan suspected this young woman could read straight from the newspaper's obituary page and all listeners would be riveted.

Dan had first met Alexa when she was admitted to the treatment facility. Since that time, her medication had been reviewed and stabilized. Now she was coherent and capable of normal interaction. Yet one area that remained unchanged was her appearance. She was as striking as he remembered. But to Dan, far more important than her physical beauty was what she did with it. As before, her blonde hair was fluffed back from her face and fell in loose waves around her shoulders. Her makeup was expertly applied—not too much, not too little. This perfection was replicated in her clothes. She wore a sleeveless cerulean outfit with matching high-heeled sandals. The neckline was trimmed with ornate silver braid, which artfully complemented her dangling silver earrings. According to his wife, Dan was the least savvy man on the planet when it came to fashion; but even he knew "expensive" when he saw it. Dan was certain the pantsuit's label boasted a prestigious designer name. As with so many of the patients he had gotten from "debutante country," Alexa came perfectly packaged. Yet her wardrobe, obviously tasteful and expensive, was ill-suited for the ranch environment. He wondered if she even owned a pair of Levis. He would ask one of the mental health technicians to locate more appropriate clothes for her to wear while in treatment. There was simply no way she could groom, much less ride, a horse while in spike heels.

Dan noticed Alexa held her arms pressed closely to her sides. He suspected she was trying to hide the self-inflicted wounds on the inside of both arms. This had been the first time she had cut on that particular location. He had reviewed the physical exam done by her primary-care physician when she first checked in. The cuts on her fore-arms were merely the tip of the iceberg; she had intention-ally mutilated herself on several other areas of her body. But the most severe, and therefore the most therapeutically relevant location, was her abdomen. What's more, these lacerations were not in a random pattern, but resembled an X. Dan had certainly seen cuts on the torso before, but never in an actual pattern. Was it deliberate, or simply con-venient? If deliberate, did she even know why? Several old burn marks had also been unearthed, leading him to sus-pect the self-injury had begun with either matches or cig-arettes held to the flesh.

Because of these findings, Alexa had been required to sign a "No Harm" contract, promising she would not indulge in self-destructive behavior while in treatment. Nevertheless, she would be watched closely. Often if patients couldn't cut themselves, they would find other ways to self-mutilate. Dan had seen everything from patients biting themselves to banging their heads against walls to cutting themselves with cactus needles. Some were restricted from riding because they might purposely fall from the horse, hoping to cause serious injury.

Of course, the medical inventory had uncovered the usual suspects: dehydration, electrolyte imbalance, minor glandular swelling. Her weight was low, but not life threatening and there was a mild case of malnutrition. Her throat had been scratched severely in the vomiting process. The report also revealed Alexa had undergone a breast augmentation, evidently, at the age of seventeen. When Dan encountered this finding, his heart sank. How many times had he seen it? Dozens. In recent years, it had become fashionable among the wealthy elite to present their daughters with implants as a high school graduation gift. New improved breasts? What happened to the traditional new car for college? Dan wondered if these parents had any idea what a profoundly negative message they were sending their young daughters regarding the importance placed on their physical appearance, to say nothing of their sexuality. He strongly felt that instantly transforming a B cup to a D cup through the marvels of plastic surgery was an obscene thing to do to an adolescent.

Dan drew in a deep breath, momentarily reveling in the sweet smell of pending rain. He flicked a glance over at Alexa, who sat with ankles crossed, painted nails tapping on the hard metal surface of the chair. He cleared his throat. "Alexa, I had some confusion while reviewing your family information. Is Loren your only sibling?"

She released a terse humorless chuckle. "Now that depends on who you ask." At his confused look, she continued, "My mother would say that my sister was my only sibling, but if placing a hand on the ever-popular King James was required, she might be forced to admit that I also have an older brother."

No wonder he had been baffled. "I don't get it. What's that all about?"

"Jackson is gay. And though the South has surely come a long way since Reconstruction, it hasn't quite fully made it into the current century. Gay just isn't allowed in refined society. At least, not according to my family. When Jackson came out, he was forced to get out. Gentlemen callers were always welcome in our home, but they were expected to come courtin' me, not him. I haven't seen my brother in years; I don't even know where he is." Alexa offered this explanation in a matter-of-fact tone. Her clinical presentation was offered without emotion.

"Alexa, I…" Dan paused as a thought suddenly occurred to him. "I never asked, do you want to be called Alexa, or do you prefer something else? A nickname?"

"As a little girl, I always wanted to be called Lexy, but my mother wouldn't allow it. She said it sounded like poor white trash."

"May I call you Lexy?"

She lifted her chin and gave him a spontaneous smile, not the beauty pageant smile he had already witnessed, but a real one. Naturally, her teeth were uniformly straight and toothpaste-commercial white. She had a deep dimple in her right cheek and her extraordinary eyes, so similar to the cerulean shade of her blouse, flickered with violet high-lights. "Please do, I would like that."

"Good. Lexy, tell me how you feel about being here."

"I don't know. It's fine." She shrugged. "It's been quite some time since I've shared a room with another woman and I don't much like having a stranger flush my toilet for me."

"But you do understand why we do that, right?"

"Sure. Y'all need to make sure no one purges while in treatment."

"Do you miss your husband, your baby?"

She bit the inside of her lip. "I know I'm supposed to say that I really do miss them like crazy."

Dan sat forward in his chair and gave her a look intended to be as direct as his words. "While you're here, when you and I are talking, please don't ever say what you're supposed to say or do what you're supposed to do. My guess is you've lived your entire life saying and doing what others want. That's not going to work here; I need to see and hear the real you."

By now, all traces of the smile had vanished; her expression metamorphosed into one of profound sorrow. "There is no real me." She lowered her gaze. "What you see is all there is. What is that expression—All the lights on and no one's home? That's me; lots of lights."

"Sorry, but I don't believe that. I think there is a real you, you just lost her somewhere along the line. And you know what? We're going to find her."

She shook her head slowly, sounding as sad as she looked. "If you find her, you won't like her."

Dan regarded his new patient and thought of all the other women who had said such similar words to him, each believing she had no value or worth; and each had been wrong. "Let me be the judge of that," he said to Lexy.

In the brief conversational lull, Dan grew increasingly aware of the gusting wind blowing in from the west. The pervasive aroma of rain now held the unmistakable fragrance of sage. The branches of nearby trees began to sway and dip. Their leaves chattered, whispering tantalizing secrets to one another. Sun-bleached grasses engaged in a languid ballet, dancing to music only plants could hear.

Dan repeated the question. "So, do you miss them?"

She tilted her head to one side in an attitude of contemplation. "Honestly, no. I don't feel anything at all. I haven't felt close to Scott for months. We haven't been physically close since I can't remember when. I know he's tired of having to deal with me and my problems. I can't blame him; I wouldn't want to deal with me, either. Whoever is taking care of Logan is surely doing a better job than I ever did. Both are better off without me, especially my son."

"Why do you say that?"

"Because it's true. I've never been a good mother. He deserves so much better than me."

Dan cocked an eyebrow. "Do you think other people feel that way?"

She slid her fingers along the blouse's silver braiding. "I don't know…it doesn't matter."

"What does matter, Lexy?"

She hesitated, still staring out onto the open desert. Her fingers stopped their idle musings; her slender sculptured nails came to rest on the bare, slightly freckled skin of her collarbone. Dan thought she would not answer, but finally she offered a flat rejoinder. "Nothing, nothing at all."

How could so much despair, such hopelessness, be captured in one seven-letter word? Dan didn't know, but there it was, no mistaking it. He had wanted to move forward and touch on her eating-disorder behavior, but knew he needed to allow some time to pass between these difficult topics. He redirected the conversation with a gesture toward the distant mountain. "Look, it's about ready to hit. When my kids were little they would make bets as to the exact moment the storm would get to our house. They were usually right on the money. Arizona storms are fairly predictable. Watch the clouds…they're really amazing."

The mountain was festooned with thick foliage: junipers, sagebrush, mesquite and cedars. The flora showcased nearly every shade of green, everything from deepest emerald to the lightest silver-flecked jade. Only occasionally was the solid green quilt interrupted by the odd brown boulder or tan scrub bush. On the opposite side of the mountain, dense rain clouds were accumulating like billowing foam in a beer mug; soon they would crest the summit and spill into the valley below. With the increased wind came the pyrotechnics, bursts of jagged white light followed by bone-jarring thunder. The sporadic lightning crackled and snapped behind the leaden clouds, causing them to glow with a gray luminescence. At times, it appeared as if the mountaintop was crowned by a halo of sheer radiance.

"They are amazing," she agreed.

"With the clouds backlit, the sky looks so ethereal. You can see it's raining just behind the mountain. With this wind, I give it less than a minute to get to us." Dan narrowed his gaze, then pointed a finger. "Look at that speedy guy; he must be late for an appointment." A roadrunner scooted out from behind a large bush, running for all he was worth. With pointed face jutting out, tiny gray-feathered wings clamped to his sides, his rigid body and straight tail, the bird resembled an arrow shot from a bow. Only, this arrow had sprouted spindly legs and feet from its underside. These appendages were now only a blur of dynamic motion. The determined bird streaked across the desert floor, dust puffing behind him like jet exhaust. He was there, then gone.

"Even though I know better, I am always on the lookout, expecting Wile E. Coyote to be hot on his trail," Dan remarked. She responded with a small laugh. Presently, the clouds crested the mountain and swept into the valley.

"It's time," Dan proclaimed. They got to their feet and dashed to the door. Inside, he went to his desk and she lowered herself into an upholstered chair near the large picture window. The storm came at them like an invading army. Water poured from the sky in torrents; within seconds the mountain was obliterated from view. Fat raindrops pelted the ground, instantly flattening smaller bushes. Tree branches bowed under the weight of the water, bending like supplicants at an altar. Rain pounded on the roof, eclipsing all sound, even the thunder. Suddenly, the wind shifted direction. Rain lashed full force into the window with a deafening crack, startling both of them. Dan reflexively jumped in his chair and Lexy lurched back in her seat.

She slapped a hand onto her chest. "Oh my," she said, elevating her voice to be heard over the racket. "Goodness, it reminds me of riding through the carwash as a little girl."

"Yes, and watch, it will be over just as quickly."

No sooner had he voiced the claim than it became a fact. The storm blew out, leaving no doubt it had visited. Water sluiced from the roof, creating deep rivulets in the ground. The patio furniture, so recently vacated, was drenched. Everything dripped.

Dan got up and cracked the door to the outside. "I love the way it smells after a rain, especially the aroma of creosote." To underscore his words, he drew in a deep satisfying breath and smiled at the fresh fragrance of clean air and wet earth.

Dan reclaimed his chair and refocused his attention on her. "Lexy, I'd like to ask you about the purging. You started it in college?"

"Uh-huh, some of the girls in my sorority showed me how. But back then, it was more like a game, something you would do when you'd eaten too much pizza. No big deal."

"Then for a while you stopped. But you started again during your pregnancy?" Dan retrieved a pencil from the desk, just to give his fingers something to fiddle with. Somehow, keeping his hands occupied helped him remain focused.

Though she nodded in agreement, he could tell she was unwilling to say any more. Undoubtedly there was just too much mortification attached to the behavior. Bulimia, by its very definition, was a disorder that engendered incredible shame and guilt. Whereas those with anorexia could rationalize certain aspects of their behavior such as dieting, exercise or vegetarianism, when bulimia was involved, no reasonable explanations existed, not a single one. It was simply impossible for anyone to justify consuming thousands upon thousands of calories, then purging them through vomiting. The more a person practiced this maladaptive behavior, the greater the shame. Then, if a woman engaged in bingeing and purging during pregnancy, when the health of a baby was involved, these negative feelings were magnified tremendously. No wonder Lexy didn't want to talk about it.

Dan moved on. "Then…"

"I started doing it even more right after Logan was born." She shuddered lightly.

He knew she practiced the behavior with great frequency, so he wouldn't ask about actual numbers; what he needed to know was why she did it. He wondered if she knew. "And you binge and purge because…"

"I need to be thin."

He figured this would be her response. It was pretty much what all his patients said initially. They weren't lying to him, they honestly had no idea what the truth was behind their eating disorder. The therapists had an expression they used often: it's not about food, it's about feelings.

Dan tapped the pencil on the knuckles of his left hand. "And if you weren't thin?"

Undisguised alarm registered on her face. She was truly horrified. You would have thought he had advocated wearing white after Labor Day. "Are you kidding? Well, that would just be unacceptable."

"To whom?"

"Why, everyone…especially my family."

"Lexy, finish this sentence for me. I cut myself because…"

A flush rose to her face, staining her cheeks a vivid pink. She averted her gaze and plucked at the buttons on the cushion of the overstuffed chair. Then, she folded her arms across her chest and gripped her elbows. She inhaled, exhaled.

He waited.

Eventually she answered in a barely audible voice. "It feels good."

He waited.

"I like watching the blood."

He waited.

"It helps. It takes my mind off of other things, things I don't want to think about."

In an equally subdued voice, Dan prompted, "It makes me feel…"

She completed the sentence with one simple word. "Something."

Only a therapist could know that her answer was right on target. Dan had worked here since the ranch had opened its doors more than a decade ago. During his tenure, much to his extreme regret, he had seen many women and girls who were cutters. Though the rest of the world might erroneously assume that they lacerated themselves with an eye toward suicide, Dan and his colleagues knew better. Often, these women did it simply to feel something, anything at all. These patients were completely shut down, emotionally void. Something, even self-inflicted pain, was better to them than nothing at all.

Dan and Lexy sat quietly for several minutes listening to the hypnotic aftermath of the storm. The steady stream of rain water cascading from the roof had dissipated into a trickle, then a series of intermittent drips. The individual droplets plinked and plunked in counterpoint into the puddle just outside the open office door. In time, Dan swung his chair around toward the desk. He grabbed a tablet of paper and drew a sketch on the top sheet with his pencil. "I want you to take a look at something. Now, I am no artist, but you'll get the idea." He swung back around, then scooted his chair closer to where Lexy sat. "Okay, this is an iceberg," he said and pointed to the rudimentary drawing with his pencil.

The young woman looked dubious. "It is?" She widened her eyes with feigned amazement. "Could have fooled me."

Dan chuckled, delighted to see how quickly she had rebounded from the previous conversation. "Look, just go with me on this. Pretend this is an iceberg."

"Okay, I'm with you. It's an iceberg." She peered closer at the paper.

"Here at the tip-top are the eating-disorder behaviors you've developed as a coping mechanism. Lets put a B and a P for bingeing and purging; C will stand for the cutting behavior." He penciled the letters in under the word *Behavior*, then drew a horizontal line just beneath the letters. "Under this waterline are what people don't see, the feelings and emotions that cause the behaviors. Notice how much bigger it is beneath the surface; what actually shows is really quite small. Keep in mind, it was the unseen part of the iceberg that sunk the Titanic." He wrote *Core Emotional Issues* under the line. "Lexy, you said you purged to stay thin. What would happen if you gained a little weight?"

She shook her head emphatically; her silver earrings tinkled with the swift motion. "I can't, I won't even go there."

"Please try." He knew he was asking a lot of her. Asking her to imagine weight gain was like asking an average person on the street to picture living without arms or legs.

Lexy closed her eyes; she lifted her hands and pressed her fingers against her temples in concentration. He could tell she was honestly trying. Suddenly, the words just burst out: "It would be awful. You don't understand; I must be thin; I must be beautiful. It's the only thing I have, the only thing that counts." As she reached over and clutched his forearm in a tight grip, she gave him an imploring look. "All my life I've been this beautiful doll that people could take out and show off. Thin is part of that. Really, it's true. Have you ever seen a fat Barbie?"

Barbie, again; Dan wanted to scream or throw his pencil across the room. If he had a dollar for every time that ridiculous doll had come up in therapy, he could retire today, a wealthy ex-therapist. Choosing to let the Barbie question go, he said, "So what I hear you saying is that if you weighed more you would be rejected? Unloved?"

She nodded. "That would be only the beginning…the beginning of the end."

Dan couldn't help but respect her fear; this woman came from a family who permanently banished a child because he was gay. No wonder she was afraid of rejection. "Then we'll just start with this." Dan penciled in an *R* and a *U* under *Core Emotional Issues*. "This right here…" He tapped the two letters. "Your fear of being rejected and unloved is why you do this." He drew an arrow to the behaviors. She held the edge of the paper, her hand quivered as she looked down, then up, and down again. Dan leaned back in his chair. "While you're here, you will not be allowed to practice those maladaptive behaviors you've depended on to help you deal with life. The more you don't do them, the more your true feelings and emotions will come to the surface. It's kind of like whacking off the top of the iceberg; what's below will just naturally push its way up to the surface."

She looked back up at him, bewildered and clearly terrified. "But I don't want to feel those things."

"I know you don't, that's why you have an eating disorder. You've been using it to keep those emotions held down, to ensure you won't have to feel pain." His tone was gentle, reflecting the deep compassion he had felt for his patients throughout all these years. "But Lexy, look where you are…" He gestured around his office with the sweep of one hand. "You're in treatment. You're here for a long time. It isn't working for you anymore. You used to control the disorder, but now it controls you. It's time to deal with what is behind all this. And really, aren't you tired of what your life has become: the bingeing and purging, the guilt and shame, the lies, the isolation, the hiding? Lexy, isn't it time?"

She visibly recoiled. "Yes," she acknowledged in the faintest whisper. She sagged into the chair and dropped the paper onto her lap. It sailed silently to the floor, unnoticed. Her enormous blue eyes stared out at him from a face that had turned as pale as winter sunlight. Alexa Kent looked as though she was about to say good-bye to her best friend; and Dan knew...she was.

———⟨o/o/o⟩———

Scott Kent fastened his gaze on the baby boy cradled in the crook of his arm and tipped the bottle of milk a little higher to ensure maximum flow. Logan clutched the bottle even tighter with his tiny hands and sucked on the nipple with renewed zeal. As if receiving an action signal from command control, his chubby legs and bare feet began to kick in unsynchronized motion. The activity caused his disposable diaper to make distinct crunching sounds. "So how soon will I have to give up this nighttime bottle?" Scott posed the question to his sister, who sprawled on the plump cushions of a white wicker chaise lounge. She peeked over the rim of a glass of sweet tea, a quizzical expression defining her features. "Gosh, I don't know...when he's a year old?"

"I'll have to find out. If somebody doesn't tell me it's time to stop, I probably never will."

"If you're still doin' it when he's a teenager, we're going to have to have a talk."

"No kidding." He made a self-effacing grunt deep in his throat. "I know he doesn't really need milk at bedtime, but

I sure do need to give it to him. It just feels so good to hold him."

Scott had arrived home from work later than usual and he and Jennifer had thrown together a quick dinner. Now they were enjoying the tranquil September evening on the screened-in porch of his Charlotte home. Just beyond the black mesh barrier stretched an enormous verdant yard. The ground was covered with a thick carpet of lush green grass and was bracketed by a six-foot-high hedge. Crickets and other earthbound insects sheltered among the strategically placed azaleas and dogwoods. They noisily chirped, buzzed and hummed the news of the day to one another. Closer in, huge winged moths banged relentlessly against the screen, coveting what they could not possess: the low-wattage light glowing just out of reach on the porch. A few of these winged creatures had managed to infiltrate the well-guarded sanctuary and now performed their flirtatious dance within striking distance of the burning bulb.

Logan took one final gulp, emptying the bottle. The nipple made a small popping sound as Scott extricated it from his mouth. The little boy looked up at his father through glazed sleepy eyes. Somewhere deep in the recesses of his baby brain, all the current sensations from his world—the satiated hunger, the firm hand securely supporting his bottom, the warmth emanating from Scott's body in tandem with the familiar sound of his voice—coalesced into a sense of pure contentment. He emitted a deep drowsy sigh, issued a tiny burp and gave his father a lopsided toothless grin. His eyelids drooped, then gradually slid shut. Scott placed the bottle on the tabletop next to his glass of tea, then dabbed Logan's mouth with the edge of his Winnie the Pooh T-shirt. When he placed an index finger into his son's palm, the miniature fingers closed around it and held on. Scott bent down and brushed his lips over Logan's soft forehead and breathed in the fragrance of his freshly shampooed hair. "I love you so much," Scott told his slumbering son.

"Who could help but love him? He's the very best baby in the whole wide world. Of course, I am not partial in the least," Jennifer said, then followed up with, "Scott, do you realize you still have your tie on?"

A look of vexation flashed across Scott's face. "I can't believe it. When I was at Duke, I swore I would never become one of those tie-wearing executives. Now look at me after only two years at the bank." He yanked off the tie that had hung loosely around his neck and tossed it onto the table. "I wonder if I still have sense enough to come in out of the rain."

"Probably not. Good thing I'm here to watch after you." Jennifer stretched out her legs on the long cornflower blue and white striped cushion and wiggled her toes. She leaned forward and inspected the shiny plum polish she had put on her toenails earlier that afternoon while Logan was napping. She had never painted her toes before in her life; truth be told, she rarely even bothered with her fingernails. But she had come across the polish shoved into the back of a bathroom drawer and decided to give it a whirl. Satisfied with the results, she redirected her scrutiny to her fingernails, also newly manicured.

Scott shifted in the wicker chair and rearranged Logan on his lap. The baby cooed softly, snuggled closer and insinuated one clenched fist into his open mouth. Scott snagged his glass of iced tea and took a healthy swallow. "Jen, I can never thank you enough for taking care of this little guy while Alexa is away. I have no idea what I would have done without you."

"You know I'm happy to do it. I was at loose ends anyway. Since I didn't score a teaching job this year, I'm footloose and fancy-free. I'll be here as long as you need me."

Scott sighed, his exhalation sounding far less content than his son's. "My guess, it will be anywhere from forty-five to sixty days. At least, that's what has been indicated."

"Wow, seems like a long time." She drew her knees up, wrapped her arms around her shins and parked her chin on her shoulder. Jennifer fixed her eyes on his, which were the identical gray-blue shade as hers. "You know, we've been kind of like ships passing in the night since I got here. We've never had the time to really talk. So, are you going to give me the straight skinny on Alexa, or am I supposed to buy that ridiculous debutante vacation story her parents are cranking out to whoever will listen? I know she went to the hospital the first night. I know she's sick—care to elaborate?"

He looked down at his hand, now cupping Logan's right ankle and foot, then over at his sister. "Did you realize she was bulimic?"

"Yep." She offered him a curt nod. "I guessed it a while back."

He blinked, startled by her rapid reply. "How?"

"Remember, I just graduated from college. You spend enough time there these days and you know about this stuff. Anorexia is easy because the girls look like the walking dead. With bulimia, it's harder to tell, but just take a stroll through the girl's dorm sometime." At his confused look, she explained, "Vomiting. You hear it in the dorm bathrooms; even when they try hard to hide it, the sound echoes a lot. It's really pretty disgusting."

Though I never saw or heard Alexa throwing up, there were other things. Like the way she always got up and left the table immediately after eating. So many girls do that; I guess they want to get to the bathroom right away before the food gets digested. I also noticed Alexa's hands. You know, they are so beautiful, but her fingers were kind of bruised and scraped. That happens a lot when girls stick their fingers down their throats."

He grimaced. "Boy, for the longest time, I never had a clue." A wry, humorless laugh accompanied his confession. "Guess the husband is always the last to know."

"How could you have known?"

Eyes closed, he threw his head back, massaged the base of his neck. The weak light spilling across his familiar features caused him to look far older than his years. "I just should have; I should have been more attentive, more aware, more…something."

She scowled at her brother. "You know what? You're wrong." Anger crackled in her voice. "From what I could tell, Alexa did an amazing job of hiding it. There's no way on God's green earth you could have known. It even took me a while to catch on."

"But…"

"But nothing," she shot back, every syllable punctuated by a blend of impatience and aggravation. "It really chaps my hide to see someone blame themselves for something that wasn't their fault, especially you. Scott, you have always been a good husband and a wonderful father. So quit with the blame thing because it really ticks me off."

He burst out laughing. "By God, I'd forgotten how feisty my little sister could be."

She joined in the laughter, just to relieve the tension. Eventually, she asked, "So was it just the bulimia, or is it other stuff with Alexa?"

"For a long time it was the bulimia and we were getting help for that. What broke the camel's back was…" He paused. Only Alexa's parents knew about the most recent turn of events. It wasn't a question of trust; he trusted Jen implicitly. It had to do with saying it. In his exhausted mind, he somehow equated saying the words with making the entire nightmare real. It was foolish, he knew. Right this minute his wife was thousands of miles away in a treatment facility. How much more real could it get? He opened his mouth, tried to form the words, but his throat constricted.

Across the room, Jennifer waited as he collected his thoughts. It took all the discipline she could muster not to fidget or gnaw on her cuticles, a nervous childhood habit that had regrettably held over into adulthood. She caught her lower lip between her teeth, ensuring she would not speak before him. She must be patient, a virtue she had found in short supply throughout her life. She had waited days for this moment, ever since the first night she arrived after Scott's frantic phone call. Though only twenty-two, she thought she was too old to be truly shocked. But she was wrong. That night she had been aghast by her brother's appearance. This was a Scott she had never seen before: nervous and distraught; his face pale and drawn; he looked as if he'd recently lost weight. Clearly, whatever had been going on in this house had taken a severe toll on him. It was time for him to tell her all of it and release that burden from his mind and heart. Once he spoke the words, she knew they could no longer own him. The truth would become something they shared and dealt with together

He licked his lips and finally murmured, "She started…harming herself…cutting herself. Apparently, it's been going on a while. I should have told you the first night, but I needed to get to the hospital."

Stunned by his disclosure, Jennifer gasped audibly. Eyes wide, she clamped a hand over her mouth.

"I know, it is really very bad." He swallowed hard, his Adam's apple bobbing up and down. "And please don't ask me why she did it because I have no idea, no answer to give you."

"Poor Alexa. Something must be really wrong for her to do such a thing."

"Evidently," he concurred tonelessly, staring down at his feet.

Jennifer tucked her legs beneath her and leaned against the back of the chaise. Arm slung over a pillow, she rubbed the cotton duck fabric between a thumb and forefinger. "I wish I could have helped her in some way, but you know I've never felt close to Alexa. I always wanted to like her and be friends because of you, but couldn't figure out how."

"I know. Whenever the three of us were together, I saw how hard you tried."

"I've never been able to see what you see in her. In fact, when you told me you two were getting married, I…" She cut off her own words mid-sentence. Her face flushed with mortification at what had almost slipped out.

"You thought I was marrying her because she was beautiful and her family had money." Seeing Jennifer cringe, he quickly went on, "No, don't be embarrassed, I know that's what a lot of people were thinking. That's because no one really knows her. There is someone deep inside of Alexa that is so completely lovable, so precious. I got the chance to see that when we were dating, when we were away from Charlotte, and especially away from her family. Now I keep thinking I should never have taken the Bank of America job and made her live here. Her family...God help us all, talk about dysfunctional." From his position on the porch, Scott could look through the glass sliding door into their living room. From this vantage point, he could clearly make out the framed wedding photo of Alexa and him propped on the fireplace mantel. He did not need to be up close to appreciate what the photo displayed: the two of them, hands joined, regarding each other as though they were the only people on earth. Absolute adoration was carved into both of their expressions.

"For a while, when we were first married, everything was as good as anyone could hope for. Then she got pregnant..." He looked down at his son sleeping so peacefully in his lap. He brushed his fingertips through Logan's wispy blonde hair and traced the outline of his delicate shell-shaped ear. "We hadn't planned it at all, it was just one of those things. That's when it started to go bad with her. I don't know why, it just did. And it never got better. Though I was aware of her bulimia, I had no idea how severe it had gotten. I kept hoping, once our baby was born, Alexa would snap out of it, but she only got worse. It got to the point where she hardly ever went out of the house anymore. I did everything, everything I could think of to help her, but nothing worked. Then, she started hurting herself..." His fingers traveled on to caress the little face pressed into his ivory button-down shirt. The skin of Logan's pink cheek was soft as a cloud.

When he spoke next, his voice was hoarse with undisguised emotion. "How could it be, Jen? How could this wonderful little guy mean the world to me, yet for Alexa…I just don't get it. And what about our marriage? I thought she loved me as much as I love her and was equally committed. Weren't Logan and I enough; couldn't she be happy with us? I don't understand any of this. I…" His words trailed off into nothingness. A huge tear splashed onto the exposed skin of his wrist, followed by another on Logan's T-shirt, landing smack in the middle of Tigger's grinning orange-and-black-striped tiger face.

Jennifer got up and crossed to her brother in three brisk paces. She hitched a hip onto the arm of the chair and placed a hand on the back of his neck. As another tear plunked onto the baby's plastic diaper, Scott leaned over and laid his forehead on Jennifer's thigh and wept. He cried for the longest time, his body convulsing, shoulders shaking. Jennifer stroked the back of his neck and occasionally leaned over and bestowed a kiss on his head. Silent empathetic tears, quickly swept away by the back of one hand, zigzagged down her face. She knew this was exactly what he needed. She could almost see the strain, the long-pent-up emotion, melting from him. Beneath her hand, she could feel the tense muscles begin to relax. Yet, listening to his sobs, she felt her own heart might shatter in her chest. She kept an eye on Logan who slept on, haphazardly cradled in his father's arm. Gradually, the tears subsided; Scott remained where he was, spent. Jennifer massaged little circles on his back, still soothing and comforting.

More time passed as the siblings pondered their own thoughts and listened to the familiar night sounds. At some point, Logan managed to squeak out a tiny gurgling noise, despite the fact that his face was wedged somewhere between his father's side and the chair cushion. Scott eased back into a sitting position, taking care not to squish his son.

"I declare I have never seen anything like that in my life," Jennifer said. "Not only does that kid sleep like a stone, but he gets twisted into the craziest positions. And he's happy."

"It's true, he's a funny kid." Scott wiped his face with the back of a sleeve. "Oh no, look at your pants. They're soaked."

"Pants are amazing things—I bet they dry." Jennifer slid to the floor and sat near her brother's feet. "Scott, talk to me—please tell me all about it. You need to tell me and I need to hear."

They exchanged a look that captured all the deep affection they had felt for each other throughout the years. She gave him a "go ahead" gesture with the wave of one hand. And moments later, he did. Words poured out like precious stones from a velvet pouch. He spoke of the many emotions that had burdened him during recent months: confusion regarding the demons that plagued his wife;

frustration at not knowing how to help her; grief over lost closeness and intimacy; love for Alexa, though little was returned; fear that she might die; hopelessness as to what their future could possibly offer. Then he told her about the intense anger. Fueled by exasperation and impotence, this resentment was aimed directly at Alexa and her problems. The truth was he was mad as hell at her. But he had been unable to tell anyone about it because it seemed so mean-spirited. The whole situation was so bizarre. Who could possibly understand? What's more, he was so ashamed of his own feelings and felt so guilty for being mad at Alexa. After all, she wasn't well.

Jennifer listened attentively, asking the occasional question, offering the odd bit of advice when requested. She remained cross-legged on the floor, rising only once to extinguish the overhead light. The relentless smacking of insects against the bulb had driven her near to distraction. With the flip of a switch, the insects ceased their irritating quest, and the porch was instantly flooded with moonlight. The absence of artificial light created a heightened intimacy. Their eyes soon adjusted to the dark. Their faces glowed like carved alabaster statues in the lunar light. They talked on and on as the enormous silvery moon arced across the night sky. Later, when Scott told his sister goodnight, then placed his son in his crib, he felt as though a tremendous weight had, indeed, been removed from his shoulders. This night, he and his son shared a common trait: they both slept like stones.

As the Kent household retired, across town, a lone individual still kept the nighttime vigil. Grayson Stockton, sat alone on a patio chair staring up at the glittering sky. The stars, so alive with flickering fire; the moon, giant, flat, luminescent. He briefly considered the moon. Basically, it was nothing more than an inert mass floating around in the heavens. Its singular claim to fame was its talent for reflecting the sun's light. He thought about his life, his wife, their circle of friends. Who reflected whom? Or did they all reflect one another, possessing no individual light of their own? But then, the question must be begged: what was the origin of the light; where did it come from in the first place?

He smirked at his esoteric mental folly and took another swallow of scotch from the squat crystal glass. Jiggling the glass in his hand, ice cubes clattered against one another like large dice. How easy it was to stare into the sky and ponder inane questions; how difficult it was to focus on what was truly troubling him: his daughter, now so far away. He remembered Alexa as a little girl, bubbly, bright, full of spit and vinegar. He called her his little sunshine. For years, she was the brightest spot in his life. Then things began to change. As Alexa moved into adolescence, the molding, shaping process began; the subtle pressures from society, and less subtle pressure from her mother, slowly transformed her into the perfect young lady. By the time her debutante season arrived, the refining process was complete and all trace of his little sunshine had vanished.

No more true sparkle, no more genuine vivacity. Just a well mannered, socially correct, cookie-cutter deb draped in a magnificent white silk gown remained.

Gray swore softly and took another generous swallow of Glenlivit, then placed the glass on the flagstone terrace beneath his chair. All those years he had seen what was happening to Alexa, had watched the calculated transformation occurring right in front of him. Why hadn't he stopped it? Why hadn't he stepped in at some point and said enough is enough? He wasn't willing to sit by and watch his little girl become something she wasn't. Why had he done nothing? The answer was so simple and so pathetic: because it was easier, far easier to simply continue with life as he knew it, spending long hours in surgery, golfing on the weekends, attending social events. Now look where Alexa was—in a treatment facility suffering from bulimia, self-mutilation and God only knew what else. Look at where they all were—Alexa in a hospital, Jackson gone and Loren working hard to become the third casualty of this family. The only one who seemingly managed to remain unscathed at all times was Pamela.

And what of him? He raked his hand through his hair. Sure, on paper, he undoubtedly looked great: successful plastic surgeon, beautiful home and wife, member of the Myers Park Country Club. But, turn that paper over and look at the underside; the blank side that was as empty and void as his life. Gray spent his days performing as a conspirator to wealthy women. For vast sums, he helped them turn back the hands of time and strive for perfection on every level. Smaller noses, fuller lips, flatter stomachs, unlined skin. It had become nothing short of an assembly line to him, with patients serving as interchangeable parts. Beautiful women coming in, beautiful women going out. How many times had he heard people joke that Gray's waiting room was filled with the most stunningly gorgeous women in Charlotte. It was true; all his patients were darn near perfect, but not perfect enough. Lately, his medical practice had become a blur. It was so very far from what he had hoped to accomplish in his life. Gray Stockton, whose original ambition was to be an emergency room doctor, who wanted to help and heal when it was most needed. Then he had met and married Pamela while still in medical school. She had encouraged him to go into plastic surgery, claiming it was the field to be in. He had done it because, back then, he would have moved heaven and earth for her, his love was that great. What's more, since it was her family money that supported them, he felt a sense of obligation to do as she asked.

So now he spent his days doing something that held little interest for him, then returned home at night to a vacant marriage and a family in chaos. All for how things looked on paper. But there was no room for self-pity here because he had made choices, bad choices, but he had made them himself. Unlike Alexa, who had made precious few decisions for herself. Her friends, her clothes, where she attended school—everything had been dictated and somehow preordained as though carved on some sacred tablet. Only upon reflection could Gray now see how wrong it had all been for his daughter. Perhaps the only real decision Alexa had ever made on her own was to marry Scott. Gray had felt such optimism when the two had wed, hoping their deep love and commitment could somehow override her upbringing. Considering where she was right now, obviously, it hadn't.

Gray took one final look out at his moon-drenched back yard, then threw his head back and reconsidered the stars. He thought about Alexa, his little sunshine, living out in Arizona somewhere under these same stars. "I am so sorry, honey. I love you so much." He spoke the words to his daughter, wishing he could hold her and tell her everything he felt. As Gray Stockton rose from the chair and trudged inside, he desperately hoped for the opportunity to someday, somehow, rectify even a handful of the many wrongs that had been done in this family.

Chapter four

Kyla closed the leather-bound book and placed her clasped hands on its black cover. Preparing for her first meeting with Abby, now only minutes away, she had reviewed some of her favorite scriptures. She focused her attention on a hand-carved oak cross displayed on the wall across from her desk. "Please help me help her," she said to the unadorned symbol as if it were not a piece of wood at all, but the living God Himself. "Please give me wisdom, give me the right words to say to this child of yours. Please guide my actions and thoughts throughout this day and everyday. I love you and need you, Lord. Thank you." She sat quietly until, from the corner of one eye, she caught a glimpse of Abby coming down the hall toward her office. The girl wore baggy blue jeans, an oversized, faded-pink sweatshirt and tennis shoes. She walked with head bent, shoulders slumped. If despair had a name, it would be Abby.

Though Kyla's office with its dim lighting, warm colors and cozy furniture was designed to be nonthreatening, she suddenly decided to change the venue for their first official meeting as therapist and patient. She rose from her chair and went into the corridor just as Abby drew near. "It's a beautiful morning. I thought we might talk outside today. That okay?"

Abby nodded her agreement and the two headed for the door. Outside, they went down a set of wooden stairs and ambled along a short dirt path. Kyla set a very slow pace, and still the girl lagged behind. Whether this was due to her physical condition or emotional state, the therapist had no way of knowing. They stopped at a pair of gray granite boulders. Kyla loved this spot because it afforded a wide-angle view of the fenced pasture. Hiking her khaki maternity skirt up a little, she hitched her bottom onto the larger of the two rocks. The hard flat surface felt cool through her clothing, in opposition to the sun, which was warm on her arms and face. Following Kyla's cue, Abby took her place on the smaller rock.

Kyla smoothed out her skirt with one palm and crossed her feet at the ankle. "So, how's it going so far?"

"Fine." Abby spoke to her hands, which rested limply in her lap.

"And your roommate? Is she all right?"

"She's fine."

During her tenure at the ranch, Kyla had grown to detest the word *fine*. By definition, patients with eating disorders were so numb, so out of touch with their own emotions that *fine* along with the ever-popular *I don't know* proved to be the knee-jerk answers to virtually every question that called for a feeling response. Kyla knew she could ask this girl if she wanted to kiss a snake or marry a worm and the answer would probably be that same four-letter word. As soon as the two of them returned to her office, Kyla would give Abby a feeling sheet. Every new patient got one. It listed emotions, everything from happy and sad to angry and annoyed. Such a simple tool, yet it helped patients to identify and put an actual word to how they were feeling at any given time. Unfortunately, what the rest of the world did with such ease, eating-disordered patients found nearly impossible to do without the aid of a list. Kyla eagerly anticipated the day when the *fine* word would be stricken, or at least sharply reduced, from Abby's vocabulary. But for now, it was incumbent on Kyla to phrase questions in such a way that this word could be relied upon as little as possible.

Abby sat huddled on the rock, trying to appear even smaller than she was. Like so many anorexics, she undoubtedly thought if she just got small enough, no one would notice her and everyone would leave her alone. The sad truth was that Abby was almost to that point. This young girl was the picture of emaciation. No fat remained on her body, every bone stuck out, her cheeks were hollow, her big brown eyes sunken and rimmed by dark shadows. She looked skeletal, as if all that was needed was a brass hook protruding from the top of her skull so she could be dangled from the ceiling in an anatomy class. Severe malnutrition had caused her hair to thin dramatically and her sallow skin to dry and flake. Though her arms were concealed beneath the huge sweatshirt, Kyla guessed they were covered with baby-fine hair. This was yet another way the body tried to keep itself warm. From her position slightly above Abby, Kyla could easily observe the bluish-purple shade of the girl's exposed fingers, a clear sign of acrocyanosis. Abby's body was struggling to stay alive by drastically slowing her metabolism. Kyla winced, contemplating how very cold Abby must be. Recent lab reports revealed her resting heart rate was a mere thirty-eight beats a minute, her blood pressure was so low it hardly registered and her body temperature was only ninety-five degrees. Nothing in Abby's labs even approached normality. No wonder she was turning blue.

"Look." Kyla pointed out to the pasture, where several horses had just been turned out after a morning ride. "I was hoping we'd see him."

Abby followed the trajectory of the index finger. "See who?"

"Sultan. He's one of my favorites. Watch him; he's great."

The magnificent chestnut gelding, his sleek coat gleaming bright as a newly minted copper penny in the morning sun, pranced out into the open field and dropped his nose to the ground. He sniffed, then pawed the patchy grass with one hoof. Appearing dissatisfied, he gazed around, then trotted to another less-rocky area and followed the same ritual.

Abby sat up a little straighter, watching. "What's he doing?"

"I call it a horse hunt and peck. He's trying to find just the right spot."

"For what?"

"Just watch."

Sultan angled a couple of feet to the right, sniffed, pawed, then gradually dropped to his knees. Lowering one shoulder to the ground, he slowly rolled onto his right side, then fully onto his back, all four curled legs held aloft. Momentarily still, he looked like a giant dead bug. A short-lived vision, though, for he began wiggling his bulky body from side to side, legs flailing, loud snorting sounds emanating from his upside-down head. He paused, took in a deep breath, blew it out in a prolonged groan, then recommenced thrashing about. Soon, the lower half of his body stopped its gyrations and he concentrated on the upper part, slowly shimmying his shoulders on the ground, his head rolling back and forth.

"He's scratching his back," Kyla explained. "Doesn't he look happy?"

Abby nodded as Sultan snorted one final time, rocked over onto his side and clamored to a standing position.

Feet firmly planted on the ground, he shook his enormous body with great enthusiasm, once, twice, and then again. Tufts of grass and clumps of dirt flew everywhere. He flicked his reddish tail onto his rump and random bits of debris fell to the ground. In a matter of seconds, the copper coat that had shone so brilliantly in the sun was gone, now effectively concealed beneath a thick carpet of dust. He tossed his mane, tilted his head and sampled the light breeze coming out of the west with a huge intake of breath.

"Hey Sultan." The chestnut's pricked ears locked onto Kyla's voice like twin radar units. He swung his head in their direction. Tail swishing, he regarded the two through deep brown, soulful eyes.

Kyla scooted forward until her feet touched the ground. "Do you like horses?"

"I don't know. I've never been around them."

"Here, let's see if he'll come over." Kyla strolled to the split-rail fence. She took a Ziploc bag out of her pocket and shook it in Sultan's direction. Used to this familiar routine, he knew exactly what the bag contained. Without hesitation, he loped across the open space and hung his massive head over the top rail of the fence. Though Abby had accompanied Kyla, when confronted by the horse, she quickly faded back a few paces.

Kyla had anticipated this reaction. Even at their initial meeting, Abby had struck her as a girl who was frightened of many things, probably most things. Nothing she had witnessed thus far had altered her initial impression. "He's a big one. Does he scare you?"

"Yes." Her timid response was barely audible, as if to speak in a voice even one decibel louder might cause the horse to leap the fence and trample her to bits. "But I like him."

"Good. And don't worry, you'll get used to these guys in no time." Impatiently, Sultan nosed the plastic bag and nibbled at Kyla's fingers with his soft probing lips. "Okay, okay," she said to the horse and poured a handful of flaky oats onto her flat palm. He ate greedily, large yellow teeth prominently displayed, then bumped her hand wanting more. "Sorry bud, that's it for today." She looked back over her shoulder at Abby. "Unless you'd like to give him some?"

The girl shook her head, clearly still frightened. Kyla stepped away, clamped the bag under one arm and dusted her hands off on her skirt. Sultan nickered softly, then extended his neck and nuzzled her shoulder, angling toward the end of her French braid. She pushed his head away and told him, "You know you can't have that." If it was possible for a horse to appear sheepish, Sultan did. "For some reason, he always thinks the little elastic scrunchy on my braid is edible. Who can figure it," she commented to Abby as they returned to their seats on the boulders.

Realizing no more treats were forthcoming, the horse sulked for a while then trotted over to where the other horses stood grazing. Kyla decided the time had come for serious talk. "So Abby, why are you here?"

Several moments passed before she answered and, as before, her words were directed toward her hands. "My parents think I'm sick."

"Do you think you are?"

"I don't know."

"When did you start losing weight?" Kyla waited patiently for the answer. When she first started working with eating-disordered adolescents, the waiting had proved challenging. She would offer little verbal prompts and encouragements, trying to get them to answer questions at a quicker pace. It never worked. The girls wouldn't respond faster because they couldn't. Malnutrition caused them to think very slowly. The protracted amount of time it took them to synthesize information, then construct a suitable response, made normal interaction impossible. The psychologists had a fancy term for it, psychomotor retardation, but in Kyla's everyday world it simply translated into waiting. So she waited.

"I don't know, a couple of years ago."

"Why did you want to?"

Abby shrugged her narrow shoulders. "I was fat."

Kyla combed several strands of hair back into her braid with her fingers. "What made you think that?"

Abby dug the toe of one tennis shoe into the soft dirt. "I don't know, I just was."

"Did other people think that, too, like your family or kids at school?"

She stiffened slightly. "No."

"So you were the only one."

"Uh-huh. But I was fat. It was awful. I hated it. I was getting all big and gross."

Kyla decided to take another tack. "Abby, when was the last time you actually felt good, you know, happy, like Sultan?"

The girl raised her bowed head and looked out to the pasture searching for the horse. She located him at the far side of the field peacefully cropping grass. "I can't remember ever being that happy. Maybe when I was a baby, but I don't know." The simple words sounded infinitely sad.

Kyla modulated her tone, wanting to appear as understanding and nonconfrontational as possible. "Abby, you realize that while you're here you will be eating more normally and putting on some weight?" When no verbal response was forthcoming, she continued. "How do you feel about that? And before you say you don't know, please try to think about it. I know it's really hard. We're talking about eating real food and gaining weight. When you think about doing that, what feeling or feelings come to mind?"

In a voice hardly more than a whisper, she finally said, "Scared."

"Good. Thank you. That helps me a lot. You know what? Most girls say they are scared."

"They do?" Abby remained focused on Sultan. When she did not retreat to her former hunched position, Kyla felt encouraged.

"Sure. A lot are angry as well. Do you feel angry?"

"I don't know. I feel…" Kyla waited, hoping to hear more. "I feel…I'm confused, I can't think. I want to go home. I miss my little sister and my cat." She wrapped her frail arms around her bony body, as though trying to comfort herself.

"I know, I know you don't want to be here. No one does, except maybe me. I want to be here right now with you."

For the first time that day, Abby looked over at her therapist. "You do? Why?"

"Because I want to help you and I think I can. While you're here we'll spend a lot of time together looking at your life. We'll talk about your family, your past and your feelings. When you've eaten a little, you will be less confused and it will be easier for you to think and understand things, I promise. Just a little nourishment will make a world of difference. In fact, you will be seeing your dietitian this afternoon. I've already talked to her. She's going to ask if you're willing to have a nasal gastric tube."

Alarm swept across Abby's gaunt face. Her huge brown eyes took on a deer-caught-in-the-headlights look. "You mean that plastic tube thing I've seen sticking out of some of the girls' noses? Why?"

"Because we really need to get your body a little healthier and that means nourishment. Sometimes having to eat that much food is too overwhelming, too difficult after not eating for so long. With the tube we can feed you at night while you're sleeping. It's much easier."

"Does it hurt?"

"I guess it feels a little funny in the beginning, but after a while most girls say they don't even notice it at all."

"Will it make me fat?"

"Goodness no. It will help you get healthier. The dietician will tell you all about how it works and the calories involved."

Abby flung one hand out in the general direction of the horses. "What's happening over there?"

Kyla shifted her attention to the opposite side of the corral and saw an impromptu game was underway. She smiled at the equine antics. "They're fooling around, having fun. Horses play games with each other, just like little kids. You'll notice Sultan, that little troublemaker, is right in the middle of it." They watched as Sultan stretched out his long neck and nipped a creamy-gold palomino on a hind leg. Provoked, the mare whirled around and lunged toward the much larger horse. Dust billowed in large puffs around her dancing feet. With the finesse of a matador tossing a red cape, Sultan ducked the charge, then darted after the mare. The two streaked across the field, manes and tails whipping in the morning air. Their hooves pounded the ground, causing walnut-sized dirt clods to fly in every direction. They ran with complete abandon, heads held high as though that moment in time had been created exclusively for their pleasure. As they galloped from view, Kyla asked, "Aren't they beautiful?"

"Uh-huh. They seem so…"

"Free?" The girl nodded and Kyla touched her lightly on the shoulder. "Someday, if you really want it, you can be just as free as they are. Right now you're a prisoner of your eating disorder, but together we can change that. It's as if for the past couple of years, you've been walking down a road all by yourself. That can be pretty lonely. But now, we're walking together. You and I are a team and we're going to work this thing out together. Sound all right to you?"

"Maybe, I don't know. I'm still worried about that tube thing."

Kyla stood, dusted off the back of her skirt with one hand. "Talk with the dietician. If you want me to come, I will. If you want me to be with you when they put it in, I can do that, too. Whatever you need, we'll do it together. Okay?"

Abby got to her feet. Obviously overcome by dizziness, she wobbled slightly, then steadied herself. "I guess."

"Now, let's go in and get you warmed up." Once again, Kyla moved slowly along the path, but this time, Abby walked closer to her side.

It was the smell that got to Mary Cardoza the most. The smell of industrial-strength cleaner, mixed with bodily fluids, mixed with aging and decaying flesh, mixed with Lord only knew what else. Each day when she returned home in the afternoon or evening, she could smell the odor in her clothes, taste it in her mouth. She could even smell it in her nightmares. Extra spritzes of Shalimar behind her ears and on both wrists failed to mask it. It wasn't as if Mary was some sort of neophyte to nasty odors. After all, she had been exposed to plenty throughout her forty-four years. Rearing Abby and Sara and owning countless stray cats had placed her on the receiving end of many challenging olfactory experiences, everything from dirty diapers and flu-inspired vomiting to nasty fur balls and rank litter boxes. But somehow this was different and far worse. Perhaps it was because she was forced to equate this hideous nursing home stench with her cherished father, who deserved so much better than this. After all his years on the bench, the thousands of hours he selflessly devoted to public service; to say nothing of being the best father a daughter could ever have hoped for, Judge Earl Shwimmer deserved better than to be lying in this bed, in this room, in this nursing home…with that smell.

Seated next to his bed Mary massaged her throbbing temples, remembering the day she had received the call while volunteering in the library at Abby's school. The judge had collapsed while speaking at a Lion's Club meeting. Paramedics had taken him directly to the hospital. The diagnosis had been as swift as it had been certain: a massive stroke in the middle cerebral artery on the left side of his brain. The anterior or frontal portion of the left hemisphere had also been involved. What did that mean in real terms? Primarily it meant paralysis of his right side and severely impaired speech. Though he could understand what was being said to him, he had difficulty responding in turn. Not only did he suffer an inability to find words, it was equally arduous for him to articulate his subsequent thoughts. The paralysis meant he was relegated to a wheel-chair. Though these ramifications of the stroke were undoubtedly the most difficult for him to endure, what Mary found most troubling were the moods.

The neurologists had explained that the damage to the front of the brain caused many patients to manifest more anger, frustration and depression than most stroke victims. This was certainly the case with him, for now her father was prone to fits of rage over the smallest things. Though she knew it wasn't his fault, his fury upset her all the same. A host of anti-depressants had been tried, with few positive results. Her father had remained in the hospital for several weeks before being moved. Though Mary had done her research and located the best possible facility in Santa Rosa, it was still a nursing home, a place where her father simply did not belong.

Now, slouching in the uncomfortable chair, Mary watched her father napping. His face, in repose, looked ancient, the jaw slack, the crêpey skin as gray as the sparse wisps of hair plastered to his scalp. The harsh fluorescent lighting caused his face to appear cadaverous. It was all Mary could do not to avert her gaze from that beloved visage that used to look upon her with such affection. Beneath the folded-back sheet, his withered body appeared shrunken and frail. His left arm and liver-spotted hand, now the only functioning appendage, lay limply on the lavender coverlet. It too, looked fragile and bony. Its diminished mass caused the ropey veins snaking across the top of the wrinkled hand to appear enormous, almost grotesque.

Mary looked away in an effort to conjure from her youth a more positive image of that precious hand. She recalled being a little girl, perhaps Sara's age, walking downtown with her daddy. The two had strolled from store to store, running errands and visiting with friends. Everyone in the whole town loved and respected the judge. He had bought her a banana split and they had laughed for hours. They held hands the entire day. With her tiny hand in his large one, she always felt safe and protected; nothing and no one could ever hurt her as long as she was with her daddy. A tear escaped from one eye at the sweet memory. She swiped it away instantly with the back of a knuckle. She would not let him see her crying; she had done much too much of that lately. He deserved to see a bright, happy daughter when he awoke, not a miserable wretch.

Across the room, a small window looked out onto the grassy yard surrounding the nursing home. Mary could just make out the outline of a lone sparrow perched on the branch of a rather tall tree. Watching, she could tell the brownish-tan creature was singing its heart out, warbling with all its might on this brisk and blustery fall day. Yet Mary could hear nothing of its joyous song, for the window was sealed shut. All she heard was the blowing air from the vent in the corner as it continuously recirculated stale air throughout the building.

Acknowledging the outside world had nothing to offer her, Mary dismissed it altogether. She slipped off her shoes and shuffled her stocking feet back and forth on the cool linoleum floor. She plucked pieces of lint and random cat hairs off the stiff fabric of her modest knee-length navy blue skirt and struggled to think of something happy to focus on. Nothing came to mind. Sitting alone, head hung, shoulders hunched, Mary knew she looked defeated. Unfortunately she felt no better than she looked.

Clair Whitlock, the day nurse, stuck her head in the door. "So you are here?"

Mary looked up and managed to manufacture a smile. "I came early today."

Clair tilted her head to one side and smiled at Mary. She was always smiling, always displaying a huge toothy grin; Mary thought she seemed to have an inordinate number of sparkling white teeth, to say nothing of a tremendous amount of hair. Clair must have had three-dozen black corn rows plaited on her head, maybe more. Mary wished she could count all of those braids, then maybe loosen them one by one and braid them again. Anything, anything at all that could provide some relief from focusing on her father. Clair, still smiling, cut through Mary's idle musings. "I was just about to bring in lunch. Can I get you anything?"

Mary shook her head. "No thanks, I'm fine."

The nurse disappeared and returned moments later trundling a stainless-steel cart stacked high with food trays. Though the cart was large, Clair was by far the larger of the two. Mary had often pondered just how much she must weigh—three hundred pounds would be within the realm of possibility. Yet, with the exception of breathing quite heavily, Clair got around with ease and never seemed put off by her bulk. "Here we go, lunch." With one enormous, meaty arm she hoisted the green plastic tray with its many covered dishes onto the bedside table. "Sure I can't get you something, Hon? Maybe a cold drink?"

"No, really, I won't be staying long, but thanks anyway," Mary said as the other woman managed to turn the cart around in the confined space and wheel it out the door, her white nurses shoes making squeegee sounds on the slick floor. The brief exchange, though spoken in low tones, caused her father to stir. He opened his eyes and glanced around the room, perplexed. He often woke like this, not knowing where he was.

Mary swiftly pinched both cheeks, hoping to infuse some much-needed color into her pasty complexion. She finger-combed her lank brown hair, but was stymied by snarls. Her father looked her way, a puzzled expression still defining his lackluster features. "Hi Daddy, have a nice nap?" His eyes cleared, then turned dull again, once he realized where he was. He let out a harsh breath. "Look, Clair brought lunch." Reaching over, Mary began removing covers from the plastic dishes. The welcome aroma of a hot chicken casserole wafted up from the plate. Fully awake now, her father grunted and pounded his good hand on the bedrail. Mary, determined to be as cheerful as he was cantankerous, asked, "Want to sit up?" At his nod, she depressed a nearby button that elevated the head of the bed. He grunted again and lunged his hand toward the tray. Mary handed him the fork and edged the table a little closer.

Though it always proved a messy affair, he insisted on feeding himself, an activity Mary never begrudged him since there were so few things he could accomplish on his own. As he made his way through the hot meal, Mary tried not to notice the pronounced droop on the right side of his face or the spastic condition of the right side of his body. Instead, she kept up a lively chatter about things at home, the girls, the weather, pretty much anything she could think of. She and Jim had decided not to tell him about Abby. It would be too difficult for him to comprehend and she didn't want to get him unduly upset. So occasionally, she told a little white lie about how well Abby was doing in school or what activities she was participating in, just to keep him from getting suspicious. She asked God every day to forgive her for the prevarication, knowing it was a sin. Occasionally, she wondered if she even needed to keep up the pretense. He never inquired about anything or anyone. He never once asked about her sister or why she hadn't been by to see him. Mary guessed that was actually a blessing, since questions concerning Ruth would probably have necessitated additional lies.

He finished eating about the same time she ran out of things to say. She cleaned his face and hands with a damp towel and nudged the tray away. He spoke to Mary and gestured toward the bedside table. His words were garbled, unintelligible. But she interpreted without him having to repeat. She knew exactly what he wanted, for it was always the same thing. It was a battle she had waged and it was a battle she had lost. Gritting her teeth, she picked up the cellophane-wrapped cigarette pack and tamped one into her palm. She inserted the nonfiltered cigarette between his fingers and struck a match. He inhaled deeply and closed his eyes, clearly savoring the experience. Mary could almost picture the filthy smoke blackening his lungs, destroying healthy tissue, seeping carcinogens into his bloodstream, hardening arteries and creating a perfect environment for a second stroke, the one that would surely kill him.

Angry, though never allowing it to show in her expression, she flopped back into her chair and scooted it away from the bed. She had never smoked in her life and found the habit loathsome. During his years as a smoker, she always made Jim stand outside on the porch when having a cigarette. Yet, such was her love for her father that she would sit with him in this small, poorly ventilated room day after day while he continued to pay homage to the god of nicotine.

For the remainder of their time together, Mary focused on shaping her father's speech. She would throw out easy questions that required little thought in terms of a reply. When he answered, she worked to help him formulate the syllables, then the entire word. He was getting better, but the process was painfully slow, primarily due to his emotional state. Mary could only work with him a little while each day, fifteen minutes at the most, before she would see that look in his eye. It meant she had better stop right away, or risk one of his rages. She would quit the exercise immediately. Nothing was worth being on the receiving end of such fury.

Two hours later, Mary sat alone in the hushed church. Because Sara had woken that day with the sniffles, she had missed morning mass. The 5:30 service had just concluded and those in attendance had left, including Father Russell. Mary had come hoping the familiar words and ancient rituals would provide much-needed comfort to her severely taxed mind and troubled spirit. She had stood, sat and knelt at all the right times, she had recited the correct responses when required, but still, peace remained elusive. Alone now, Mary wanted desperately to pray, but found she couldn't. Her rosary beads dangled uselessly from limp fingers; the words she had routinely repeated for years and years would not come. She felt utterly bereft. The rosary slipped from her fingertips and plopped silently to the carpeted kneeler. Mary did not pick it up. Instead, she clasped her hands loosely in her lap and gave her weary eyelids permission to close.

She concentrated hard on the tranquil atmosphere: the lovely fragrance of candle wax and highly polished wood tinged by a hint of dust; the precious silence; the peace. Then she shifted her attention inward. She concentrated on her breathing, drawing the air in slowly, feeling her lungs expand, then release. She grew aware of her heart beating methodically in her chest, forcing life-giving blood around her body. She felt the skin of her feet press against her navy blue leather pumps and the waistband of her skirt pinch marginally at the flesh just below her ribs. She felt the individual vertebrae of her spine bump against the hard wood of the pew. But the moment her conscious mind ceased focusing on her physical body, Mary was overwhelmed anew by emotional pain. The truth was, she had never felt such misery in her life, not even as a young girl when her mother had died. Perhaps it was because Daddy had explained to her and Ruth that Mommy, after years of being an invalid, had gone home to be with God. Mary hadn't even experienced such anguish when time after time she had failed to conceive or miscarried the desperately wanted babies. But now, she had no father to provide reassuring words and one of the two children God had allowed her to keep was far from home in a treatment facility.

For the millionth time, Mary posed the unanswered questions: Why was God punishing her? Why was His wrath directed at her? What had she done that was so bad that she deserved such pain? Throughout her life, Mary had always tried to be good, follow the rules and do everything right. Hadn't she always attended church, taught Sunday school and given faithfully? Hadn't she tried to be a woman of good character, a loving wife, a good mother? Then why? Suffering through her father's stroke had been hard enough, especially since she was the only family member involved. Her sister had let her down, again, refusing to come to Santa Rosa even once to help. Mary had never understood Ruth's long-held enmity toward their father. Why couldn't she see how good Daddy had been throughout their lives? It hadn't been easy for him, taking care of a sickly wife and rearing two daughters. He had been the best. Yet, when she turned eighteen, Ruth couldn't get out of the house fast enough. And she never looked back, not even when Daddy went to the hospital and Mary could have used some help.

Wrapping her arms around her body, Mary hugged herself. She opened her eyes and peered at the intricate stained glass mural at the front of the cavernous building. The rays of the setting sun brought the darkly hued pictures of biblical saints to life and cast jewel-tone shadows onto the floor below. She lowered her gaze to rest on the sculpture she had always treasured. It was Mary, the Blessed Mother, cradling Jesus in her arms. Head bent, she looked down on her dead son. Unnoticed, tears of grief and bewilderment streamed down Mary's own face. The Blessed Virgin knew the pain of loving a dying child. Then why didn't she help Mary, whose daughter was so close to death? She had lit dozens of candles, prayed countless prayers asking Mother Mary to intercede on Abby's behalf, seemingly, to no avail. "Why won't you help me?" she pleaded aloud in the vacant church, feeling her chest tighten. But the marble Madonna just continued to stare silently at the marble Messiah.

Mary took in a ragged breath and retrieved her beads. Once again, she tried to pray for her daughter. Again, words eluded her. She struggled to picture Abby in Arizona, but having never seen the ranch, she could create no image. She balled her right hand into a fist and brought it to her mouth. She bit down hard on her knuckles; the wooden beads clacked together, the simple crucifix swung like a miniature trapeze. Abby, her daughter, in an eating disorder facility, diagnosed with anorexia nervosa. But how, how had it happened? Mary had watched plenty of entertainment shows on TV and had seen the tabloid headlines at the grocery checkout counter. She knew about eating disorders. They were like nervous breakdowns and medication addictions; they happened to the rich and famous, Hollywood stars, and fashion models, not small-town girls. And even if they did, it would surely be the prom queen or the head cheerleader, not a quiet, shy girl like her Abby. Even the therapist had characterized Abby as being behaviorally compliant, which was just a fancy way of saying she was a good girl.

A soft purring sound came from Mary's purse on the floor. She reached down and fished out the cell phone Jim had given her for Christmas last year. She had never wanted the darn thing, but it made him feel better knowing she had it. She flipped it open, spoke for less than a minute, then dropped it back into the purse. It had been Jim, reminding her of their appointment with the realtor in twenty minutes. She had forgotten. On purpose? Probably. She and Jim were signing the closing papers on her father's home, which had finally sold. Though they had waited for months after the stroke to place the house on the market, eventually they had been forced to post a "For Sale" sign, due to the enormous cost of the nursing home. Fresh tears coursed down Mary's face as she realized the magnitude and widespread implications of this sale. An entire piece of her life and that of her family would be over, gone for good.

She and Ruth had grown up in that house, Abby had played there as a little girl, as had, to a lesser degree, Sara. Now it would no longer be theirs, but belong to another family altogether, strangers. Never again would Mary breeze through that front door without even bothering to knock, rummage around in the refrigerator or kitchen cabinets for a snack, or clip flowers from the backyard garden for a fragrant bouquet. In addition, it meant her father was never, ever coming home. Though Mary had known this in her mind, the message hadn't quite filtered down yet to her heart. The moment she and Jim signed those papers, the reality of his situation could no longer be avoided. Daddy was never coming home; he would remain in the nursing home forever, until the day he died.

Leaning forward, Mary crossed her arms on the back of the pew in front of her. Pain radiated in her chest; her heart beat wildly, flip-flopping about like a fish kept too long out of water. She dropped her head onto her folded arms, now so overwhelmed by sorrow, exhaustion and pain, she almost wished she could die herself, just to make it all stop.

Chapter five

Robin stormed into Tom's office for their first meeting and flopped into a wingback chair. She carried the patient notebook that was given to all adolescents. She hooked a leg over the padded arm and tossed the binder on the floor. She glowered at the therapist. Tom smiled back. As her eyes raked the office, he quickly evaluated her emotional state. Robin's entire demeanor could be summed up in one word: rage. Seething anger radiated from her like heat from a high-wattage lightbulb. Not for the first time, he wondered what event or series of events in her relatively short life had caused her to feel such anger.

Her gaze eventually came to rest on the bookshelf. "So what's all that weird junk you have next to those books?"

"Most are things given to me from patients."

She thought about it, then smirked. "They give you gifts? What, trying to buy their way out of here?"

He shook his head slowly. "No, most of the time it just has to do with forgetting. Either they don't want me to forget them, or they want to forget their eating disorder and leave it behind. Like this mask..." Tom retrieved an object and held it aloft for her to see. It was a hideous flaming-red face with swirling black snakes poking their fanged mouths out from the top of the head.

"Gross."

"It is gross. One girl made this in art therapy. It represents her eating disorder. Notice how the mouth is sewn shut and the eyes are gouged out. That's because her anorexia kept her from speaking the truth and seeing things clearly."

"That's stupid." Robin rolled her eyes and clamped her forearms across her chest. The fingernails of both hands dug into the bare flesh of her upper arms. "I think therapy is totally a waste of time. So don't expect any presents from me—ever."

"We'll see." Tom replaced the mask on the shelf, then settled back in his office chair. His strategy had always been to remain relaxed during the initial session, regardless of how obstinately or belligerently a patient behaved. Remaining sedate had never proved too difficult, since most patients spoke so slowly and their reaction time was so stunted. He idly wondered if that was one of the reasons Robin utilized rage so frequently; perhaps it helped her to not only maintain control but to feel more normal.

"So, I suppose Snow White was a gift?" Her tone mocking, she tossed a hand in the direction of the window. "Let me guess…she was leaving behind her virginity?"

Tom considered the colorful fairy-tale figurines lined up on the window sill. Snow White, in her trademark dark blue and canary-yellow frock, headed up the line, a bluebird perched on one outstretched hand. She stood gazing back at her seven diminutive cohorts. Tom rearranged Dopey a bit, so his goofy grin, plump cheeks and flapping ears faced out toward the room. "Actually she and the dwarfs came from a patient's father. Since we are always talking about feelings here, he thought these guys might come in handy. Happy, Sleepy, Grumpy…so which one are you today?"

Robin regarded the little glass characters, her foot swinging back and forth like a manic pendulum. "Do you have a ticked-off and want-to-be-out-of-here dwarf?"

"Afraid not."

"Then shucks, I can't play."

"Robin, that's the second time in fewer than five minutes you've mentioned being out of here."

She issued a small snort. "Well, duh. Is that like some huge surprise?"

"No. But you do understand there's nothing you can do about it, right?"

She flipped her light brown hair over one shoulder with the back of her hand. Tom was certain the action was designed to reflect the same bravado displayed in her words. "I could run away. You know, it's not like I'm chained down or anything."

"And where would that get you? First, you'd be lost out there in the desert all alone, then we'd send people out to find you. Your parents would be called back so we could process the behavior together. But they would not take you home. You'd remain here, with even fewer privileges than you have now."

She grunted in disgust. "Is that even possible?"

"Sure. Look, I'm just putting this out on the table because the faster you realize you're in a no-win situation, the better. Like it or not, you're seventeen years old and your parents have legal guardianship over you. You are a minor and they are calling the shots. If they want you here, you're here, regardless of how you feel about it."

Robin leaped to her feet and began pacing around the small office like a caged animal. "This is so lame. I hate this," she hissed. Only now, with her standing once again, did the therapist have a real opportunity to see how she was dressed. As with all things—word choice, eye contact, body language—what a patient wore said a lot. Today, Robin was in baggy white shorts that hung off her bony hips and a clingy cranberry-colored shirt with spaghetti straps. Some type of silver beaded choker was slung around her narrow neck, accentuating her protruding collarbone. The shirt fit so tightly it was possible to count every smooth rib. Her white bra straps were visible. Though displaying bra straps was certainly the fashion these days, Tom had absolutely no idea why anyone would find that look attractive. The fact that Robin showed more skin than what was concealed beneath clothing suggested she was quite proud of her severely underweight body. Especially considering how cold she must be; clearly, when it came down to which mattered most, comfort or appearance, Robin chose the latter.

Tom had discovered that patients frequently fell into one of two categories: either they wore huge clothing in an effort to disguise a skeletal appearance, or they wore as little as possible, trying to garner attention. Many girls would dress like Robin, because they thought they looked good, even sexy. This amazed him. Anyone in the real world would take one look at this painfully skinny girl and think that she should be in the hospital. And they would be right.

Tom noticed she was still digging her nails into her skin as she stomped back and forth. If she kept that up, blood would soon be trickling down her arms. Robin was working her way to a major meltdown. He stood up. "Come on, let's take a walk." Knowing she would object to anything he suggested, he gave her no opportunity to respond. Tom flung open the door and walked out, forcing her to follow.

They went along a narrow gravel path in a slow, measured gait. He said nothing, wanting to give her time to settle down a bit. Control was clearly important to her; he would let her decide when to speak. And eventually, she did. "I hate this," she repeated the earlier claim.

"I know," he acknowledged, keeping his voice low and level. Though he wanted to validate her feelings, he remained unwilling to get into a spitting match with her.

They walked on toward the stables, the silence of the late afternoon punctuated by the crunch of their shoes on the gravel. Tom savored the dry air, redolent with the distinct aromas of desert vegetation. The weather was unusually mild for this season. When the time seemed right, he ventured, "So, is Tucson like this, or is it different?"

"Different."

"How?"

"Hotter."

Tom kept his tone steady. "Are there hills and trees like we have here?"

Robin gave a labored sigh. "No."

Forced to concede that that particular topic was dead in the water, Tom searched for another approach as Robin smoldered. His goal was simply to get her talking, to get her started on a dialogue with him. A therapeutic relationship started with basic interaction, then progressed from that point. He looked up at the huge expanse of blue sky above, praying for conversational inspiration. Before a new topic could be found, the scruffy bushes far off to the right of the path began to rustle and shake. The two stopped in their tracks. Suddenly, a baby jack rabbit bounded lightning-fast out of the bushes. Pebbles and bits of dirt scattered in every direction. It leaped in a tremendous arc across the path only five or six feet in front of them, then came to an abrupt stop and hunkered down near an overgrown desert shrub.

"Wow!" For once, Robin forgot to be angry and sullen. "Did you see how high he jumped?"

"Yeah." Tom shaded his eyes with one hand and squinted into the nearby foliage, trying to see what had spooked the little animal. "I wonder what scared him. Do you see anything?"

She scanned the surrounding area. "No."

Everything remained silent, nothing stirred. They drew nearer and bent toward the bunny, which was roughly the size of a child's tennis shoe. His disproportionately long, floppy ears were flattened on his back; his front paws, no bigger than miniature asparagus stalks, were clamped together, tucked beneath his tiny chin. The bunny's enormous black eyes were open wide, fixed with a glassy stare.

Tom couldn't help but smile as he whispered, "Isn't God amazing?"

"God?" Robin whispered back, clearly baffled by the question.

"Yes. Just look at that little creature, look at how his speckled brown fur blends in with the ground. He is completely disguised. Honestly, if it wasn't for that twitching nose, would you have seen him, even knowing he was there?"

"No, but what has that got to do with God?" she asked, her tone now peevish.

"God created that little guy, didn't He?"

She shrugged, indifferent. "I don't know. I've never thought about it."

They resumed walking. Tom, unwilling to let go of the newfound rapport, however fragile, asked, "Do you have any pets?"

"We have a golden retriever, Lute, short for Lute Olson."

"Who or what is a Lute Olson?"

Robin was incredulous. "How can you not know that? Did you just move to Arizona, or what? He's the basketball coach at the University of Arizona. Everyone knows Lute."

"Well, what do you know. Guess I've never been much of a basketball fan. I used to live back east—ice hockey's my game." Tom continued to amble along the path, thumbs hooked in the empty belt loops of his Levis. He darted a covert glance at Robin, trying to gauge her physical condition up close as she shuffled along beside him. He could easily recognize the signs of dehydration: brittle hair and parched skin. Her lips and the skin of her hands were severely chapped. As he had come to expect from most of his patients, her fingers were chalk white, tinted bluish-purple at the tips. Even though she was in profile, the swollen glands beneath her jawbone were highly defined. Second only to dental damage, these "chipmunk cheeks" were the most obvious overt indicator of excessive purging.

Yes, Robin Hamilton, his newest patient, hadn't missed a single eating-disorder trick. Her skinny body clearly demonstrated her commitment to restricting food intake, while her teeth, skin and glands suggested more than a passing flirtation with bingeing and purging. He knew from the inventory that she was an obsessive swimmer. Odds had it, she probably abused laxatives, too. A pang of dread streaked through him as he considered the implications of her extreme behavior. For a patient to have anorexia or bulimia was bad enough; to have both struck real fear in the hearts of therapists and medical doctors alike. Subjecting the human body to such trauma was a recipe for disaster, often death. Already Robin had been hospitalized more than once due to her deteriorating health. This was precisely why everyone needed to help this girl and help her fast.

So consumed was Tom with thoughts of Robin that he actually flinched a bit when she suddenly blurted out, "So how long do I have to be here?"

"Adolescents stay at least sixty days."

"I so can't believe this. I…"

As a rule, Tom rarely interrupted a patient. But he could tell by her inflection another tirade was pending. He needed to stop it before she gained momentum. "Robin, do you love your dog?"

"Lute?" she asked, bewildered. "Of course."

He glanced sideways at her. "If he was hurt, would you take him to a vet?"

She nodded her head, still striving to figure out where he was going with this.

"Whether you think so or not, your parents love you. They think you are hurt and they're trying to help you. It's no less than you would do for Lute."

Not missing a beat, she countered, "He wouldn't have to stay at the vet for two months."

"Good point." Tom laughed at her rapid comeback, so unusual in a patient. "How about this. When we get back to the office, let's start over, let's look at your notebook together, you and me. We can talk about what you need to do in order to get through the next couple of months as easily and successfully as possible. I don't expect you to like any of this, but I want to help you, and I can if you'll let me."

Though she remained silent, still reluctant, not wanting to give an inch, Tom somehow knew he had gotten through to her. They turned and began the short journey back to the office. When they passed the spot where they had stopped, the bunny had vanished.

One hour later, Tom picked up his office phone and punched in the familiar four-digit number. When it was answered on the other end, he said, "I just got done. Can you come over?"

Moments later, the office door swung open and Kyla stepped in. "How did it go?"

He gestured to the couch. "Sit and I'll tell you."

She settled into the cushions and tucked a puffy throw pillow behind her back, then waited expectantly.

"At first it was exactly how I thought it would go. She was recalcitrant, angry, sarcastic, defiant. No kidding, she was awful. So I took her outside, hoping that would help. Still, I couldn't get her to engage. I kept thinking, 'Please God, help me with this girl.'"

Kyla arched an eyebrow. "And…"

"Suddenly, a little brown bunny ran across our path as though it had been shot from a cannon. It gave us something in common, something that had absolutely nothing to do with eating disorders or treatment. We started talking and she stayed with me, albeit reluctantly, but she didn't shut down."

A look of sheer delight suffused Kyla's face. "It's just like Abraham and the ram."

"Yep, but this time He used a baby jack rabbit." Tom threw his head back and laughed out loud. "Guess rams are a little hard to come by in Arizona."

"He uses what's available."

"Well, it did the trick. I don't know what I would have done if that bunny hadn't popped up during our walk. We'd probably be halfway to Utah by now, still walking in silence."

"How do you think you'll do with her?"

Tom scratched his head and thought about it. "Hard to say. She's a tough one. But someone or something has got to get through to her pretty soon or her life could end almost before it's gotten started."

Kyla nodded in commiseration. "I know, I've got one of those, too."

"Abby?"

"Uh-huh."

"Her name came up today, Robin mentioned her."

Not surprised in the least, she drummed her fingers on the arm of the couch. "Bet you a million bucks I know what the context was."

"No way." He shook his head. "That's a sucker bet. You and I have both seen this too many times before with our girls."

"Then let me guess. Robin thought Abby looked great and wished she could be that skinny. Right?"

"On the money." Tom spread his hands out wide, palms up. "No wonder I never bet with you."

Kyla gave him a small smile, yet the deep concern she felt for her young patient continued to flicker in her eyes. "Of course, as you know, Abby looks terrible. At this point, the only thing that has saved her life is that bulimia somehow never entered her mind. If she had gotten into that along with the anorexia, she never would have made it here."

"I know," he agreed, his expression serious. We'll just have to keep both of them in prayer."

"Got that right." Kyla stood and headed for the door. "Better go; I still have a ton of paperwork."

"Me too. See you tomorrow." He gave her a little wave and turned back to his desk, edging his keyboard closer, preparing to record his notes on Robin.

⫷◉/◉/◉⫸

The classroom, located on the third floor of the University of Arizona's Social Science building, was a study in visual tedium. The room was monochromatic to a fault. The ceiling and walls were a dingy greenish gray color, with no dash of color here, or bright spot there, to break up the drab landscape. Only a beige corkboard, with its many flyers and student notices, offered the slightest relief. Even the scuffed flooring was cast in the same nauseating shade. The three windows on the south wall looked out onto a parking lot. The hum of the air conditioner was constant as it waged a temperature war of chilly whispers against the late summer heat radiating from the windows.

Inured to the dismal surroundings, Dr. Natalie Grant-Hamilton stood at a black metal podium. She swiftly reviewed her lecture notes as a handful of graduate students filtered in and took their seats. Social Movements was one of her favorite seminars to teach, not only because of the challenging topic, but, particularly, because of the low student-teacher ratio. With drop-add now over, it appeared as if this class would come in at twenty-one students, twenty-two if her final add showed today. Natalie did a quick count of the assembled students. Twenty-one; perhaps the additional student the registrar's office had told her to expect wouldn't make it after all. She flicked a quick glance at the clock, then out to the group. Twenty-one pairs of eyes looked back at her, waiting, expectant. She cleared her throat and launched in, picking up right where she'd left off the previous week.

Fifteen minutes later, the professor was fully engrossed in her topic, as was her audience. Students often stopped their vigorous note-taking to ask probing, often insightful, questions. Natalie loved this give and take; it energized her to see inquisitive minds at work. She paused in her lecture, directing her full attention to Elliot Gibbons, a student she'd taught as an undergraduate. As he struggled to clarify an important point, the classroom door opened and closed quietly. Assuming it must be the extremely tardy twenty-second student, the professor glanced over her left shoulder at the door. The young woman, visibly embarrassed, took a few tentative steps toward the podium, her high-platform sandals clacking on the hard floor. She handed her add slip to Natalie, murmured a brief apology about being late, then slid into the nearest vacant chair.

Natalie, her outstretched hand clutching the slip, stood still as a wooden post, eyes fixed on the new student. Though the Tucson University was known nationwide for its beautiful female population, this young woman was in a class of her own, looking far more like a high-fashion model than a student. She was very tall and striking; her short black hair cut in an avant-garde style reminiscent of glossy magazines; her large eyes emphasized by smudgy dark makeup; her lips and fingernails glazed a vivid red. This dazzling creature was as out of place in this sterile classroom environment as a rottweiler at a cat show. Yet, as Natalie continued to gaze with a steady intensity, she was oblivious to the contrived glamour. All she saw was the hollow cheeks, the bony shoulders, the twig-like arms, the legs as thin as cornstalks, the complete absence of breasts beneath the copper sundress. She stared at the young woman…and saw her daughter, Robin.

Clearly uncomfortable with the continued scrutiny and incorrectly assuming it had to do with her late arrival, the new student said in a timid voice, "I'm Megan Stillwell. I'm sorry I was late. I had a shoot, a job, downtown that ran over. It won't happen again." She bit the edge of her lip, now sounding a little desperate. "Really, I promise."

Elliot, sitting at the opposite end of Megan's row, his question now forgotten, twisted in his chair and craned to get a better look. Like everyone else in the room, he was perplexed by the professor's strange behavior. He inadvertently elbowed a textbook and it toppled to the floor. The subsequent thump startled Natalie from her trance-like state. She returned to her notes, tried to find her place, started, stopped. Stammering, she tried again. The approving nods from the group confirmed she had finally located the correct spot. Though she endeavored to reconnect with the flow, teach with enthusiasm, she couldn't manage it. She kept peering back at Megan, seeing Robin. Her daughter who was so skinny and sick, far from home, who could die at any moment. Natalie would never know until it was too late. Her daughter. So skinny. So sick.

Natalie, suddenly seized with irrational panic, lost all sense of reality. Her heart stuttered in her chest, a film of cold sweat broke out on her brow and underarms, her hands trembled. Dizzy, she wobbled from side to side as though riding a bike with one bent wheel; she grasped the edge of the podium for support. Breathing through her open mouth, she couldn't manage to catch her breath. She had to help Robin right now…or her daughter would die. She dropped her notes as if they were radioactive. Megan's add slip fluttered to the carpet like a dead leaf falling from a tree. Without another word, Natalie walked out of the classroom. Dumbfounded, the students stared after her. The professor sped down the empty corridor at a rapid clip heading for her office. She had to get there and, and, and…As she drew near the office door, the panic began to gradually ebb like air released from a party balloon. Rational thought reasserted itself.

She went inside and sank into the chair behind her desk, still breathing hard. What was happening to her? A panic attack? Was she losing her mind? She couldn't help Robin; she couldn't ever help Robin with anything. What kind of mother was she? Overwhelmed by pent-up emotion, she burst out crying and dropped her face into her hands. Tears seeped through her fingers and dripped onto her lap unnoticed. Her office door arced open and Dr. Eve Lambert sidled in. "Natalie, I'm here," she said in a hushed tone, not wanting to startle her closest friend in the department. Natalie nodded, signifying she'd heard, but didn't look up.

Eve, a marriage and family counselor and part-time instructor, took a seat and waited. She sat quietly, giving

Natalie the time she needed to cry. She hoped this emotional blood-letting would result in a positive dialogue between the two. Years ago, Eve had concluded the world was filled with two types of people: those who loved to talk *ad nauseam* about themselves and those who were genuinely more interested in others. Natalie fell solidly into the latter category. Therefore, most conversations seemed to focus on university issues, Eve's life or the lives of friends or students, pretty much anything but Natalie herself. Throughout the tenure of their friendship, Eve had accepted and respected her reticence, but now felt it was time for a little healthy self-disclosure.

She watched the digital clock on the desk, red numbers on a black field, silently herald the passing time. An object near the clock caught Eve's eye. It was a CD. She picked it up and read the label. Her eyebrows shot up in surprise. It was a praise and worship disc, not unlike those she often listened to at home and in her car. But Natalie...a worship CD? A small smile flickered across Eve's face as she considered the positive possibilities this music might represent.

Finally, the tears subsided. Natalie looked up at Eve, face blotchy, eyes red. What little makeup she wore to work had washed away. "I walked out on my students."

"They'll live. When you flew by my room, obviously trying to break some land speed record, I went over and dismissed them. I got your notes and briefcase." She waved a hand at both items on the floor.

"Thanks. But what about your class?"

"I gave it to my TA; he can handle it." Eve held up the CD. "Where did this come from?"

Natalie momentarily regarded the item, trying to place it. "Oh, that. Tom, Robin's therapist, sent it to me. It's the kind of music she'll be hearing in chapel. I haven't had a chance to listen to it yet."

"Mind if I put it in?" Not pausing for an answer, she reached over to a CD player on the desk, popped in the disc and hit the play button. Seconds later, the small office was filled with rock music.

A look of astonishment flashed across Natalie's tear-streaked face. "Boy, Tom told me it was lively, but I never would have guessed this. Obviously, church music has come a long way since I was a kid. What happened to 'Bringing in the Sheaves'?"

"They're all in," Eve replied and chuckled. "Frankly, I wouldn't know a sheave if I sat on one. My guess is, no one else in this century knows either. I keep telling you, everything's changed since the last time you were in church…you know, back in the day when women stuck fancy feathers in their hair and boot-leg hooch was all the rage."

Natalie smiled, appreciating her friend's sense of humor. Easy with one another, the two women sat and listened for a while, Eve's tapping foot keeping time with the beat. As the music transitioned to a more sedate song, Eve asked, "So what's going on?"

Natalie explained what had happened with her new student. "And the most ridiculous thing about it is, she doesn't even look like my daughter, except for that one area."

"That's a pretty critical area for you these days. Tell me, are you seeing a counselor?"

Natalie sniffed, grabbed a tissue and dabbed at her nose. She shifted her focus to her computer monitor, where the screen saver displayed a school of brightly colored fish swimming languidly in a tropical sea. "Stanton won't hear of it. In his economy, this is Robin's problem; family counseling would just be a waste of time and money. And one thing is true: even with our insurance, the ranch is costing a tremendous amount."

Eve sat back, anchored her elbows on the arms of the chair and clasped her hands together. "How is he dealing with all this?"

"Now? He's shut down. Back when this all started, Stanton was the self-appointed fixer. Fixing Robin became his mission. He was going to make her eat and put an end to all this foolishness. He would make her shape up and fly right." She shook her head slowly back and forth. "What I always knew, but he didn't, is that no parent can make a child eat. You can't force them to eat peas as babies and you certainly can't force them to eat pot roast as teenagers. The only difference is, when a one-year-old spits peas back at you, somehow you find it absurdly adorable." Her expression softened at the memory and she murmured in a voice burdened with sorrow, "Robin never did like peas."

In her private practice, Eve had dealt with many families living with an eating disorder. Time and time again, she had witnessed parents, usually fathers, take a similar approach. It never worked. And as long as parents like Stanton continued to think their child's illness was exclusively about food, it probably never would.

"It was awful," Natalie continued, glancing up as if the past were replaying itself on the cracked off-white surface of the ceiling. "Every night it was like a world war at the dinner table. Stanton and Robin would yell; then Robin would cry and Stanton would yell even more and threaten her with everything he could think of. This would go on for hours. And of course, Robin never ate. Stanton made a battle out of it, and frankly, he lost. He isn't used to losing; the word isn't part of his personal vocabulary. So, his response was to quit coming home. He would stay at the office late every night well past dinner time." She stretched her neck this way and that, then massaged the muscles at the base of her skull as though the intense stress of those difficult days was revisiting her body.

"So he left it to you."

"In a nutshell."

Eve removed her wire-rimmed glasses and tapped one stem against her bottom teeth in concentration. She felt completely comfortable in the role as counselor and wanted so desperately to help Natalie, now that she was finally opening up. "So, why the tears today? I know what triggered your reaction, but what were you feeling?"

She thought it over. "Guilt." Natalie relocated her fingertips to her forehead and rubbed just above her eyebrows. "I feel so guilty about what's happened to Robin."

"Because…"

Natalie eased forward on her seat and shrugged out of her summer suit jacket. She tossed it dismissively in the direction of a nearby chair, not bothering to see if it hit the intended target. It didn't. The lightweight tangerine jacket landed half on, half off the seat before succumbing to gravity and oozing slowly onto the floor. "The eating disorder is my fault. I've never been a good enough mother to Robin."

Eve regarded the puddle of orange fabric on the carpet, briefly considered picking it up, then dismissed the thought. This was yet another thing she and Natalie had in common: a complete disinterest in clothes, especially their care and maintenance. Shifting her attention back to Natalie, she asked, "Never?"

"No, not since the day she was born. You see, when I got pregnant with her I was teaching a full load and trying to complete my dissertation. It was so stressful. The timing couldn't have been worse. Everything seemed to go wrong. Robin came early and the delivery was so hard they finally had to do a section. She had terrible colic and wouldn't nurse. My milk dried up and I had to put her on formula, which exacerbated the colic. She never slept. All she did was cry."

"It sounds ghastly."

"It was."

Eve slid the wire eyeglass frame along the edge of her lower lip. "But Natalie, why did that translate into you being a bad mother?"

Surprise registered on Natalie's face as though the answer was more than obvious. "Because…because I should have done it better; I should have…" Her words faded.

Eve frowned in mock anger. "Have I ever mentioned how much I detest that 'should' word?"

Natalie smiled sheepishly like a kid caught in a lie. "Only about two or three thousand times. I can't believe the dreaded "s" word actually slipped out of my mouth."

"Twice," Eve corrected. She took a moment to digest what she had just heard. "So, you were a young woman, a new mother, trying to hold down a job while finishing your doctorate. What's more, you were recovering from major surgery and had a difficult baby. Surely, I must be missing something here because I fail to see the bad mother part."

"Okay, Eve, maybe you're right about when she was first born. But the problem is, and this is where the guilt really comes in, Robin and I have just never clicked, never been close like a mother and daughter should be." Eve cocked an eyebrow with deliberate exaggeration and Natalie interpreted the gesture immediately. "Sorry, the way mothers and daughters often are."

Eve gave her friend a curt nod. "That's better."

"I don't know if our temperaments and personalities are just so different or what, but we've never been able to truly get along. It's the oil and water thing. She is far more like Stanton than she is like me. Then, what makes it worse, is that I am so close to her brother. Unlike her, Josh was a happy, content baby, a joy from the moment he was born."

"And he came at a much easier time," Eve suggested, placing her spectacles back on her nose.

"Much. Josh was planned. Stanton and I were teaching and he was involved in research. We didn't have money troubles. And then as Josh grew, he was just so easy to parent, easy to get along with. Unlike Robin, where everything was a struggle, an argument waiting to happen."

The worship CD had ended and clicked off. Though the office was still, the hall outside was teeming with activity. Eve often thought you could simply close your eyes and imagine yourself in Pamplona, Spain, during the annual running of the bulls—honestly, the students made as much racket as a herd of stampeding animals once class was let out. "And how has Robin reacted to the relationship between you and Josh?"

Natalie plunged a hand through her hair, then grabbed a fistful of the auburn curls. "Badly. She gets mad. That's pretty much her standard response to everything. She claims she hates both her brother and me. I've gotten used to it, but I know it hurts Josh. Of course he acts like a tough guy and gives as good as he gets, but I know deep down inside, he loves his big sister and secretly wishes she would love him in return." She released the death grip she had on her hair and sighed heavily. "So there we have it: Stanton bailed out, Robin and I can't seem to get along, Josh is a great kid whom Robin can't abide, and then there's me in general."

"What do you mean by that?"

Natalie waved an open palm in the direction of her torso. "Come on Eve, just look at me. I'm not what Robin wanted. I'm not pretty and thin like some other mothers. I'm not fashionable or stylish. I'm a complete disappointment to her."

Stunned by these words, incredulity flashed in Eve's heart. Natalie…a disappointment? Because she wasn't beautiful, and even more ludicrous, because she wasn't thin? The very idea of it made her want to scream, to verbally lash out at the unseen Robin, the source of all this grief and pain. Instead, holding her emotions firmly at bay, she drew in a deep calming breath and allowed her rational mind to synthesize this information. She knew her rage was misdirected. After all, it wasn't Robin causing all this anguish, it was the eating disorder. During her years as a therapist, she had grown to loathe anorexia and bulimia with a passion boarding on mania. She had seen marriages end, families destroyed, lives torn apart and worst of all, she had seen intelligent, talented, lovely, often gifted, adolescents and young women so addicted to the disorder that it eventually killed them.

And as the death toll continued to mount, the rest of the world went right on believing that an eating disorder was simply a diet gone too far, or a clever little game teenage girls played to get attention. If they only knew the mortality rate for eating disorders was higher than for any other mental illness, even depression. Eve did know. It was that knowledge that kept her awake at night worrying about clients and friends such as Natalie.

Now, needing to respond to what had just been said, Eve sat erect in her seat. "Natalie, you are a brilliant woman with an impressive career, you have the integrity, morals and ethics of a saint, you are a true friend with a heart of gold..." She ran out of air and began to sputter.

Natalie's face flushed. "Thank you." Though abashed by the praise, she was touched by her friend's words. "Unfortunately, in Robin's world, those things don't matter."

Eve shot forward and slapped an open palm on the desk. "Maybe not now, but someday they will. When Robin gets better, she will be so proud of her mother and all of your accomplishments."

"I hope so."

"I know so," Eve countered. "And until then, I don't want you to dwell on that piece of this particular equation. There might be a lot to hammer out in terms of your family dynamics, but your appearance is not one of them. You are who you are, and frankly, those of us who know and love you are completely satisfied with you."

"I'll try to let that go." Natalie dropped her head on the back of the chair and pressed her palm to her eyes. "All of this is such a mess."

Eve couldn't disagree—this family was a mess. Not without hope, but a mess all the same. In her role as quasi-therapist, she wondered if she should caution Natalie concerning her relationship with Josh. Certainly, nothing untoward was going on, but the dynamic was unhealthy all the same. With Stanton effectively bowing out in the midst of such turmoil, Natalie was undoubtedly turning to Josh more and more for comfort and companionship. In essence, Josh was functioning as a pseudo-husband to his mother—a situation many professionals would label emotional incest. A relationship of partnering, not parenting, could ultimately prove developmentally deleterious to the boy. Eve thought about it for a while, then decided against it. Natalie had enough on her plate; it wasn't the time or place to burden her with more. But what could Eve do, what could she say right now to give her friend a modicum of help? The question was rendered moot when Natalie abruptly pushed away from the desk and stood. "Gosh, I lost track of time. I need to pick up Josh at school for a dermatology appointment."

Eve hoisted herself to her feet. "Let's talk more about this soon."

Natalie bent down and retrieved her jacket from the floor. She gave it a hard shake, like a woman snapping a freshly laundered sheet, and put it on. "Can we?" She sounded hopeful. "But you must get so sick of hearing everyone's problems."

"You're not a client, you're a friend. That's different."

Natalie embraced the other woman in gratitude. "Thank you. I always need your friendship and now I could really use your help."

"How about Sunday? We could go to church together, then have brunch afterward and talk."

Buttoning her jacket, Natalie gave her an arch look. "If you think you're being sly by sneaking God into the equation, you aren't."

"I know. I give you credit for being a whole lot smarter than that." Eve propped a shoulder against the doorjamb and crossed her feet at the ankle. "Come on Natalie, it won't kill you. Come with me just this once and if you don't like it, I'll never ask again."

"Promise?"

Eve held up one hand. "Girl Scout's honor."

Natalie wrinkled her nose. "You were never a scout."

"Lawyers aren't the only ones with loopholes."

"Okay, it's a date. I guess if Robin is going to chapel every day, I can go with you to church at least once."

"Good enough—it's a deal," Eve concluded as the two women walked out of the office and said good-bye. Natalie went right, Eve went left. One woman consumed with thoughts of her son; the other, consumed with thoughts of her Father, her heavenly Father.

Part Three

Chapter Six

Kyla typed in a few final notes before closing the patient file. After spending nearly three months at the ranch, Trista Delgado would be going home a happier, healthier sixteen-year-old. Trista, who had come to them from Texas, had been a victim of the system, a system that endeavored to shape young girls into something instead of someone. In the case of this willowy teenager with the long black hair and far longer legs, the something was a ballerina. Because she had shown such aptitude as a small child, her parents had made sure she took all the right classes, got all the right training.

Eventually, they placed their daughter's future into the hands of a highly respected and revered coach. What Joseph and Nora Delgado had seen was the impressive results he got on the stage; what they didn't see was the lengths to which he would go to get a star performer. They never saw the daily weigh-ins; they never heard the strict lectures regarding caloric intake, fat grams and the non-negotiable necessity to stay thin—thin to win. But Trista had, and she shared her parents' goal for her to be a famous ballerina. So she dieted and danced, dieted and danced, until one day the stringent dieting caught up with her; she danced, collapsed during a performance and nearly died. One by one her vital organs had shut down due to dehydration, electrolyte imbalance and malnutrition. It took a week in the hospital just to build her body up enough to travel to Arizona for treatment. And the initial days and weeks at the ranch hadn't proved any easier, especially for Kyla. Trying to convince this lovely young girl that her adored coach did not have her best interest at heart, and that being a great ballerina was not a goal worth dying for, was no small task.

Kyla shifted position in her swivel chair, trying to get comfortable, a goal that proved harder and harder to accomplish as her pregnancy advanced. She gazed at the now-blank computer screen, thinking of her struggles with this teenager. Not surprisingly, Trista's adoration for this man had gone past the crush stage and moved well into blind infatuation, which made the coach/student bond that much harder to break. How easy it had been for him to make her toe the line, to place thinness before all else. But where would he be when Trista was grotesquely hunched over with debilitating osteoporosis at the ripe old age of twenty-five, if she even lived that long? Probably involved with another handful of talented young girls, similarly enraptured, eager to please and fully prepared to do anything to achieve fame. Though Kyla had never met the coach, it took all the Christian commitment she could muster not to despise him for how he had injured this precious young woman.

Kyla shook her head in disgust at him as well as the world at large. At least today she could chalk one up for the good guys. She had met with Trista that morning and truly believed she would be all right. This girl would make it through the difficult process of recovery. Kyla swung around in her chair and faced the office window. Her small satisfied smile of moments earlier dissolved as she observed a patient whose outlook may not prove quite as bright. Through the large pane of glass she saw Abby Cardoza standing in the stable yard just outside the barn. She was grooming one of the geldings. Kyla squinted, trying to make out who it was. Sundance? Narrowing her gaze a little more, she focused on the horse's rump and spied the long flowing tail. That was Sundance all right; he alone possessed such a magnificent mane and tail.

Growing thoughtful, the therapist took a deep breath, held it, then blew it out. "Abby, Abby, Abby, what am I going to do with you?" Kyla asked herself as she watched the girl brush the chocolate-brown horse. Abby loved to groom, but she would not ride. This worried Kyla; this worried everyone involved with Abby. The simple truth was that the professionals, from therapists to equine staff, realized what it meant when a girl refused to mount a horse. And unlike most patients, Abby was the very model of compliance. She would do almost anything to please those around her...but she wouldn't do this. Kyla sighed heavily, felt her heart sag in her chest. She wondered when she and Abby would finally get to it, when the moment would arrive that this girl would face her demons head on. Kyla thought it was coming, and soon. Without active anorexia to dull emotion and push down the pain, the truth about her trauma must come to the surface. And the therapist knew that's exactly what it was: trauma, some kind of abuse had taken place in Abby's early life. Kyla had guessed it during her initial interaction with Abby's father. Sadly, to a mental-health professional, the signs were there: the hoarding of food, the excessive neatness, the obsession with all things being in their appropriate places, the isolation. Each was a huge red flag; she had seen these seemingly odd behaviors manifested before in her patients.

Yes, with the eating disorder in remission, the day of reckoning was pending. Abby knew it, too, but only on a deep, unconscious level. In therapy sessions together, Kyla felt as if the two of them were inquisitive cats crouching outside a mouse hole. In Kyla's mind, the little gray mouse hiding just inside was representative of the truth. At times, it would poke out its tiny whiskered nose and Abby would dart forward, take a tentative swipe at it, then swiftly retreat. She wanted, needed the truth to come out; yet wanted, needed it to stay safely tucked away in the dark where she had kept it for so many years. Impotent, Kyla merely watched Abby's advance and retreat with the symbolic mouse. Certainly, she offered affirming body language, positive eye contact and verbal encouragement, but these therapeutic tactics consistently failed. Up to this point, Abby simply wasn't ready to face the truth and forcing her was not an option. Kyla just had to wait.

This was not to say that Abby had not made significant progress, for she had come a long way. She had allowed them to insert an NG tube, which had helped her to gain weight faster. Between nighttime refeeding and nourishing meals throughout the day, her cognitive function had been nearly restored. Abby's renewed ability to think was crucial. It afforded Kyla the opportunity to process many issues with her and help her make significant strides in understanding the function of her eating disorder. Abby, like most patients, believed her anorexia was driven by the desire to be thin. It wasn't. Whereas a skinny, lithe body was definitely the motivation for a dancer like Trista, with Abby it was far more complex. Kyla felt certain it was more about the denial of puberty, rebellion against physical maturation and the deep desire never to grow up. And of course, it had worked. The anorexia had effectively retarded the development of breasts and hips and the advent of menses. What's more, the eating disorder held at bay any threatening thoughts or feelings. But now, one by one, emotions were returning and, with help, Abby was learning to correctly identify them and understand what they meant. As healthy cognitive and emotional processes returned, Abby's initial shyness dissipated, which was an unexpected bonus. She got along well with the other girls and even spoke up from time to time in group therapy. Though not destined to be a social butterfly, she was certainly a distant cry from the diffident girl Kyla had met weeks ago.

On a whim, Kyla got up and located Abby's recently completed life timeline. She unrolled the white butcher paper and, with the aid of two books, anchored it open on the desktop. Kyla smiled, contemplating the hours the two of them had sat cross-legged on the floor working on it together. It had been an intimate time of talking, giggling and sharing stories. Kyla told Abby about the time in kindergarten when she had laughed so hard at recess that she wet her pants; Abby told Kyla about the little boy with the enormous coke-bottle eyeglasses who picked his nose then chased the girls around the playground. This type of interaction between therapist and patient was invaluable because of the trust built and the bond established.

Plus, at such times when all guards were down, precious nuggets of information and insight could be mined, especially with a patient like Abby. Unlike most of the adolescents, this girl was without guile and not well-versed in the art of deception. She was basically transparent as a pane of clear glass. A perfect example was her reaction to the gender of Kyla's unborn baby. When told it was a boy, her relief was as obvious as it was genuine. Probing, Kyla discovered this was based on her belief that people didn't hurt little boys the way they hurt little girls. A therapist dead for a decade would have gleaned the significance of that statement.

Kyla stood, arms folded habitually across her huge stomach, and stared down at Abby's timeline. The sheet included all the usual milestones: her birthdate, starting school, Sara's birthdate. All of these factors had been committed to paper first, then as their time together went on, Abby filled in less-significant items and events. Little markers such as the acquisition of pets and special family vacations eventually found a home on the timeline. Taking in Abby's life as a whole as Kyla was doing now, allowing her gaze to sweep from left to right, it was impossible to miss the informational imbalance. Virtually nothing was recorded in the segment between birth and about six years of age. When Kyla had pressed her on this point, Abby could not provide additional information. All she could come up with were a couple of anecdotal tidbits, obviously told to her by others.

Even when Abby told her life story—an assignment every girl was required to do in home group—she had little to report reguarding those early years. The other girls also pressed her on this, but despite their encouragement, she provided nothing more. She was not being belligerent, for that particular character trait was simply not in her nature. The long and short of it was that Abby possessed precious few memories of her own regarding that time in her life. Recognizing another huge red flag, Kyla was certain that was when the trauma or abuse took place. Leaning over, she stabbed the relevant place on the time-line with an index finger as if she could poke the truth out of the white paper. The question was: Who else knew? Frowning, Kyla worried this question like a dog with a bone. The answer became increasingly relevant the closer they got to family week when Abby's parents would join them at the ranch. The truth had to come out. Kyla prayed it would be soon, in order that she and Abby could face it and deal with it before her parents entered the mix.

Lifting her gaze to the window, Kyla stared out at the stable yard where Abby was grooming Sundance. She bit a knuckle as she watched this girl of whom she had grown quite fond.

Standing at the hitching rail, Abby ran her hand down the gelding's smooth, strong neck and onto his girth. With the late-afternoon sun blazing down from a cloudless sky, the horse's dark coat was toasty warm. She had never encountered such a massive animal, but she wasn't afraid. He had that fabulous mane and tail that Abby just couldn't wait to get her hands on. Maybe, if she had time, she would braid his tail and stick a few colorful wild flowers in it just for fun. Briefly, she rested a cheek against his shoulder. Even though he remained motionless, she could feel the tight muscles just beneath the skin press against her face. She closed her eyes, breathing in the scent of him. Abby thought the smell of horse was wonderful, a blend of dust and sweat and earth and...horse. It conjured images of the rustic barn with its rows of leather saddles, bridles and stacked bales of sweet-smelling hay.

The sound of hooves tramping dirt caused her to look up. The rest of the patients were returning from a trail ride. Abby waved to several as they trotted by. Robin reined in, flung her right leg casually over the saddle horn and propped an elbow on her knee. "Hey Ab, where's Belle?" Everyone had gotten used to seeing Abby with the mare. Belle belonged to one of the therapists and was boarded at the ranch. Girls who didn't ride spent time with her. Belle was in the final days of her pregnancy and couldn't be ridden by the therapist, so Abby was with her a lot, talking, grooming, and sneaking her an occasional treat. She adored the mare's gigantic belly. Sometimes, it distorted crazily as the baby moved around in there. Belle never even glanced down, as if oblivious to the wild gyrations going on inside her body. The horse had enormous dark eyes, fuzzy ears and a nose as soft as flower petals.

Abby looked up at Robin, shading her eyes from the glare of the sun. "She's in labor. She's having her baby, her foal, like right now." Abby had been waiting for the others to get back so she could share this exciting news. She bounced on her toes in anticipation of the upcoming birth.

Her jubilation was infectious. Robin let out a whoop and pumped her balled fists in the air. "That rocks. Do you think they'll let us see her foal when it comes? I've never seen anything newly born before."

"I haven't either." She hesitated, thinking about it. "I bet they'll let us. I'll ask."

"Cool. Better go; you know how they get when you're late, we're talking panties in a serious wad." Scowling, Robin rolled her eyes and swung her leg back over the top of Lucky's head and jammed her booted foot back into the stirrup. The worn leather of the saddle creaked familiarly with the swift motion. Retrieving the reins from the horse's neck, she nudged Lucky in the direction of the rail where the others were dismounting.

Abby smiled, watching Robin maneuver Lucky into the appropriate slot. The truth was she really didn't know "how they got when you were late" because, unlike Robin, Abby followed the rules. Maybe that's why she liked the older girl so much—the two of them were just so different. Robin got in trouble all the time. In fact, if Abby had any money, she would bet it all that her friend would get in trouble again today for the way she groomed Lucky. Robin, who openly resented having her physical activity curtailed by the staff, approached grooming like an athletic event. She stretched and reached and brushed the gelding with such vigor it nearly blurred Abby's vision. Poor Lucky; it was amazing he wasn't bald by now. The patients knew she was trying to burn additional calories through the exercise.

But the staff was wise to her, too. She had already gotten called on the carpet more than once for exercising while in the shower.

Standing on tip-toes and peeking over Sundance's back, Abby saw Sally, one of the mental health technicians, sidling over to where Robin stood. Sally knew all the tricks. Posted next to Robin, she wouldn't let her get away with a darn thing. Abby laughed a little and returned to her horse. As she brushed his neck and moved on toward his flanks, Abby hummed a song to herself and occasionally sang a few random lyrics. It was a praise song she had learned recently from their worship leader. She loved chapel; it was the very best part of her day. They sang great songs and always had a speaker who taught them something about the Lord. Abby was learning so much about God, Jesus, the Bible and prayer. She was learning about grace and forgiveness and mercy, all kinds of neat new things. Time and time again, she wished her mother had been there with her so she could learn, too. It seemed like her mom, who always felt guilty or ashamed about something, had gotten God all wrong.

When the worship was over they spent time in prayer. A lot of girls prayed for themselves and one another—out loud. Abby had held back a long time, thinking it would be too embarrassing, but last week she had finally tried it. She had sat right there, next to Robin, no less, and prayed to God out loud, asking Him to help her and her friends and to watch over her little sister Sara while she was gone. As it turned out, Abby wasn't embarrassed at all; in fact, it felt kind of good to be praying like that with the others.

Having groomed Sundance's entire body, Abby moved on to the horse's mane. Cautiously, she combed her fingers through the long strands, then brushed it out. She was careful not to snag on any knots or tangles. She retrieved little bits of hay, plenty of burrs, and even the occasional small twig. Once his mane lay soft and glossy on his neck, she headed for his tail, remembering what she had been taught about always staying in contact with the horse, so he wouldn't be surprised or scared. Her left palm remained flat on his side, sliding along his sleek coat as she moved down his torso. From her position a few yards away, Sally called over to Abby in a teasing voice, "Better be careful, you're going to get splashed."

Simultaneous with the woman's warning, Abby heard the sound of urine pelting the ground right beneath Sundance. She hopped away from him just in time. That was when she first saw it. Abby's eyes grew wide, then wider still as she stared. Synapses fired in the girl's brain, opening first one door, then another, then another. Memories flooded Abby's defenseless mind. She tried to force them back behind the doors where they belonged. They refused to go. The pictures flashing one by one before her mind's eye were so vivid, so real, so awful. A small whimper escaped her lips.

"Abby, you okay?" Sally called, concerned. Momentarily abandoning Robin, she walked toward this girl who looked as if she was staring straight into hell.

Now standing at the window, Kyla knew something was wrong, very wrong. She could tell by Abby's hunched posture, the anxious expression on Sally's face. Not hesitating a moment, the therapist flew out of her office, down the vacant corridor and out the door. She slowed only slightly when encountering the wooden steps, cautiously, yet swiftly, taking them one by one. Supporting her stomach with both hands, she ran across the open space to Abby. Kyla exchanged a worried look with Sally, who stood near Abby, but did not touch her. The girl was still as death, one clenched fist pressed to her parted lips. Kyla tracked her line of sight and saw what Abby was staring at. "Abby," Kyla said, breathless from the short jaunt. She reached over and clutched the girl's shoulder. The spell broke. Abby looked at Kyla, eyes haunted, her face as pale as skim milk, then swung her gaze back to a point just under Sundance's belly. She moaned softly and pointed. "Look, it's huge. It's just like when I was little. He made me touch it. It was hard like rock. Then he touched me. And then, then…"

Kyla wrapped her arms around the trembling girl. She had to bend slightly to accommodate for her large abdomen and Abby's shorter stature. Holding her close, she could feel Abby's heart fluttering in her chest. "I know, Abby, I know," was all she could say. Gently, she turned the girl away from the horse and guided her in the direction of her office. Abby followed Kyla's lead, as obedient as a sleepwalker. The therapist spoke in low, reassuring tones. "I know. You and I are going to talk about it now; we're going to talk together. And it is going to be all right, I promise. Everything will be all right." As they scaled the stairs, Kyla glanced over Abby's shoulder and gave the MHT a significant look. Sally offered a curt nod in return, indicating she understood what was going on and would take care of everything on her end. Still embracing her young patient, Kyla managed to finesse the door open and ease the two of them through. The solid wood door closed soundly behind them.

——⊰०/०/०⊱——

"Come on, Daddy, we gotta go," Sara yelled over her shoulder as she sprinted toward the front door. Peeper, diligently grooming his gray fur, glanced up from his position in the middle of the carpeted hall. Alarmed by the little girl's speed and trajectory, Peeper leapt to his feet and scampered away at a fairly rapid clip for a cat of his immense size. He sought safe refuge beneath an upholstered chair, circling in the cramped space in order to keep an eye on family activity. Sara hit the screen door at a full run, burst through it and bounced down the front steps. The metal door slammed behind her. Finally running out of steam on the sidewalk, she whirled around and planted both fists on her nonexistent hips. "Daddy," she called again in the loudest voice she could muster. Briefly, she considered stamping her right foot on the pavement, even though Abby had always told her that particular gesture had zero impact on her father's haste. As it turned out, additional action proved unnecessary because there he was poised in the doorway.

Jim Cardoza looked down at his pint-sized daughter standing with her back to the street. She had struck a pose of extreme vexation, one that always made him want to laugh. "By chance, did you forget something, young lady?"

Sara scruntched up her face. She glanced down at herself and took inventory. Shoes and white lacy socks, fancy red party dress. She patted her head with one hand. Yes, her sparkly hair bow was in place. She had even remembered to put on clean underpants like Mommy always said. Then what? Standing on one foot crane-like, she locked one ankle behind the other. Perplexed, she bit the edge of her lip.

From his position at the top of the steps, Jim watched his youngest daughter go through the predictable mental machinations, to no avail. "How about Beth's present?" He held the brightly wrapped box up for her to see.

Never without a dramatic reaction close at hand, Sara gasped and slapped her forehead with one hand. "Oh no," she exclaimed breathlessly and scooted back up the walk, her red patent leather dress-up shoes slapping the hard cement. She bounded up the stairs and relieved her father of the gift. "Let's go." And with that, again she was off.

"Slow down, honey, you'll be exhausted before you even get to the party." His words fell on deaf ears for Sara had already bolted down the sidewalk in the direction of

Beth's house. Not to worry. Jim's ace in the hole was the intersection at the end of the short block. Sara was not yet allowed to cross the street alone, so he knew she would be forced to wait for him there. Unhurried, he locked the front door, checked it, then dropped the key ring into his pants pocket. He walked at a reasonable pace, not wanting to show up early. Approaching his daughter, he noticed she had now adopted vexation pose number two, this particular stance designed to convey an even greater sense of disappointment and aggravation. She stood with a stern expression pasted on her face and arms folded across her meager chest. Weight thrown onto one leg, the other was extended to the front and side with toes tapping impatiently on the ground. Though he knew it was a mistake, Jim laughed out loud. He couldn't help himself, it was just too funny. Sara was only four years old. Where did she get this theatrical behavior?

She pursed her lips, demonstrating her escalating angst. "Sara, don't worry, we will get there right on time." He took her hand, the one not gripping the gift, and stepped into the street. Crossing together, he walked, she skipped. Regaining the sidewalk, he continued to hold her hand, just to keep her in check.

Jim understood her excitement. It was Sara's best friend's fifth birthday party—pretty heady stuff when you were only four. Sara had been looking forward to this important event for weeks. Mary had bought her a brand new dress and matching shoes. And now, she looked as cute as she could be as she strutted along at his side, her satin hair bow shining in the bright morning light. She chattered on nonstop about the party: who would be there, the games they would play, the food they would eat. It lifted his spirits to see her so happy. It used to be, Sara was always animated and cheerful. Unfortunately, of late, this had been the exception instead of the rule. Sara missed Abby with an intensity hitherto unseen in her young life. The truth was, Sara loved her sister more than anyone, even her parents. Though Mary was occasionally distressed by this situation, believing parents should be first in a little girl's heart, Jim didn't mind in the least. He had grown up without siblings, therefore, the close relationship between his daughters delighted him to no end. Only now, with Abby gone, did this attachment to one another prove problematic. Sara was often listless and lethargic, at loose ends without her sister. She had shifted her dependence to her teddy bear, and was seldom seen without him clutched in her arms. Jim frequently heard her crying in bed late at night. It broke his heart. He did everything he could think of to fill the void left by Abby, but his efforts did little good. Sara simply would not be the same until her adored sister returned home.

"So can I have a horse doctor, too?" Too late, Jim realized he had lost track of the ceaseless monologue. Sara had obviously shifted topics.

"What's that, honey?"

"Like Abby. She has horse doctors at the hospital she's at. She tells me about them all the time. Belle is having a baby pony soon." Sara's expression turned disgusted, as if she had just swallowed something bad. "I don't want to go to old Dr. Betler anymore. He's cranky and smells bad. I want a horse doctor, too."

Jim chuckled softly, finally catching the drift of the conversation. He and Mary had told Sara that her sister was at a hospital in Arizona, recognizing "treatment facility" would not register in her young mind. "Oh baby, the horses Abby talks about on the phone aren't doctors."

She wrinkled her nose, a sure sign of confusion. "Then why are they there at the hospital?"

"Because they help the girls in different ways. They help them practice new things that they are learning, things like patience and communication and being assertive. That last one is a pretty big word, probably too hard for me to explain to you right now. The horses are very important, but they aren't medical doctors."

Sara cocked her head to one side, still skeptical. "Are you sure?"

"I'm sure."

Sara grew silent. She was obviously giving this entire topic some serious thought. Suddenly, animation returned to her face and she blurted out, "Then can I get a horse of my own...like a pet to play with? It could help me be sertive, too."

Jim thought if Sara got any more "sertive" he and Mary would be forced to lock her in her room. Though fully prepared to launch into an explanation of how a horse wasn't possible for a variety of reasons, Jim was saved, not by the bell, but by proximity. At that very moment, they rounded the final corner and Beth's house came into view. Such was her considerable zeal regarding the birthday party, Sara didn't even wait to hear the fate of her mythical horse. Off she went, dashing toward the mailbox with the helium balloons affixed to it. Following at his same steady pace, he watched her go, long hair flying behind her, fancy ribbon already askew. Jim's love for this little girl was so great. By the time he made it to the driveway, she had already disappeared inside. Beth's mother, now holding Sara's gift, stood at the front door. They greeted one another, he confirmed the time he would return to pick Sara up, then he left. Retracing his steps, he passed by the balloon bouquet tethered to the mailbox by glittering grosgrain ribbon. The festive pastel-colored balloons swayed this way and that in the gentle breeze, looking like a giant floating ice cream cone.

Jim turned left at the sidewalk, heading in the opposite direction of his house. There was no reason to go home— no one was there but the cat. As usual, Mary was at the nursing home with her father. So he had a few hours to kill before picking up Sara. Hands shoved in his pants pockets, Jim ambled along with no destination in mind. Without Sara's constant conversation, his thoughts were his own, which was not necessarily a good thing. Lately, he had tried hard not to think, not to have time to think. He endeavored to distract himself by his surroundings. With each passing house, Jim took in the landscaping, analyzing what materials were used, the plants and shrubs involved. When that grew tiresome, he considered the weather and how far off winter might be. In no time at all, he found himself standing outside Abby's old elementary school, where Sara would attend kindergarten next year.

A handful of cars were parked in the administrator's lot, but no one was in sight. He strolled onto the familiar, now deserted playground and over to the swing set. How many times had he pushed Abby on this very swing when she was no older than Sara? Far more than he could ever count. She had always been so daring, wanting to go higher and higher, believing it was possible to touch the sky. Then, before returning home, she would beg him to wind her up in the swing. He would turn her around and around until the chains were twisted together all the way up to the frame. Releasing her, Abby would spin at roughly the speed of light, hair whipping out, feet flying, Abby squealing with delight until the swing finally came to a shuddering stop. Inevitably, she would stagger drunkenly from the seat, too dizzy to navigate, so he would scoop her up in his arms and carry her home.

Shaking his head in an effort to rid himself of the bittersweet memory, he lowered himself onto one of the slatted wood swings suspended by two dingy silver chains. He stared down at the ground beneath him with its deep parallel grooves made by thousands of sneaker-clad feet. Unfortunately, the monochromatic dirt and gravel had nothing to recommend it, nothing to rescue Jim from his own thoughts. He tried to focus on Sara and her engaging vivacity, but that again only inspired images of Abby at her age. Abby, his first child, the daughter of his heart. He remembered holding her as a newborn; she was so very little. To Jim, she was a miracle. On the very day she was born, he promised to always love her, always protect her; he vowed no harm would ever come to this small defenseless creature. Then where had he gone wrong; how had things turned out so badly? He thought he had been a good father, done the best he knew how. Could Jim have ever imagined she would end up harming herself?

And now, the girl he had pledged to provide for and protect was in a hospital, due to an eating disorder. How had it happened? Jim shook his head in bafflement, recalling the day so many months ago when Mary had returned from the latest doctor with the latest diagnosis: anorexia nervosa. The problem with this particular diagnosis was that unlike the plethora of others that had come from any number of specialists, this one happened to be correct.

Anorexia? His precious daughter was starving herself? Even now, months later, he still couldn't quite take it all in. He knew it was real because Abby was almost near death by the time they got her into treatment, but he still could not understand why. His mind had gone around and around in circles trying to comprehend what could have caused this. In his darkest moments, usually late at night when sleep wouldn't come, he worried if the same thing might occur with Sara. Though the doctors had told him the odds were against it, he continually begged the question: why not? After all, Sara came from the same set of parents, was growing up in the same house. What would prevent it from happening to a second daughter? If he had to go through this again, his marriage wouldn't make it...he wouldn't make it.

Sitting in the empty playground, shuffling his feet in the dirt trenches, he slumped over in sheer exhaustion. He didn't know how much longer he could hold everything together; the burden was getting too big for him to handle. He felt old, far older than his years. Only that morning he had noticed how many gray hairs were cropping up in his moustache. It wasn't just Abby, it was everything. It was Abby and her illness; Earl and his stroke; Mary and her grief; Sara and her loss. Just last night, Mary had wept for hours in his arms, primarily about Abby, but with a little Earl thrown in for good measure. As always, she needed, expected him to be strong for her. He must reassure and console her, tell her repeatedly that their daughter would be all right. He had done it, because he had to. Yet later, he had felt such resentment, actual bitterness directed toward his wife. It wasn't that he begrudged her the need for comfort, but did it ever occur to her that he might need a little comfort, too? After all, who consoled him; who offered him words of encouragement when he was exhausted or overwhelmed? No one. It seemed he was carrying everyone on his back.

He thought about his relationship with Mary. When was the last time either had said "I love you" to the other? When was the last time they had laughed together, gone out on a date or made love? It had been months. They could have weathered the situation with Earl, they could have successfully supported one another, but this eating disorder was threatening to not only kill Abby, but destroy the entire family. It was as if a dark unseen force had entered their home and all thought, all energy, went into fighting it. To say nothing of financial resources. Jim dragged a hand down his face, contemplating all the money he owed. He was working as hard as he possibly could, taking on every electrician job that came his way. He had been forced to let his part-time gal go to save money and now had Mary doing the books. Still, he didn't see how he could make ends meet. The sale of Earl's home had helped with his care, but Abby…the cost of the ranch was so high. He had already dissolved her college fund, figuring it better be used to help her now, or she might not live long enough to even see college. But the bills were piling up.

As these thoughts flooded his mind, Jim could feel the weight of all his worries pressing down on his shoulders. He compressed a little more and leaned his head against the chain supporting the swing. The large iron links felt cold against the skin on his balding head. Planting his feet firmly on the ground below, he rocked gently, forward and back, forward and back. He wanted a cigarette. If he had a pack in his pocket, he would have lit up without a moment's hesitation, promise or no promise.

Jim sighed heavily. If only he had someone to listen to him like he listened to others. If he could just talk out his fears and concerns to someone, anyone, he felt certain the burden would somehow lessen. But there was no one. Everyone in his world was counting on him to be strong. At least, Mary had her religion, though it seemed to be letting her down lately. He threw his head back and stared up at the sky, which today was a clear robin's egg blue and appeared so vast. Was there a God up there hiding among those wispy white clouds? If so, could He perhaps help Jim, maybe just this once?

A dark shadow unexpectedly fell across the man on the swing. "Are you Abby Cardoza's father?" The voice came from directly behind Jim. Startled, he lurched in his seat, craned his head around to see who was speaking to him. The woman was tall, dressed in a lightweight Kelly-green pantsuit and carried an extremely large black purse. She wore a single strand of pearls around her neck, something he hadn't seen in quite some time. Jim could not place her to save his life.

"You are Abby's father. I was heading for my car and thought I recognized you sitting here. I shouldn't have snuck up on you like that. I'm sorry I startled you. I'm Betty Staton, the principal here."

Jim's memory finally kicked in. Of course, Abby's principal. He had seen her at a dozen different school events—bake sales, Halloween parties, talent shows—all the standard grade-school fare. "Yes, Betty, I'm Jim." He edged forward on the seat, preparing to stand.

"No, don't get up." She waved a hand in the air. "Instead, why don't I join you for a minute. I've been locked in a meeting all morning; it's refreshing to be outside in the open air. Unless I am disturbing you. Did you want to be alone?"

"No, no I don't. Please join me."

The principal eased her somewhat considerable bulk into the swing alongside Jim's. "My, it's been a long time since I've sat on one of these. Is it my imagination, or have they shrunk over the years? It certainly couldn't be that my backside has gotten bigger."

Jim smiled at the elderly woman. "I had a pretty snug fit myself. There's no doubt in my mind, they've shrunk…a lot…it's probably all the rain we've been having."

They chuckled at the shared joke, before Betty grew serious. "How's your daughter doing? I think about her a great deal. She was always one of my favorites."

"Thank you. Best I can tell, she's doing better. Her therapist seems positive, but maybe, they always have to be. The alternative, well, isn't so good." Jim hunched his shoulders, wishing he had more to offer in the way of good news.

"I understand." She rocked a bit on the swing. Above, the chains made plaintive creaking sounds where they connected with the frame. She swung her gaze over to Jim, studying his face. He could actually feel the intensity of her stare. Yet he did not flinch under the scrutiny for her face was suffused with so much warmth and compassion. Eventually, she spoke again. "How are you doing, Jim? The strain on you must be tremendous. I can't even begin to imagine how difficult this has been for you." Reaching across the short distance between swings, she brushed his shoulder lightly with her fingertips.

Somehow, the simple touch completed the connection between the two. Now, he not only saw the compassion in her expression, he felt it in his heart. Looking into her kind eyes, his throat constricted. He opened his mouth, fully intending to speak. No words came. Instead, he felt something deep inside his soul shift, and then give way. Without warning, tears flooded his eyes and began streaming down his face unchecked. Prior to that moment, Jim could never have imagined crying in public, especially with a relative stranger. But it seemed as if he had no choice in the matter. So he simply gave in to the deep-seated anguish and let the tears come. Betty continued to rock sedately, never saying a word. At some point, the principal rummaged around in her leather handbag and came up with several fresh white tissues. She handed them across to him, and as he pressed them to his face, he sobbed even harder. Once the tears subsided, he blew his nose and finally spoke. At her encouragement, he opened his heart to her, sharing all that had troubled him lately; all the fear, anxiety, pain, worry. He told her about Sara, Mary, even Earl. She listened. They sat together talking—two large people on two little swings—until the time came to go.

Standing, Jim struggled to convey how much he had needed her at that exact moment, how much her being there had meant to him. Though he tried so hard to thank her, mere words failed to express his gratitude. She also got to her feet, straightened her jacket and slung the handbag's long strap over one shoulder. "You're welcome. I'm just glad I was here to help. It's so rare—being in the right place at the right time. When I got out of that meeting, I looked over and saw you there. I said to myself, 'That man needs a friend.' I don't know how I knew, I just did."

"You were absolutely right. Thank you so much." He gave her a crooked smile, then leaned over and embraced her, yet another thing he had never, ever done. They parted; she to her car, he to the street. Jim was a little late in picking up Sara. Beth's mother told him it was fine and that the party was a complete success. As expected, Sara was completely done in. Jim picked her up, hoisted her onto his shoulder, and carried her the few blocks back home. After the time spent with Betty Staton, this burden did not feel heavy in the least.

—⁂—

The antique clock on Kyla's desk registered every passing second. Tick. Tick. Tick. It was the only sound in the room. Abby sat pressed into the corner of the couch, knees drawn up to her chest, arms wrapped tightly around her legs. Her chin was tucked deep into the hollow between her still-bony knees. She had made herself as small as she could possibly get. It saddened Kyla to see her regress to this tight, safe posture. Her patient hadn't felt the need to "be small" since their initial meeting together weeks ago. But she clearly felt the need now. Kyla understood and respected it.

Perched on the couch alongside Abby, the therapist scrutinized the now-silent girl. Her skin resembled paste; her eyes were red-rimmed and puffy from crying. She appeared shell-shocked and gazed blankly at the carpeted floor. Jesus had said that the truth would set you free, but he never said that freedom would come without pain. And this precious child had experienced enough pain for several lifetimes.

Briefly, Kyla closed her eyes while Abby collected her thoughts and prepared to go on. The girl had spoken nearly nonstop for an hour, pausing only when her strangled sobs obliterated her words. She had finally told Kyla everything about that dark period in her early life. It was exactly what Kyla had waited for, hoped for, needed to hear. And now as she allowed all this information to settle into her mind, there was a piece of her heart, albeit a very small piece, that desperately wished she had never heard a word. Kyla had been on the listening end of many abuse scenarios. All of them were bad, but this was particularly difficult to hear. Such a very small child; such very horrific abuse. Abuse that stretched far past inappropriate touching or watching, and into the realm of oral sex. From a trusted family member, no less. Kyla drew in a deep steadying breath and touched Abby's elbow lightly with her fingertips, wordlessly encouraging her to continue.

Abby picked right up on the nonverbal cue; she went on with her narrative. "He always said it was our special secret and I should never tell. But I knew it was wrong and I felt so much...shame. It was kind of like embarrassment, but worse. I didn't know it was called shame until I came here and we talked about feelings.

"It was like I was living two lives. There was the real life where everything was normal, then there was the time alone with him. I knew it was wrong, but I didn't want him to be mad. And I still wanted him to love me." She paused. "Then, all of the sudden, it stopped."

"How old were you then?"

Abby's shoulders twitched, trying to manifest a shrug. "I don't know."

"Maybe around six?"

"Yeah, maybe."

Not only could Kyla have guessed her age due to the timeline, but she had seen pedophilia like this before. A certain type of offender often began to lose interest in his subject when she was about six. Either the girl had grown too big, or the man grew too fearful of exposure. Kyla had no way of knowing what the motivating factor was in this situation, and it didn't really matter. "And then?"

"Then I felt like I was living one life instead of two. But it was still all wrong. Everything in the family was normal, but it wasn't. I still knew something that no one else but he knew. He acted all normal, but I felt scared and funny all the time. After a while, I told myself it hadn't happened, that it was just like a bad nightmare. I think I might have believed it a little, but I was still scared. I only felt really safe locked in my room."

"And then when you were nine, Sara was born."

Abby jerked her head up. Her dark eyes were saturated with naked fear. "I couldn't keep pretending it wasn't real, because it was. I had to protect her. I was so afraid he would hurt her, too."

Kyla noticed the knees of Abby's jeans were now painted a dark blue due to the many tears shed. She knew the denim would dry far faster than this heart would heal. "So you kept Sara safe. Then around eleven years old, you…"

"I stopped eating. I wanted to die."

Kyla knew it was the advent of puberty and its commensurate emotions that triggered the eating disorder, but she was pretty sure Abby could not currently make the connection. The therapist had several weeks to explain it to her, but right now, she needed to know Abby's thoughts. "Abby, why did you want to die?"

Abby looked bleak, defeated. She spoke in a soft murmur, yet in a tone that was utterly matter of fact. "Because I'm bad. I don't deserve to eat. I don't deserve to live."

Kyla blinked, stunned. Although she had heard similar words before, spoken by any number of patients, she couldn't remember a time these statements had been uttered with such absolute conviction. And of course, she couldn't help noticing that Abby spoke in the present tense: "I am bad," instead of, "I was bad." This meant, on some level, she still believed she deserved to die. Striving to keep her own emotions under control, Kyla concentrated on maintaining a level voice and steady expression. "Why do you think that?"

"Because it's true. If I had been a good girl, he never would have done those things to me."

This was precisely what made childhood trauma so difficult. A child's worldview was so narrow, so one-dimensional. Often, the only perceived individual in that world was the child herself. Therefore, when something went wrong, she automatically blamed herself. This was exactly what Abby did then and was continuing to do now.

Kyla leaned closer, retained significant eye contact and spoke every word carefully. "Abby, what he did was wrong. He was an adult, you were a child. Adults are supposed to protect children, not harm them. If anyone is bad, it's him. You were not bad then and you are not bad now."

It was as if the therapist had not spoken at all. Abby averted her gaze and repeated in the same apathetic voice, "I am bad. I was born bad. I have always been bad."

Kyla would not debate the point. Abby had held on to this conviction for far too many years. To her, it was truth; indeed, a fact. She would not give it up without a real struggle. In time, Kyla felt certain she could get her to see the lie, but not today. "You've been learning a lot about God in chapel, haven't you?"

Abby, her face now anchored between her knees, offered a small nod.

"God is a God of love. He loves all His children because He created every one of them. He doesn't make bad children; it is not in His nature. He created you and He loves you." When Abby failed to respond, Kyla reached over and retrieved the worn leather Bible from her desk. She laid it on her lap and flipped through several pages looking for a specific passage. She located it quickly. It was Psalm 139, a beautiful scripture she referred to often with her patients. "Here, listen to these words." Kyla read: "…You created my inmost being. You knit me together in my mother's womb. I praise you because I am fearfully and wonderfully made. Your works are wonderful, I know that full well. My frame was not hidden from you when I was made in the secret place. When I was woven together in the depths of the earth, your eyes saw my unformed body…"

Kyla closed the book and rested her hands on its cool surface. "He, God, knit you together in your mother's womb. He made you exactly how He wanted you. As it says, you are fearfully and wonderfully made."

The girl shrugged. "Then something went wrong somewhere."

Kyla placed the Bible on her desk, then turned back to the girl. "Abby, is Sara bad?"

"My Sara?" She was visibly aghast by the question. "No. She's the best thing in the whole world."

"Right now Sara is the exact same age you were when the abuse began. If he had done to her what he did to you, would that make Sara bad?"

In her mentally and emotionally depleted state, Abby didn't see where Kyla was going with the question. "No, never. Sara is just a little girl."

Now, the therapist just waited, knowing silence was her most powerful tool. Even though dusk had fallen outside the office window and Kyla had not bothered to turn on a light, she could still clearly discern Abby's expression. She was making the connection. Still she said nothing. Eventually, the girl looked up. Kyla spoke, "And nine years ago you were…"

Abby hesitated, confused. Her face contorted with clashing emotions. Kyla could tell she wanted so desperately to climb aboard the life raft the therapist was tossing out to her. But she had spent so many years thrashing around and nearly drowning in the turbulent water of shame, the thought of rescue was nearly unfathomable. "Just a little girl, too?"

"Yes." Kyla infused the simple one-syllable word with all the power and conviction she could muster.

That was enough for today. It was time to stop. They had come a long way and Abby was exhausted. Kyla smiled. "Abby, it took a lot of courage to tell me all this. I am very proud of you. Could you maybe use a hug about now?"

Abby also attempted a smile. She unfolded from her consolidated position and fell into the therapist's waiting embrace. They hugged and Kyla whispered affirming words into the girl's hair.

Kyla recognized the need for closure. She could take Abby for a short walk before returning her to the group, but she tried to think of something special, something that might really lighten Abby's heart. All at once, it came to her. She rose from the couch, explaining she must make a quick phone call before they left. She punched in a few numbers, turned her back to Abby and covered the receiver as she spoke softly to the person on the other end of the line.

"Oh thank you God," Kyla said aloud as she swung back to the girl, heart filled with joy. "Guess where you and I are going right now?"

"Where?" Responding to Kyla's obvious elation, a spark flickered in her voice as well as her expression.

"We are going over to the barn to see Belle's new baby. It's a little filly."

Abby's eyes grew huge. "She had the baby? It's a girl? We get to see it?"

Kyla grabbed her briefcase and headed for the door. "Yep. And we are the only ones who will be allowed to see her tonight. Better get going before they change their minds."

Demonstrating the amazing resiliency of youth, Abby hopped to her feet and followed along. Yet, resiliency could only go so far. In deference to what the two had just experienced together, she continued to clutch Kyla's arm in a tight grip all the way to the stables.

Chapter Seven

I hate my body. Look at how fat I'm getting." Robin jumped up from her seat and turned sideways. She pulled her T-shirt taut across her slightly rounded abdomen and glared down at it. "Look at my stomach. It's disgusting. Gross, I look like I've got a beer gut. "

Kate Dixon, the center's body image therapist, dutifully examined the patient's stomach. "Robin, who is your dietician?"

"Sherry." Releasing the stretched-out fabric, Robin slumped back into the chair.

"I know she's explained that the bloating and constipation you're having is completely normal and will dissipate in time. You've got to understand, you have abused your body for years; right now you are experiencing the negative consequences of that behavior. We're trying to get your digestive system to function normally again. The human body is not like a car that you can just switch back on and have it run perfectly. It's going to take a while for everything to work right again."

Robin, always one for worrying a topic to death, said, "You know the nurses won't even let me see how many pounds I put on when they weigh me." She scratched her arm, then bit a cuticle. "Even when I was still at home and my parents took all the scales away, I still knew exactly how much I weighed."

The therapist cocked an eyebrow in question and Robin explained, "It was easy. I would go to drug stores or department stores where they sold bathroom scales and stand on them. So I always knew. Now, who knows? I've probably gained like a hundred pounds."

Kate wanted to chuckle at the girl's dramatic exaggeration, but of course, stifled the urge. Considering the average patient gained between one and two pounds a week while in residential treatment, Robin was in little danger of having to join Overeaters Anonymous. "Trust me, you haven't gained a hundred pounds."

Robin grunted, by way of response, then lifted her right hand to her head. Only when her fingers encountered the many clips in her hair, did she realize what she was doing. The hand reluctantly returned to her lap. Observing this, Kate recognized what had just transpired. Early on in treatment, Robin was diagnosed with trichotillomania, an impulse-control disorder defined by recurrent hair pulling. About 11 million people, mostly women, suffered from the disorder. If not controlled through mood-stabilizing medication, patients often ripped out their hair until they were bald and forced to wear wigs. Kate had seen girls who compulsively yanked out both their eyebrows and eyelashes. Fortunately, this girl had come to the ranch before the problem had become severe. Though patchy in places, her hair was already starting to grow back. Tom, Robin's primary therapist, had encouraged her to wear something on her head to serve as a reminder. Some girls chose baseball caps, others barrettes. Usually Robin wore a variety of bright hair clips. It had been a while since Kate had seen Robin resort to hair pulling, a behavior illustrative of a high level of anxiety.

The truth was Kate was close to ripping out her own hair over this patient. She had tried nearly every trick in the book to help Robin, but she remained recalcitrant. Kate wasn't trying to get this girl to love her body; she was simply trying to find some way for her to live in her own skin without hatred, anger or abuse. She knew Robin was a smart girl, therefore, when the negative ramifications of refeeding were explained by Sherry or her, she definitely understood. The problem was Robin believed what she saw; and what she saw was a lie. Like so many patients at the center, Robin suffered from severe body image distortion.

When she looked in the mirror she literally did not see what the rest of the world saw. When gazing at Robin, as Kate was doing now, she saw a tall, skinny girl with a plethora of mismatched clips in her hair. Yet, if Robin were to stand, pivot and regard herself in the mirror, she would see the exact same height and hair adornments, but she would not see skinny. What Robin truly saw, Kate couldn't know, but it wasn't the bony frame seen by everyone else. It was this extreme distortion that inspired this one-on-one between Kate and Robin. Today, they would do a body tracing. This exercise often proved effective with such distortion. Robin would draw what she thought her body looked like, then Kate would do an actual tracing; they would then compare the two.

Robin glowered at her legs. "By the time I get out of here the friction caused by my fat thighs rubbing together will probably make my underwear burst into flames."

Kate slapped her hand to her forehead and laughed out loud. This girl was really too much.

Robin, scrutiny returning to her stomach, reiterated, "I hate my body."

"Well I don't," Kate said as she stood, came around the table and gave Robin's shoulder a gentle squeeze. "It's the body God gave you." Expecting no response and receiving none, Kate went to a closet and retrieved a short stack of spandex items. "Here, find a top and bottom that work for you. You can change in the bathroom. While you're in there, I'll lay out the paper." Robin picked through the clothes, selected two and left. She did so without a single complaint or derogative comment. This surprised and relieved the therapist, since most patients reacted to spandex as other people might react to live toxin. The last thing they wanted to place on their "fat" bodies was spandex. But for an accurate body tracing a snug material was necessary—street clothes simply would not do.

Kate unrolled a six-foot length of white butcher paper on the hardwood floor and grabbed a handful of colored pencils. Waiting, she ruminated on Robin and smiled. In their first meeting together, Kate would have drop-kicked this girl out of the body image session for a nickel, maybe less. Yet, as time went on, the therapist grew to like her, even though she could be a major pain in the rear end. When the two were alone together, Kate could see the Robin with so much potential hiding behind the eating disorder. She was bright, clever, articulate, assertive, feisty and funny. The other girls, sensing a natural leader, liked and gravitated toward her. A tall girl, she had strong facial features and excellent bone structure. Robin, once set free from the eating disorder, would be an extremely attractive, and Kate believed, highly successful young woman.

When Robin returned barefoot in a raspberry top and white bottoms, she looked as though she had just swallowed rat poison.

"Hey, I'm proud of you. I know that wasn't easy; thanks for putting those on."

Robin feigned a pout. "I look like a blimp," she muttered, a comment the therapist chose to ignore.

"Here, pick a color, any color." Kate held out the pencils and Robin selected a vivid fire-engine-red hue. "Okay, now I need you to lie down on this paper." After Robin lay flat on her back, Kate explained, "First, you will sketch what you think your body looks like. To help you, I am going to mark key areas such as the top of your head and shoulders, the end of your fingertips, your elbows and knees and the bottom of your heels. These will provide some guidelines once you get up." Using the red pencil, the therapist marked the paper as she spoke, then Robin stood and looked down at the various points Kate had made on the paper.

Kate handed her the red pencil. "Now, go for it. Draw your body, and if you need help, I'm right here. Start by scribbling your name at the top of the paper, so we will know it is you." For the next ten minutes she watched as Robin, now on her hands and knees, drew.

When finished, the therapist asked her to lie back down in the same spot she was originally. "I believe I shall use black—always a dazzling complement to red," Kate said as she began to outline the girl's body in black pencil. "Robin, I want you to pay attention to what you're feeling. Notice how I am moving this pencil right along the edge of your body. You can feel my hand. I just want you to know that this will be an exact representation of you. I never cheat. Understand?" Robin nodded.

"While I'm doing this, let me tell you what body distortion isn't. It isn't a problem with your brain or your eyes; it isn't a psychiatric problem that's treated with meds. When people say, 'It's all in your head,' they're right. If you feel a certain way about how you look, that is what you'll see. In essence, you are validating your own feelings. To one degree or another, everyone has some distortion. In your case, it is just a little extreme. Does that make sense?"

Robin remained petulant. "Maybe."

Kate paused in her journey around Robin's left ankle and glanced briefly at her most therapeutic mirror. It was a fun-house mirror designed to drastically alter the way people appeared. The most powerful example of body image distortion occurred when using that tool. Earlier, she and Robin had stood together in front of the mirror. What each of them saw proved decidedly different. Whereas Kate saw two elongated, skinny reflections, Robin saw only one—Kate's. To Robin's eyes, Kate was comically thin, but she wasn't. Because Robin decided she was overweight, that's what she saw, even when peering into a mirror that caused her to look skinnier than she was already. It was an incredible phenomenon and if Kate hadn't witnessed it dozens of times already, she wouldn't have believed it was possible.

Robin wiggled her toes, refocusing Kate on the task at hand. Quickly and efficiently, she completed the tracing. As Robin got to her feet, the therapist lifted the paper and lightly folded it over itself. Before Robin could squawk in protest, she said, "You change your clothes, then we'll look at it together."

While Robin was changing in the bathroom, Kate tacked the paper up on a board, then stepped back a few paces to examine the results. The two outlines were shockingly dissimilar. The red body, Robin's drawing, was far larger than the black. Moments later, Robin, redressed, stood alongside the therapist and scanned the paper. "No way," she blurted out caustically. "That's not my paper. You switched it with someone else's."

Fully anticipating this reaction, the therapist pointed with an index finger at the scribbled name. "Look up in that corner. Isn't that your signature?"

Frowning, Robin eased closer, the better to scrutinize. She stayed silent. Since reticence was not her strong suit, the condition spoke volumes. Kate also stepped up. With a bright yellow pencil she drew an arrow from the red line to the black line at approximately the waist area. "One theory suggests that every quarter of an inch translates into about ten pounds. And you think you've gained at least a hundred pounds since coming here. Well, well, well—imagine that."

Robin continued to stare. A small sound, something between a gasp and a groan, escaped her lips. "Wow," she finally uttered, clearly dumbfounded. She dragged a hand down her face, as if that simple act alone might change the reality of what she saw. "I can't believe it. That's not what I see. It's not even close."

"I know."

"It's like…it's like…," Robin stammered, still trying to make sense of it, then find words to clarify her thoughts.

"It's like you telling me that my shoes are white when I know they're blue." Accordingly, she gestured to her royal blue running shoes, then lowered herself to the floor and crossed her legs. Her eyes remained pinned to the board. "You know what I mean?"

"Absolutely." Kate hunkered down beside her and sat back on her heels. "But that's what distortion is. And why in God's name would you perceive yourself as so much bigger than you truly are when all it does is cause you such pain?"

Robin, flummoxed, shook her head. "I don't know." Several moments slid by. "Do you?"

Kate waited a few moments to ensure complete attention, then spoke concisely. "I think it's the payoff. If you can convince yourself that you are fat, you can continue to justify your behavior. You can go on restricting, go on bingeing and purging, always believing that if you are thin enough, perfect enough, you will get what the eating disorder promised in the first place. So, what *did* it promise you?"

Robin dropped her gaze, spoke to her undeniably blue shoes. "Everything. I'll be everything I want to be. I'll have everything I want to have." She sounded infinitely sad, her voice little more than a whisper.

Kate lowered her voice to the same hushed register. "You'll get your needs met."

A nod.

"Such as…"

"Everyone will like me...I'll finally be good enough for my father...I'll never, ever be teased again for being fat...my mother might love me the way she loves my brother, Josh."

"But Robin, look at that tracing—you are thin. What's more, you have been thin for a very long time." Kate reached out a hand and clutched the girl's forearm. She felt the gravity of this moment as though it were a tangible thing. Robin must get this; if she didn't get it right now, Kate thought she probably never would. "Tell me, did being thin get you those things?"

Robin's eyes welled with tears. Eventually, she whispered her answer, giving voice to the one word the therapist longed to hear. "No."

⸺⋘◦⦿◦⋙⸺

Tom leaned toward his office window. With two fingers, he separated the dusty horizontal blinds and peeked out. In less than a minute, he observed Robin off in the distance trudging along the gravel path toward his office. Even if Kate hadn't called to report how the session went, he would have known by her posture and demeanor. A marble statue exhibited more bounce in its step than did this girl.

Allowing the blinds to snap shut, he brooded a while. If there was such a thing as a classic textbook example of an eating disorder, it was this patient. Robin was extremely intelligent, performance oriented and perfectionistic. Her self-esteem was inextricably linked with always being the best at everything she did. She must get the highest grades, must be the best swimmer. Because individual achievement was so valued in her family, she saw personal excellence as the exclusive vehicle to gain approval and love, especially from her father.

Earlier in her life, Robin had been pudgy, a fairly normal condition as a girl grew and matured into womanhood, especially with someone destined to be as tall as Robin. In her situation, it just took a little time for her height to catch up with her weight. Unfortunately, youth extends precious little grace to its own. Her peers, particularly boys, ridiculed her. It wounded her deeply. Yet, perceiving this as weakness on her part, she never expressed this hurt to anyone, and therefore, the wound never healed. Just prior to puberty, when adolescent emotions ran high and teenage girls were often at their most vulnerable, her father, a man dedicated to fitness, made the occasional negative comment about her weight. Her insecurity grew. When her first high-school boyfriend dumped her for a prettier, thinner cheerleader, that did it. The eating disorder, which already had a firm foothold, took over completely. Inch by inch, it invaded every aspect of her life. It became her god, in which she placed all faith and trust. It gradually seduced her into believing if she just did the eating disorder right enough, her life would be perfect. Unfortunately, what everyone at the ranch knew, if Robin did it right enough, she would be dead. This alone was the exclusive goal of the eating disorder, its only agenda.

After an admittedly rocky start, Tom and Robin had worked well together. Unable to vent through her eating disorder, Robin had been forced to express her emotions, then deal with them. The problem with addressing emotion, especially if it had been suppressed for a long time, was that pain was always attached. Robin had successfully avoided experiencing discomfort for years. Which was why she remained unwilling to give up the eating disorder. When negative emotions such as anger, hurt, rejection or frustration arose, Robin would rather rid herself of them through purging than experience pain. It was her way of coping with unpleasant feelings. Though they had tried to teach her a number of new coping skills, she preferred her strategy. Unfortunately, her technique worked. The human body perceived intense vomiting as a traumatic event; therefore, immediately following the act, the brain flooded the bloodstream with endorphins in an effort to soothe. No wonder Robin felt so much better after purging.

By this point in the therapeutic relationship, Robin should at least be considering recovery. She wasn't. None of her therapists could hit on the right argument to make her actually desire change. Today's body tracing was just one more attempt in the ongoing effort to chip away at the tenacious grip the eating disorder had on this girl. Tom and Kate had labeled it the one-two punch: first Kate would shed light on body distortion, then Tom would do the same with thought distortion; or at least, that was the plan.

Hearing footfalls right outside his door, Tom rolled his head from side to side, trying to relieve the accumulated tension in his neck. Robin came into his office and wordlessly handed him the rolled-up white paper. He shook it, encouraging the sheet to unfurl. He held it up with both hands and gave the drawings a good once-over. "I sure don't have to ask what color you used." He draped the paper over his desk, then reclaimed his chair. "Yep, it's about what I had expected."

Silence fell over the room like a fine layer of dust. Robin sat hunched in her usual seat, fingers interlocked across her middle, chin nearly resting on her chest. She gazed blankly into space. For once, she failed to fidget or twitch, something he had encouraged her to gain control over for weeks. Though her exterior appeared calm, Tom knew an interior war was being waged, a take-no-prisoners battle between Robin and her eating disorder. It was a fight to the death. Eventually one combatant would live, one would die.

"God, please help Robin to be the victor," he prayed silently, then asked aloud, "Robin, what is your eating disorder telling you right now?"

She tossed her head, striving to manifest her usual bravado. "That all of you are lying to me; that none of what Kate said was true. All of you are trying to trick me. Her tracing was a hoax. My drawing was the accurate one."

Tom took in a breath, then blew it out. Throughout his years at the center, he had grown to hate that eating disorder voice. However, he had also learned to treat it as a very real and fundamentally important aspect of the illness. The voice inhabited the minds of patients and harped at them constantly, whispering lies, undermining the truth. They genuinely heard it speak. What the voice said to his patients was as real to them as what Tom heard from the Lord. "Robin, you were right there. You saw it all, didn't you?"

Robin chewed on her lip as she cast about for a reply. "Well, I know, but..."

Tom sat forward in his chair, rested his elbows on his knees. "Have Kate or I—or anyone here—ever lied to you...ever?"

She slumped deeper in the chair. "You want to take everything away from me," she mumbled.

"Answer the question, please. Have we?"

Robin shook her head.

"Then if we haven't, who has?" He waved a hand back and forth in the air. "No, forget it, don't bother to answer. Both of us already know. Your eating disorder has been lying to you since day one. Remember Robin, remember all the wonderful things it promised you? Wait, hold on, I have your list right here."

In one of their first sessions together, Robin had carefully delineated the many benefits she expected to receive from her disorder. Now, Tom extracted the sheet of yellow lined paper from a manila file folder on his desk. He perused the first few items. "Okay, how about this. It said it would give you control over your life. Do you have control now? No. And don't blame that on us. Even before you came here, you had lost it. The truth is you forfeited all control to the disorder a long time ago. Those last few months, was there a single decision you made without considering the eating disorder first? I doubt it. If you ate, you had to purge; if friends or family wanted to go out, you had to say no since food consumption might be involved. You had to exercise how many hours a day—was it four? You call that control? I call it bondage."

Robin continued to stare at the carpet. Tom couldn't remember the last time he had lectured a patient—it just wasn't his style. What's more, he knew his words were blunt. But "warm and fuzzy" wouldn't stand a chance against her well-fortified shield of resistance.

Tom returned to the paper. "And speaking of friends— here's number two on the list. The eating disorder would make you popular…you would have so many friends because you looked so good. Friends? Robin, at last count, you had one friend left. And according to what happened the night before you came here, Amber may also have called it quits. So now you are left all alone with your eating disorder, which believe me, is no friend at all."

Still gripping the sheet, Tom stood, briefly wandered around his office, then perched on the corner of his desk. "Now, let's see here…item three. Your father. The eating disorder promised he would give you attention, love you. In fact, he would probably be proud of you for demonstrating such strength in overcoming the need to actually eat food like weaker mortals. Sure, you got attention, and it came in the form of anger, disappointment and disgust. And now? Nothing. He hardly says a word in our teleconferences. Robin, you may have gotten attention initially, but was it really the type of attention you wanted anyway? I don't think so. You didn't want anger, you wanted love. You didn't want disappointment, you wanted respect and to be valued.

"Robin, I could go through this entire list and it would all sound the same." He rattled the sheet of paper in the air. "The eating disorder made promises it had no intention of keeping. And lies? It lied to you at every turn, saying if you just got thin enough you would be happy, strong, and enviable. Lies. Look what it's stolen from you—your happiness, your health, your ability to swim, your friendships, your position of trust in your family. And what do you think is next on its list? Your future—that's what."

The diatribe was over. Tom had either made his point or he hadn't. He flung the list onto his desk, then jammed his thumbs into his back pockets. "Robin, how many times have I told you—there is nothing wrong with what you want and need; what *is* absolutely wrong is the way you are going about getting those needs met. Not only is it slowly killing you, but it just isn't working. Can't you see that?"

The argument was made; the question was posed. And Robin said…nothing.

The basketball whipped through the black metal hoop. "Swish," Josh Hamilton yelled out. "Nothing but net." The lanky teenager raised clenched fists in the air, a victory gesture unwittingly picked up months ago from his sister, Robin. He then bounded forward, snagged the ball out of the air, pivoted, and threw it back toward the imaginary free-throw line. Mike, Josh's best friend, caught the ball and bounced it twice on the cement. He kissed the fingertips of his right hand for luck, then shot. The ball sailed through the air, hit the white backboard and caromed off.

Josh grabbed the top of his head with both hands, then threw his head back and howled with laughter. "Dude, you gotta stop that finger kissing. It ain't working for Jason Kidd and it sure ain't working for you."

Mike swore. "Come on, it always works for Kidd. It's just that…my rhythm was off."

Mike hustled down the driveway in pursuit of the ball. Clamping his hands like a megaphone around his mouth, Josh called after him, "Right, yeah, that's it—your rhythm. Like you have any."

Mike executed a long bounce pass and Josh leaped to catch it. Spinning, he dribbled around in a figure-eight pattern, then charged in for a fancy double-pump layup. Missed by a mile. Now, both of them burst out laughing.

Hoping to make the freshman basketball team, the two friends had practiced regularly in the front yard of the Hamiltons' Tucson home. Today, they'd been shooting baskets for the past hour. Sweat streamed down their faces and bare chests and plastered back their hair. Their oversized and ridiculously long, baggy shorts drooped even more than usual off their slim hips. Lute Olson, eager and alert on the grass, served as the official cheerleading section, offering up the occasional high-pitched whine or low woof. Panting vigorously, he never took his eyes off the ball. It might be quite a bit larger than his tennis ball toys, but to a golden retriever, a ball was a ball, and always worth watching.

They shot a few more times. As Josh was driving toward the basket, his back to the street, Mike called, "Yo dog, your dad's coming." The boys joined Lute on the sidelines as the silver Ford Explorer pulled into the driveway, Stanton behind the wheel. The automatic garage door went up, the man offered a token wave, then parked. The door went down and the boys returned to their practice. Minutes later, Stanton came out clad in a University of Arizona Wildcats t-shirt and matching gym shorts. A blue and red sweatband striped his forehead.

"I'm going out for a run," he informed his son while engaging in elaborate stretching exercises. He darted a glance over at Josh. "You should be wearing a shirt and sunscreen." The statement was rhetorical. "Where's your mom?"

Josh, hands poised in the air, carefully judged the arc and thrust required between ball and hoop. "She said she was going with Eve to some kind of fellowship thing at the church." He tossed the ball, hit the shot dead on. Stanton didn't notice.

"Uh-huh...church," Stanton echoed, tone flat. His expression reconfigured into one of distaste, then meta-morphosed into a look of vague disgust. He waved a hand dismissively in the air as though swatting at a troublesome winged insect. "Well, I'll see you boys in a while." Stanton took off down the driveway, jogging at a slow trot, shoes slapping on the pavement.

Mike swiped a forearm across his face. "Bro, he looks majorly ticked."

Josh shaded his eyes from the final rays of the setting sun and squinted over at his friend. "Yeah, sure does. Nothin' new." He shrugged one shoulder, resigned. "If it's not my sister, it's my mom. Hey, as long as it's not me." The two friends, by unspoken consent, drifted over to the grass and sat down. Lute belly-crawled over to Mike and poked his wet nose into the boy's palm, inviting attention.

Mike obliged and scratched the dog behind the ear; Lute's tongue lolled out of his mouth, a sure sign of canine bliss. "So what about that whack-job sister of yours? She ever coming back?"

Josh yanked a tuft of grass out of the ground and sifted the blades through his fingers. "Yeah, she'll come home, sometime."

"Man, before she left, she was lookin' scary. I'm talking 'poster child for a concentration camp' scary."

"I know, it was getting bad."

"For real." Lute, capitalizing on the extended conversation, gradually eased over onto his back like a huge fish executing a slow roll in the water. Now, forepaws crooked limply in the air, as Mike's hand slid quite naturally onto the dog's stomach and started scratching, Lute acknowledged the favor with an upside-down grin. "Is she like getting any better?"

"I guess. Yesterday I talked with the dude who's treating her at the center." Josh spun the basketball on the tip of one index finger.

"You're getting pretty good at that," Mike commented, watching the rotating ball.

"You talked to him?"

"Yeah, on the phone. He wanted to know what I thought about our family and why I thought Robin was sick."

"Bro, that's heavy."

"No big deal. He's the guy we'll hang with when we go up there." Josh twirled the ball again, but it tipped off his finger. Wanting to change the subject, he said, "Hey, watch this. I've been working with Lute on this trick for a while." Josh leaned over and gently bopped the dog on the nose with the ball. "Mr. Olson, my man, how 'bout it?" Obviously understanding what was coming next, Lute wiggled around on his back, clawed the ground with one paw, then scrambled to his feet. Eyes pinned to the basketball, he shook his torso and fanned the air with his golden tail. Josh held the orange ball aloft. The dog, visibly vibrating with excitation, stared at it with an intensity that defied human understanding.

"You know, I think I could light his tail on fire and he would never even notice," Josh remarked and gave the ball a light toss down the driveway. It bounced, two, three times then settled into a rapid roll. "Go get it, boy." Lute streaked after the swiftly moving object. "Now watch what he does." The retriever overran the ball, whirled around and whacked it with the side of his snout, causing it to career in the opposite direction. He bounded after the ball and whacked it again, clearly striving to curtail its speed. The ball finally slowed and Lute began nudging it with his nose.

Mike chuckled. "Cool."

"Yeah, he is totally into pushing it around, but I'm trying to get him to bring it back to me. He hasn't gotten that part of the trick yet." Though Josh hailed the dog several times, returning his newfound toy was not part of Lute's agenda. Temporarily deaf to his own name, he continued to push the ball this way and that around the driveway with his nose. Only when the game started angling toward the street, did Josh jump to his feet to retrieve both the slobbery ball and prancing dog.

The boys decided to call it a day and Mike headed for home. Josh dropped his butt on the grass; within seconds, Lute was again on the receiving end of teenager affection.

Petting the dog's neck, Lute's chain collar jingling like silver coins, Josh propped his chin on his raised knee. His thoughts drifted to his sister. Though he would never admit it to his friend, it kind of bothered him when Mike called Robin a whack job. Sure, she was a little messed up, but it wasn't like she was really nuts or anything like that. She just wanted things that were hard to get—like love from their father. That's what he had told Tom, Robin's therapist. Josh had been watching her trying to get their dad's attention and approval all his life. First, she'd earned high grades, then, she transformed herself into an awesome swimmer. But no matter what she did, it never quite accomplished what she wanted. So she got all skinny and gross looking, which admittedly was a little weird. But even weirder was that for a while, Josh could see that it had actually worked. For a time, their father had paid a lot of attention to her. Josh figured, in Robin's mind, that must have qualified as success.

Personally, Josh had never worked all that hard to get anything from his dad. After seeing Robin struggle, why bother? Josh figured his dad maybe loved both of them on some level, but he just didn't have it in him to show it. Of course Josh also recognized it was easier for him because he had his mom. Robin didn't have anyone to love her, which was probably why she was mad all the time.

Gazing at his dirty shoe laces, Josh fondled the silky fur of Lute's ear. Suddenly his vision blurred as his eyes stung with unexpected tears. He blinked furiously. Brushing them away with the back of one hand, he assured himself the tears were the result of salty sweat trickling off his forehead.

He sniffed. Another thing he would never have told Mike was how much he missed his sister. He had always wanted Robin to like him. When she won the state spelling bee or kicked butt in all those swimming races, he had been really proud of her, proud to be her brother. He should have told her that. Maybe if they had been closer, like friends, she wouldn't have gotten so sick. Now, everything was all screwed up. His mom and dad hardly spoke to each other; each was going in different directions. He was still tight with his mom, but saw her less and less. Maybe this was how Robin had always felt…alone.

Chapter Eight

In Charlotte, Grayson, eager to escape the horrendous humidity, hurried into his Myers Park home and slammed the front door behind him. He squinted at the harsh white light showering down from the multi-tiered chandelier on the vaulted ceiling. Flinging his car keys on a nearby table, he crossed the marble floor and went directly into the living room. Moving silently across the plush carpet he headed straight for the wet bar, not pausing to shed his jacket or loosen his silk tie. He needed a drink and he needed it right now. The quicker he could officially put the day behind him the better. From a crystal decanter, he poured a generous amount of Glenlivit into a monogrammed tumbler and added ice. As far as he was concerned, this was the only good reason to have a full-time maid: the ice bucket remained well-stocked. He drank deeply, relishing the familiar burn as the liquor slid down his throat, then lifted the bottle a second time and topped off the glass. Only then, did he loosen his tie.

The day had been a disaster from beginning to end. Nurses called in sick with the stomach flu, the OR got backed up, then one patient failed to appear altogether for a long-scheduled surgery. To top it off, the final procedure of the day had gone wrong, terribly wrong. What should have been a routine face lift had turned into a medical nightmare. Inexplicably, the patient had experienced an adverse reaction to anesthesia so severe that she suffered a myocardial infarction right on the table. Surely, throughout his years of practice, he had seen anesthetic complications, but never anything as life-threatening as an MI . The surgery was halted, the patient was stabilized and admitted to the Carolinas Medical Center. She would recover, but it remained to be seen how the lift would be completed, since local anesthesia was simply not an option in a surgical procedure this complex.

Grayson turned slightly, propped a hip against the bar and swirled the amber liquid in his glass. His gaze slid naturally to the impressive spotlighted portrait of Alexa at her coming-out ball. It was this picture that had been featured in the society pages. How many times had he stood right here examining it without seeing the truth?

Now he saw his daughter with new eyes, new knowledge. Without a doubt, she was a vision, truly exquisite. But where was his daughter? He couldn't see her at all.

Grayson believed the past few weeks had changed him more profoundly than the previous twenty years. He had taken serious stock of his life and that of his family. He had spent time with Scott discussing Alexa and what was transpiring in Arizona. Scott shared information gleaned from the weekly teleconferences among him, Alexa and her therapist. His son-in-law felt positive about the progress being made and he, Scott, was looking better than he had in quite some time. He had put on a few much-needed pounds, appeared rested and far less stressed. Grayson was so thankful for the young man's tenacity in this difficult situation and continued devotion to his daughter. He had seen colleagues of his, other doctors, abandon and divorce their wives for far less than this.

Grayson let out a small breath and took another healthy swallow of the single malt. Already, he could feel the liquor soothing his frazzled nerves and ushering in the mild euphoria he desperately sought. A sound from the hall caught his attention; he looked over toward the door. "Loren, is that you?"

His youngest child poked her head around the door. "Yeah, I'm going out." With that, she was gone.

Knee-jerk irritation swept through him at the cavalier dismissal. He spoke again. "Will you please come here?"

She reappeared in the doorway, now looking put upon and more than slightly peeved. "What?"

He modulated his voice, kept his tone light. "Will you come in here?"

She heaved an exaggerated sigh. "Dude, I'm supposed to hook up with Melissa in like ten minutes."

"Loren, I'm not a dude, I'm your dad. Can't you talk to me for just a minute?"

Grudgingly, she smiled a little at the dude comment and ambled in. Looking at her, Grayson's soul sank at her appearance. The word disheveled immediately came to mind, but the truth was, slovenly would have been more accurate. No makeup, unkempt hair, baggy sweatshirt and worn jeans. His youngest child was undeniably chubby. It was all he could do to not flick a quick glance over to Alexa's portrait to compare the two. But he kept his eyes steady on Loren, knowing if he even looked in that direction, she would pick up on it immediately and resent it. "What are you up to tonight?"

"Melissa and I are just gonna hang." She twirled a tendril of long hair around an index finger. As with Alexa and Jackson, it was an arresting shade of golden blonde. She also had Alexa's eyes, with the same violet-blue shade and fringe of long black lashes.

He lifted an eyebrow. "Going out on a school night?"

"Dude...Dad, chill—it's Friday."

He gave a self-deprecating shrug. "Oh, that's right, I lost track. I was sort of hoping maybe you'd stay in tonight.

I'm going over to see Scott and Logan a little later and thought you might join me."

Loren had never been one for hiding emotion; what she felt always registered clearly on her face. After issuing the invitation, Grayson watched as an astounding number of emotions flashed across her countenance. He could plainly see the love she felt for Logan, even the deep fondness she had always had for Scott. But what clearly eclipsed all was the paradoxical love/hate she harbored for Alexa, who remained the unmentioned link between the two families. Yet as quickly as they manifested, the various emotions vanished. Clearly, Loren was also becoming expert at tucking feelings safely away where they went unseen and in time, unfelt. Grayson had witnessed that same ability in Alexa, only at a far younger age. Perhaps that was due to the pressure Pamela had always placed on Alexa to be the perfect Southern daughter.

Similar expectations had never been levied on Loren, because she simply wouldn't have it. Early on, probably around puberty, she had asserted herself. Loren had made it abundantly clear that she would not be groomed and refined; not be paraded about in a chic white gown; not be a Southern Belle candidate-in-the-making. Most of all, this particular daughter could not be counted on to become a sophisticated young lady who would please her mother and society at large with a good marriage. To ensure her desired outcome, she had swiftly transformed herself into what stood before him: the antithesis of her sister. Could

Loren right now be as lovely as Alexa had been at her age? Absolutely. But she was bound and determined to guarantee that would not occur.

But as Grayson regarded his youngest, he knew her situation was all wrong, too. Perhaps not as immediately life-threatening as Alexa's, but wrong all the same. Loren, in her rigid rebellion, was also being hurt. He had watched as she clamped down on her emotions. How long before she would also become an artificial person, not knowing who she really was or what she felt? Loren's effort to be Alexa's diametric opposite might very possibly render similar results. Alexa had always been the good girl. Did that mean Loren was destined to be the bad girl? Would she turn to drugs, alcohol, or boys to ease her pain the way her sister had turned to bulimia and self-harm? Had she done so already? As that thought and its many ramifications coalesced in his mind, a bolt of sheer terror streaked through him. So blindsided was he by fear for his daughter he literally staggered under the weight of it.

"Dad, are you all right?" Loren took a couple of steps toward her father, anxiety reflected in her expression.

Grayson wiped away a film of sweat that had suddenly appeared on his brow. "Yes, Honey, I'm okay, but do you really have to go out tonight?"

She frowned, bewildered by the question. "Yes, why?"

"I just want to be with you. You know, spend some time together. Talk about important things. Could we do that sometime soon, just you and me? Please?" Pushing away from the bar, still a touch shaky, he lurched awkwardly over to his leather armchair and sank gratefully into its cushioned depths.

She hesitated. "Sure, I guess…I guess we can," she said, still looking and sounding perplexed. "Maybe this Sunday; or are you golfing?"

He winced. A fresh sadness washed over him. Golfing. How many weekends had he spent on the links, relying on legitimate recreation for escape as others might rely on a drug? "No, not this weekend. Let's plan on spending the day together. We'll talk."

"Okay."

Grayson realized Loren's confusion was now melting into suspicion. And why not; suddenly her father was displaying all kinds of interest in her—who wouldn't be leery? Trying to lighten the mood and quell her anxiety, he smiled and gave his knee a small slap. "Then it's a date. You and me, we'll hang. Okay dude?"

"Okay." Loren tilted her head and gave him a huge smile, looking so much like Alexa at that moment, he wanted to weep. I can't lose this one, too. The thought flashed through his mind with the rapidity of a single heartbeat and he knew it was true. The mistakes made in the past could be rectified with love and time. He could and would change the present and the future. Unexpectedly, Loren leaned over and kissed him on the forehead, the action seeming to surprise her as much as it did him. "I'm gone. See you tomorrow, Daddy. Kisses to Logan." She pirouetted and disappeared with a wave.

Stunned, Grayson settled back in the chair and flung one leg over onto the matching leather ottoman. How long had it been since his daughter had voluntarily kissed him, no less called him Daddy. Too long was the obvious answer. He desperately hoped that her level of affection toward him might also change. It would start with him being more routinely affectionate with her. In time, perhaps she would follow suit.

Scratching his head, he yawned expansively, then drained the rest of his cocktail. His eyelids felt heavy as though each supported huge weights. The chair, his chair, was encouraging him to settle in a little deeper and catch a quick catnap. If not for the plan to see his grandson later, he would have taken the chair up on its subtle invitation. As he engaged in private musings regarding the evening ahead, Pamela swept into the room. Though draped in a floor-length silk robe, her hair and makeup were freshly done. He immediately recognized this for what it was: a very bad sign. "Gray, Rita has laid out your tux and cufflinks. I'm going up to get dressed now. Better hurry along; we need to leave in fifteen minutes." She pivoted, the diaphanous periwinkle robe billowing like a wind-bloated sail, and sauntered toward the door.

Apathy engulfed him. "Leave for where?" he drawled, not bothering to disguise his feelings.

She glanced back at him over one shoulder, her left hand resting lightly on the door jamb. "The hospital fundraiser at the country club. You remember, I told you about it weeks ago."

He thought about it a moment, then made a decision. "Pam, I can't go. I have had the worst possible day and I told Scott I'd be over tonight to see Logan."

Now he saw where his youngest daughter got her emotional transparency. Pamela's feelings regarding this current situation were clearly cast on her face...and they weren't good. "Grayson, the baby will be there tomorrow and the next day. The fund-raiser is tonight."

He set his jaw. "I know. I'm sorry I forgot about your plans, but that doesn't change how difficult my day was or where I want to be this evening, and it isn't at the club." He rubbed his forehead just above his eyebrows, trying to relieve the residual tension. "Pamela, I am dead-dog tired. I simply don't have it in me tonight to make inane conversation with people I don't know and couldn't care less about."

She turned slowly to face him, folding her arms beneath her breasts and narrowing her gaze. "But it's the hospital. Everyone will be there."

"Darlin', I don't care if Elvis himself is making a special trip over from 7-Eleven to be the keynote speaker, I'm not going."

"You want me to go alone?" She gripped her elbows with both hands, as though endeavoring to contain her escalating anger. The negative electricity crackling between the two of them was nearly tangible. "Do you know how that will look?"

He shook his head and swore under his breath. "Don't know, don't care. You don't have to go either. Why not come with me and play with your grandson? It's been a while since you've seen him, hasn't it?" But no answer was forthcoming because the doorway was now empty, seemingly as empty as their marriage.

Hours later, as Gray strode up and down the Kent porch gently patting the sleeper-clad bottom of a fussy little boy while conversing with Scott, Loren was miles away relaxing in a convertible. She and Melissa had pulled off the highway and parked on a little-known and less-traveled gravel road. This was a favorite spot of theirs when they wanted to drink or get high. A thin slice of silver-white moon hung in the sky and the heat had fled with the sun. The cool night air possessed just enough nip to suggest winter wasn't far off. Tree frogs chatted to one another and traded rumors in surround sound.

Loren slouched comfortably in the passenger seat. Her back was propped against the car door and her feet were anchored on the dash, crossed at the ankle. She held a near-empty beer in one hand. They'd been drinking and talking for nearly an hour. Loren had just told her friend about the peculiar interaction she'd had earlier with her father.

Melissa took a final long drag from her cigarette, then wedged the butt into her empty can. It made a faint sizzling sound as it encountered the few remaining droplets of beer. "That's like way weird. What do you think he wants to talk about?"

Loren shrugged, the gesture unseen in the dark night. "Who knows? But I don't think it's a bad thing; like he wasn't ticked or anything. More than anything, he looked kinda whipped and like…bummed out."

Melissa reached into the brown paper bag and pulled out two more brews. She passed a can over to Loren, then flipped open one for herself. Both girls tossed their empties onto the floor, already littered with several dead soldiers and a half-eaten bag of tortilla chips. "Bummed? Do you think it's something to do with your sister? God, she hasn't like died or anything, has she?"

Loren took a long satisfying pull from the can. She felt a little buzzed. "No, nothing like that."

"So what's the 411? She getting better, or what?"

"I guess. No one says anything."

"That bites. You guys never talk at all. Your family is like totally messed up."

"Tell me about it."

"You know, I always kinda liked your dad. But your mom, I got to tell you, she totally creeps me out. I think she hates me."

"She hates everyone, especially kids."

"Then why did she have like three of her own?" Melissa fumbled another cigarette from the pack and flicked her butane lighter. The flare ignited a splash of yellow light into the dark night. She cupped a hand around the tip and sucked on the filter. It took a moment for their night vision to return.

"I wonder that all the time. Maybe back then they couldn't help it, you know, the pill hadn't been invented yet. Or maybe having a ton of kids was like the thing to do to show you had money, like you could afford them or something."

Melissa burped loudly. They laughed uproariously, then squealed in tandem, "Gross," and laughed even harder. Eventually, Mel asked, "Did you know your sister was into the puking thing?"

"I never know anything. Not only because no one tells me jack, but it's not like she and I have ever been tight."

"True." She took another drag, the tip glowing reddish-orange in the darkness, then flicked ash onto the ground. "If it wasn't for the kid, you'd probably never see her at all."

Loren grunted her agreement and took another swig from the can. The two fell silent, each consumed with her own thoughts.

Mel was Loren's closest friend, but even she didn't know everything. Loren had never told her that, as a little girl, she had loved Alexa, actually worshipped her. So in awe was she of her older sister, Loren wanted to grow up to be just like her. She would sit on the carpeted bathroom floor watching Alexa put on makeup in front of the brilliantly illuminated mirror before going out on a date. She was so beautiful and could apply black eyeliner perfectly, without a single smudge in the sky-blue eye shadow. The two would talk and laugh constantly. Even when she went away to college, the sisters stayed close. Then when Loren was about thirteen, something happened and things changed. She saw Alexa one weekend and she was normal and the next time she saw her, she wasn't. From then on out, Alexa was more like a mannequin than a real person. She had abandoned Loren and it had broken her heart. Then Jackson, whom Loren also loved, was gone and she was left alone with her mother. What a bust. Talk about a hate-hate relationship.

Another thing Melissa didn't know about was the self-harm. Truth was, Loren wasn't even supposed to know. She only found out by eavesdropping, which she frequently did to find out what was going on in her family. Somehow, Loren could get the puking, but Alexa cutting herself up? Even she, who actively cultivated enmity toward her sister, had trouble with that one. But she wasn't going to get sucked in—no way. If she let herself feel bad and actually started caring about Alexa again, she'd get burned, she just knew it. Loren had touched that old love stove one too many times— it just didn't pay. All she had to do was keep picturing Alexa as a mannequin, like one of those fake women she saw showcased in store windows. She couldn't feel anything, especially not love, for a person made out of plastic.

———⟨∘∕∘∕∘⟩———

"Lexy's on her way," Dan told his colleague on the phone. "Right, let me know. Thanks." He plunked the receiver back into its cradle and sighed. As Lexy's therapist, Dan prayed the next hour would garner positive results regarding his understanding of this young woman.

Throughout the past several weeks, Lexy had worked hard in their therapy sessions. Once they jointly established the bulimia was not about being thin, she had endeavored to understand the true purpose of her eating disorder. Dan and Lexy had examined the influence of several important factors on her emotional development and self-concept: the Southern society in which she was reared; her family of origin; the perfection-driven media; the impact—both positive and negative—of affluence; even her father's chosen profession of plastic surgery. Together, they thoroughly analyzed each topic and how it related to her throughout her life. They also discussed emotions at great length: how to define, understand, and label them. A battery of psychological tests had been administered to Lexy shortly after admission. They revealed she was alexithymic. This meant she was totally out of touch with her emotions, a condition frequently observed in eating-disordered women.

Considering her upbringing, alexithymia was no surprise. In her family, individual thoughts and opinions possessed no value; and in fact, were suppressed. What mattered was speaking, thinking and doing what was expected, what was socially correct. Lexy had played the role so long, she became the role. Dan knew if emotions were suppressed long enough, they fell dormant. His goal was to reawaken these feelings and get her reconnected. It wasn't easy. To date she remained stunted, rarely expressing anything deeper than surface emotions.

While at the center, Lexy had done remarkably well. Unlike the adolescent patients, she forced herself to stand back and honestly evaluate how drastically the eating disorder had consumed and damaged her life. With Dan's help she recognized this illness would ultimately destroy her. Everything was on the line: her life, her marriage, her relationship with her child—everything. Lexy wanted recovery; she wanted to be set free from the bondage of her eating disorder and get her life back. But the professionals on her treatment team were in agreement—it must be an emotionally healthy and grounded life predicated on things of real value and worth, not the synthetic, perfection-oriented existence she had lived for the past twenty-two years. This meant expending a huge amount of effort in learning new skills and adopting new behaviors.

Dan had given Lexy many assignments that challenged her old behaviors, such as going an entire day without wearing makeup. Lexy without makeup was like Dan without clothes. But she had done it and in the process, discovered that the degree to which she was valued by the therapists and patients had nothing to do with her appearance. If anything, they liked her more, knowing she was not hiding behind the artificial mask of expertly applied cosmetics.

What's more, Dan was delighted to see Lexy's response to the spiritual component of treatment. Throughout her life, she had attended the occasional Sunday service to be seen, relegating church to a social, never a spiritual, experience. While at the ranch, she had attended chapel and Bible study with a genuine seeker's heart, earnestly trying to embrace Jesus.

During her stay, she experienced the same physical complications suffered by most patients. Lexy had abused laxatives far longer than initially thought; therefore, complaints about constipation were high on her list. Dan felt certain, if given enough time, her body would function normally again; unlike others whose bodies never would. How many women had he seen go through the program who had taken upwards of two hundred laxatives a day? He couldn't begin to count…there had been so many. Women whose bodies had been so burned out by over-the-counter medication that colostomies had to be performed.

Despite her effort and commitment, Dan remained deeply concerned about the cutting behavior. Whereas Lexy had addressed the bulimia head-on, she remained unwilling to go in-depth regarding the self-mutilation. She would skirt around the topic, provide incomplete answers when questioned, and practice every possible avoidance technique. He believed this abuse was driven by self-loathing, but what motivated it? The truth was, Dan was now no closer to understanding why she harmed herself than at their initial meeting. Clearly, she was unwilling to relinquish this aberrant behavior. This frustrated Dan. He recognized that while the eating disorder and the cutting were two distinctly separate behaviors, they stemmed from the same core issue. Both must be dealt with while in treatment. Talk therapy simply wasn't working, which was why he had requested help from Rebecca Green today. The art therapist had already done excellent work with Lexy in group sessions.

Dan swiveled around in his chair, opened his large office cabinet and extracted a box. It was Lexy's Inside/Outside box; all patients were required to create one in art therapy. The idea was to decorate the outside of the white box with the person she presented to the world; the inside was to represent what she honestly felt. Lexy's box was festooned with beautiful pictures and words clipped from slick fashion magazines. She had cut and connected words together to build phrases, not unlike what would be seen in a ransom note. "Be perfect," and "look happy," and "smile, smile, smile." Of course, it was the inside of the box that captivated the therapist. She had painted the entire inside black. When asked why, she simply stated it was because she was void, empty. But Dan suspected there was more. When he held the box up and scrutinized it in the rays of the waning afternoon sun, as he was doing now, he saw the black paint had been applied in strokes that resembled an X—just like the lacerations on Lexy's abdomen. Odds had it, she hadn't even realized what she'd done. But he had definitely noticed and believed it was significant. Drumming his fingers on the desk, he contemplated the box and continued to wonder what it all meant.

———⊂∿∿⊃———

Lexy slipped into the art therapy room and pulled the door shut behind her. She fanned her face with a sheaf of papers. "My oh my, how do y'all stand it? The temperature's dropped at least ten degrees since I first got here and I still find it stiflin'."

"But remember, it's a dry heat," Rebecca, the therapist, responded. It was a common joke around the ranch, since everyone knew hot was hot, regardless of how dry. Lexy laughed, causing her dimple to become even more pronounced. "Come on in and have a seat," Rebecca invited.

The young woman slid into a metal folding chair and continued to fan herself. The air-conditioned room soon grew redolent with the aroma of her light floral perfume. She lifted her abundant mane of blonde hair off the back of her neck and fanned beneath it. "What's up? Dan just told me to head on over here."

Rebecca was gratified to see Lexy was wearing a simple sleeveless crimson blouse and blue jeans. And only a pair of gold earrings and one matching bracelet. Now that alone was nothing short of a miracle. Considering the stylish outfits and elaborate complement of jewelry Lexy had felt compelled to don every day when first at the center, she had come a long way in overcoming the need to always be dressed to the nines.

Responding to the question, she explained, "I often do one-on-one work with patients. Sometimes the therapists request it and sometimes I am the initiator. It often gives us an opportunity to go a little deeper with certain thoughts and emotions. Is that okay with you?"

"Yes ma'am…I guess." Lexy was compliant, if a shade doubtful.

"Today, I thought we might play around with a little clay." Rebecca hoisted herself to her feet and went over to the opposite side of the room to retrieve a large clay wad. Returning, she plopped it down on the table immediately in front of Lexy.

The patient stared at the grayish rectangle, obviously not liking what she saw. Rebecca knew she wouldn't, which was precisely why she had selected this particular medium. It was called earth clay and it was wet and very messy to work with. Patients plagued by perfectionism often had an extreme aversion to getting dirty. Lexy was no different. Working with this clay would prove highly challenging.

Lexy wrinkled her smooth brow. "Clay is fine, but couldn't I use some of that other stuff; you know, the pretty clay you keep in those cans?" She flung a hand in the direction of the cupboard that housed most of the art supplies.

Rebecca had anticipated this suggestion. Sure, she had plenty of that colorful, putty-like clay. She also had no intention of using it during this session. It was far too easy to remain separate from it. That clay was so tidy, it was almost impossible to become connected with it. Conversely, earth clay was so mushy, most patients couldn't tell where their hands left off and the clay began. "No, not today. I want you to use this. It's more malleable."

Lexy grimaced and didn't even try to conceal her disgust. "What do you want me to do with it?"

"I want you to make a sculpture that represents you and how you are feeling."

"But I'm not an artist. I can't…"

Rebecca cut her off mid-sentence. "Girl, you've been in my groups enough to know I don't want to hear excuses." She gave her a mock frown. "Now, what do I always say?"

Lexy sighed, then recited in a contrived monotone, "There are no mistakes in art, it doesn't have to be perfect, and…I forgot the third one."

"There is no right or wrong. And don't forget, once you start, you must continue and finish your project. So have at it. Let's go."

At the age of sixty-four, Rebecca could easily be the grandmother of many of her younger patients. Tall and bulky, she looked quite a bit older than she actually was. People had described her as "matronly" since the age of thirty. Though this failed to thrill her on a personal level, it proved beneficial when working with the patients. Because they thought of her as elderly, they perceived her as safe, non-threatening.

She and Lexy had always gotten along well. Right now Rebecca was counting on this positive rapport to see this project through. She didn't have to participate. She could leave any time. Lexy placed her fingers on the clay, testing.

Then she turned her hands over palms-up and scowled. "I declare…" she murmured. Her lovely long fingers were defaced by wet gray smudges.

"It's a little messy," the therapist said, stating the obvious.

"Now that's a fact." Lexy's genteel Southern voice sounded even more beguiling than usual in the quiet room.

The patient bit her lip; the therapist held her breath. Lexy, resigned, slowly embedded her hands into the clay. In mere seconds, her beautifully painted fingernails had vanished into the ooze. The expression on her face could not have registered greater repugnance if she had been submerging her hands into a vat of sewage. But she was doing it. That was all that mattered.

Satisfied, Rebecca settled back in her cushioned seat, steepled her long fingers and watched. Unlike other therapists who learned about the patient through constant verbal interaction, Rebecca gleaned what she needed to know through observation. She analyzed the patient's posture, hands, and most of all, her facial expressions. In Rebecca's therapeutic approach, what she saw, especially in the patient's face, was far more important than what she heard. Facial expressions, like art, rarely lied. This was particularly true when a patient was consumed with something outside of herself, such as an art project. When externally focused, she forgot to guard her expressions. Currently, Lexy's face was, indeed, an open book. Though she continued to manifest a look of abhorrence and discomfort, Rebecca knew that would soon change.

The room remained silent, save for the occasional squishy sound as Lexy manipulated the clay. Concentrating on the task, she separated a good-sized hunk from the original rectangle and began molding it. She pushed it this way and that for several minutes, clearly possessing no designated course of action or game plan. Rebecca watched intently. No matter how many times she observed a patient in a one-on-one, she found the process fascinating. Without any conscious awareness of doing so, Lexy was slowly becoming one with the clay. Already, it showed in her face. Her expression had first melted into one of neutrality, and now was evolving into a look of bewildered curiosity. She gazed at her hands as though they were no longer a part of her. Rebecca recognized what was transpiring. Lexy was gradually, and quite unwittingly, transferring thoughts and emotions from her heart to her hands. Equally important, she was wordlessly giving her fingers permission to create, in essence, to speak.

More time went by. She smoothed, molded and shaped. Her hands were covered with the gooey clay; a few thick gray drops had spattered her wrists and slender forearms. They went unnoticed. The piece was slowly taking shape. It looked like a funnel, an ice cream cone. Lexy cleared a space and sat it down, the tip pointing toward the ceiling. Using both palms, she compressed the base of the cone slightly. Then she concentrated on the narrow portion. Supporting the base with her left hand, she encouraged the upper third to arch over somewhat, as though the figure was succumbing to a strong tailwind.

Her face underwent another change. Frowning, she pressed her lips together in a hard line. Her facial muscles grew noticeably tense. Her shoulders hunched, reflecting similar strain. She formed her right hand into a fist and ground her knuckles into the clay, a couple of inches above the base, creating a hollowed-out area.

From her vantage point, the therapist found the clay work to be uncannily reminiscent of the shrouded Madonna so often displayed in nativity scenes. Especially the way it hunched over reminded her of how Mary hovered over the baby Jesus. "Is that you?" Rebecca whispered the question.

Lexy nodded, then bent closer, her hair falling forward. Her face suddenly drained of all color. Her eyes appeared huge and glazed, as she stared at the object, transfixed. Releasing her fingers from the balled-up fist, she began aggressively poking and scratching at the hollow area she had created in the sculpture; Rebecca suspected this was her symbolic abdomen. Going strictly on instinct, the therapist suggested, "It looks empty. I wonder if something belongs in that hollow place."

Lexy knew. She ceased the jabbing motions. Using the back of one hand, she flung her hair back over her shoulder. Random flecks of moist clay clung to the wavy strands and speckled her exposed neck. Without a word, she reached over and scooped another small clump of clay. Clasping it between both palms, she held it close to her face as she manipulated it. Rivulets of gray fluid seeped through her trembling hands and trickled toward her elbows. Finally, she tucked the golf-ball-sized mound in the crevasse.

Rebecca began to realize what that benign lump represented. As she looked at Lexy's anguished face, she felt deep concern, genuine dread, for this patient. "Lexy?"

The young woman did not respond; she merely stared back and forth from the large object to the small. She began to breathe rapidly through her parted lips.

Rebecca pointed to the little mound of clay. God knew, she didn't want to hurt this woman, but the therapist in her recognized Lexy must identify it; she must say the words for healing to begin. "Lexy, what is this?" Much later, when Rebecca reflected on that crucial moment, she would remember it was like watching a volcano explode; yet the reality remained that it was a deeply troubled young woman finally expressing the accumulated and suppressed pain and fury of years.

Lexy started to hyperventilate. Shoving her chair away from the table, she leaped to her feet. The chair tipped over behind her and clattered to the painted concrete floor. Suddenly enraged, a feral cry tore from her throat. Leaning over the table she smashed the large object with the flat of her hand, then pounded it repeatedly. "I hate you," she hissed at the sculpture through clenched teeth again and again as she systematically destroyed it.

Knowing she would soon be out of her therapeutic league, Rebecca picked up her phone and punched in

Dan's extension, then the emergency 911 code. "Lexy, tell me what it is," she repeated in a sympathetic, yet no-nonsense voice.

Lexy kept pounding the now-flattened clay, panting through her open mouth. "It's my baby." Her voice was high pitched, bordering on hysteria, nearly unrecognizable.

"What baby?"

The pounding stopped. Lexy flailed her hands in the air as though batting at a swarm of bees. Bits of moist clay flew in every direction. Then, she slapped her hands over her face, staggered back from the table. "The baby I killed. Oh God, it's the baby I killed," she shrieked. She threw her head back and emitted a wail of the most infinite sorrow. Tears, tinged light gray from the clay, streamed from beneath her hands. Rebecca came around the table and enveloped the keening woman in her enormous arms and rocked her back and forth. Lexy hung on to her, pressed her forehead into Rebecca's well-padded shoulder and sobbed. In fewer than five minutes, Dan rushed into the art room. He found the two women poised there, Rebecca supporting nearly all of the young woman's weight, each of them liberally spattered with wet gray clay. Soon, he too, would wear the clay…and finally know the truth.

Part Four

Chapter Nine

Autumn had finally come to the arid Arizona desert. Daytime hours were cut short while nights grew long and chilly. Dawn unveiled landscapes of scraggly vegetation sprinkled with frosty dew, which shimmered like mirror shards in the sunlight until long after the morning mist had dissipated. Afternoons often brought gusting winds and the occasional shower.

Kyla and Dan stood together in a patch of bright sunlight on the front porch of the main lodge. She leaned with elbows resting on the rail while he stood next to her with arms folded across his chest. The cool morning breeze was scented with the fragrance of wood smoke from some distant fire. It was the first day of Family Week. A few sets of parents, husbands and siblings had already drifted in. Most had flown in or driven to the center the previous day, providing the opportunity to reunite with their family member on Sunday evening. Tom had greeted Robin's family and shepherded them into the building. Kyla and Dan were still waiting for their groups to arrive.

Dan flicked a glance at the vacant gravel road, then back to Kyla. "So the plan is for Tom and me to hook up today for art therapy?"

She nodded, unconsciously fingering the chunky links of a silver chain worn around her neck. "I have to do a one-on-one with the Cardozas this afternoon, which means they will miss it. I thought it would work out well for your groups to go together. Lexy and Robin are fairly close in age and the numbers worked out. Lexy has four, right?"

"Yep. Her husband, sister and parents."

"With Robin's brother and parents that should be just about right. I take it you haven't met any of Lexy's family yet?"

He shook his head in the negative. "Nope, she came out alone. But this is a family I am certain to know on sight."

She understood. After working so intensively with a patient, often you just *knew*. She swung her gaze back to the road at the sound of an approaching vehicle. A beam of sunlight bounced off the shiny chrome of the oncoming car and Kyla squinted, striving to make out the occupants within. "What do you think—yours or mine?"

He raised a hand to his face, shading his eyes, narrowing his gaze. "Can't tell quite yet."

The large luxury car, obviously a rental, drew up alongside a squat green compact and parked. All four doors opened at once. As the front passenger door was flung wide, Dan caught a glimpse of a glamorous woman stepping out. She looked a great deal like Lexy, especially when the young woman had first arrived at the center. It had to be Pamela. She was wearing a spectacular Western buttondown blouse spangled with silver and turquoise stars; matching denim slacks; and fashionable, but in no way functional, high-heeled cowboy boots. The ensemble was the height of Western chic, lacking only a designer Stetson to complete the look. Somewhere along the line, Lexy's mother had clearly gotten the treatment facility confused with a dude ranch. Dan wasn't fazed in the least. He had seen it happen before, especially when parents were affluent. He grinned at Kyla. "They're mine." Reaching over, he gave her shoulder a gentle squeeze. "Look, I'll see you later today. Hope it goes well with Abby's parents."

Kyla tilted her head, smiled at her fellow therapist and sometimes mentor. "Boy, so do I. Thanks."

Dan descended the steps and strode over to the family, now assembled into a tight cluster at the rear of the car. "Good morning, I'm Dan." He extended his hand to the young man whom he assumed was Lexy's husband.

"And I'm Scott," he verified as he clasped Dan's hand in a firm embrace. "Good to finally meet you in person. This is Alexa's father Grayson, mother Pamela, and sister, Loren." Scott gestured to each in turn and Dan shook hands all around. Unlike Pamela, the others were dressed much more appropriately for the situation: the men in neutral-colored slacks and open-neck sports shirts, Loren in ill-fitting jeans, T-shirt and running shoes. Dan had conjured a mental image of how each member of Lexy's family would look. He had been right on the money with her decidedly overdressed mother. What's more, he had fully anticipated that Loren, now lounging against the trunk, snapping a stick of chewing gum, would be somewhat sloppy in her dress. Right again. The singular exception proved to be Lexy's father, not regarding appearance, but behavior. Grayson, an undeniably urbane and handsome man, surprised Dan by his warm handshake and direct eye contact. His demeanor was one of genuine sensitivity and humility. Immediately upon meeting Dan, Grayson expressed positive feelings regarding being at the ranch and told him how much he was looking forward to the week. This was not often the case with parents. Though they might truly want to help their daughter, so great was their trepidation regarding the content of the upcoming week, they were rarely eager to get underway.

Before entering the lodge and joining the rest of the group, Dan briefly explained the morning's agenda. "We always have plenty of breaks throughout the day in case you want to call your sister and check on your son," he told Scott before consulting his watch and darting a sideways glance out toward the street. "Lexy and the rest of our patients will be joining us soon. They'll remain here until lunchtime."

Pamela arched a perfectly contoured eyebrow. "Lexy?" She said the word with noticeable disdain. "Are you referring to Alexa?" Listening to her speak, Dan could imagine how effortlessly that lovely, cultured voice probably slid into a Southern simper when called upon to do so. Not today. In fact, her tone and words only served to trigger a vague recollection regarding how Pamela felt about this nickname. Now what was it that Lexy had told him? It was something about garbage, or trash, or...that was it: white trash. Her mother thought the abbreviated name sounded like poor white trash. Not terribly flattering. But how Pamela felt about this moniker concerned him little. The reality was that everyone at the treatment facility had been calling her Lexy for weeks and they weren't going to stop now. He turned to Pamela. "Yes. Ever since your daughter came here we've called her Lexy at her request. The nickname seems to suit her."

Pamela brushed a speck of lint off one blue cuff. The motion caused a single shaft of sunlight to spill onto the front of her ornate shirt. The pearl buttons and silver stars glistened as though illuminated from within. "Really...Lexy," she repeated, tone unchanged. She might have been saying "vermin."

"That's right," he concluded. Just over Pamela's left shoulder, he saw Loren's mouth twitch with amusement at her mother's indignant dismay. So, there *was* someone home behind that sullen mask. Dan would keep that in mind as the week progressed. But now, he shifted his attention back to the rest of the family. "So, unless you have any other questions or concerns, we can go in now." When no additional comments were forthcoming, Dan pivoted and led the way back toward the lodge. The group scaled the stairs, leather loafers and rubber-soled shoes shuffling silently, snakeskin cowboy boots clumping loudly on the scarred and weathered wood planks.

Kyla was now alone, waiting. She moved her head from side to side, trying to work out a kink that had developed in her neck. Then she closed her eyes, tilted her face up to the soothing rays of the morning sun. Somewhere far away, she could hear the chug of a locomotive and plaintive peal of the freight train's whistle. She tried to embrace the tranquility of the morning. "Be still and know that I am God," she whispered the comforting scripture to herself. She felt peace ripple through her at the reassuring words. He was God and she, like all the therapists, had complete faith in Him. Sure, she felt distinctly uneasy about how the day would unfold. It would be hard on everyone. Abby, Jim, Mary, even Kyla herself...no one would get off easy today. Kyla must keep reminding herself not to focus on what she felt, but to focus on what she knew: God was good, trustworthy, loving, full of grace and mercy. He was with Kyla always. What's more, He would generously extend all these attributes of His character to the entire Cardoza family...if only they would let Him.

Finally, a little white economy car pulled up and parked. Kyla recognized Jim immediately as he climbed out of the driver's seat. She went down to greet the two. Mary, in terms of appearance, was much as Kyla had expected: a somewhat homely, modestly attired woman who probably always wore sensible shoes. With her brown hair coiled in a tight bun at the nape of her neck, she looked exactly like what she was, a traditional librarian, perhaps a touch more dowdy than most. Jim appeared little changed since their first meeting. Kyla wondered if she would even recognize Abby's father if he were not haggard and strained. As she got closer, Kyla noticed a rectangular-shaped item outlining the breast pocket of Jim's short-sleeved plaid shirt. It was a pack of cigarettes. So, Jim had finally succumbed to the temptation of smoking. Who could blame the guy? Certainly not her; indeed, who knew better than a therapist how often people returned to old habits when the going got particularly tough. And this was tough going, no doubt about that.

Kyla introduced herself to Mary and the two women fell into easy conversation, discussing Kyla's pending baby and Abby's sister, Sara. Because of her youth, Sara could not take part in family week, so had to remain in California. She would be spending the week at the home of her closest friend. According to Mary, though Sara had wanted to come along, staying with Beth had been viewed as a real treat. As the conversation naturally segued into talk of pending events, Kyla escorted the couple up the stairs and ushered them into the building where the long week would soon begin.

—◈◈◈—

Rebecca swung the heavy door wide and propped it open with a brown and tan glazed ceramic puppy. The day had warmed up just enough to make an open door an inviting prospect. The therapist loved allowing fresh air into the art room whenever possible. She leaned a shoulder against the doorjamb and drew in a deep breath, savoring the crisp clean air. Just across the way, the wind whipped along the desert floor, creating a dust devil. It looked like a mini-tornado. It scurried this way and that, flinging detritus and bits of grass in every direction until it slammed straight into a bristly tumbleweed. Instantly, the two-foot-high air funnel disintegrated, dissolving into a fine sheet of gritty dirt. Rebecca caught a glimpse of the ranch's people mover about a block away. She stepped back inside the large room and prepared to meet her families. Presently, Dan and Tom, along with the various fathers and mothers, sisters and brothers began filtering in. Of course, Rebecca had worked with both Lexy and Robin extensively; she acknowledged each with a little wave. The rest of the group was new. Knowing little more than names and family affiliations, Rebecca enjoyed studying the parents and siblings as they straggled in. When the group was particularly large, she sometimes played a private game with herself, trying to guess who was who and who belonged to whom. Today, she scanned the room, forced to immediately forfeit the game. This small group would present no challenge whatsoever. The adolescent boy, wandering aimlessly around the room looking befuddled, had to be Robin's brother, Josh. Poor kid. Not only did he look painfully shy, but the therapist could clearly see he was smack in the middle of that awkward stage most boys went through. He was long and lanky, his arms and legs, hands and feet looked as though they belonged to someone else altogether. His cheeks and chin, aflame with barely controlled teenage acne, were showing signs of sparse beard growth. Rebecca would bet money his voice frequently cracked, probably causing extreme embarrassment to this already self-concious boy. And now he was spending time at a treatment facility, undoubtedly caught up in something he couldn't possibly understand.

Moving on, Rebecca considered the other sibling, recalling her name was Loren. She studied her. Wouldn't this young woman be surprised to discover that Rebecca actually felt greater empathy and concern for her than she did for Josh. What currently plagued the boy was temporary; time would eventually resolve his testosterone-induced difficulties. Not so for Loren. Just looking at this adolescent with her somewhat shabby clothes and surly demeanor told Rebecca so much. Upon entering the room Loren had immediately distanced herself from her family. She slumped into a chair, legs stretched out before her, rubber-soled toes tapping randomly against one another.

One thumb was hooked casually into a belt loop on her baggy jeans, while the fingers of the alternate hand fiddled with a small hoop earring. This girl was bored beyond belief and wanted everyone to know it. Gazing off at nothing in particular, Loren wore her smug aloofness like an invisible cloak.

Observing the two sisters, it was clear that Lexy had opted to deal with her family situation and upbringing one way, while with Loren, the pendulum had swung dramatically in the opposite direction. And no wonder—just look at their mother, who Rebecca could have easily identified if the room had contained a hundred people. Currently, she was prancing around, giving everything the once-over, secure in the knowledge that she looked like a million bucks, which of course, she did. The mother was as arrogant as her youngest daughter was apathetic. Idly, Rebecca wondered what this woman must be thinking. When she heard art therapy was on the docket, she probably thought it would translate into an afternoon spent fashioning clay ashtrays or weaving straw baskets. Occasionally parents, when learning of this activity, thought exactly that. Little did they know or even suspect that this "experiential" would probably offer some of the most revelatory therapy they received throughout the entire week.

Rebecca assumed the distinguished looking gentleman must be Lexy's father, while the younger man, sitting next to Lexy, tenderly holding her hand, had to be her husband. He had a kind, if tense and troubled, face. By default, the remaining two were Robin's parents. She, not unlike her son, was ambling around the room peering at the items on display with open curiosity. Robin's father, in opposition, was seated, hands clasped tightly on the table in front of him, elbows pressed closely to his sides. He appeared uptight, shut down. He looked like a man who was worried that someone would try and steal his wallet. The fact that Robin had elected to occupy a chair on the opposite side of the room from her father was certainly telling. Rebecca wondered where the other two family members would choose to sit when the time came. And, consulting her watch, she realized the time *had* come. She quickly encouraged everyone to take a seat in order that they might get started. Having other patients to meet with, Tom and Dan slipped out. She would review the session with each later that afternoon.

⚜

The small office was comfortable for two, a bit crowded for four. Kyla could have convened this meeting in a larger room, but ultimately decided against it. Abby felt safe here, and right now, that was worth a lot. The four occupants sat facing each other, Abby and Kyla on the couch, her parents on upholstered chairs. Jim, agitated, tapped the palms of both hands on the chair's padded arms, while Mary remained still, back straight, feet crossed at the ankles. A few errant strands of hair had escaped from the severe bun and lay limply on her shoulders.

In their final teleconference, Kyla had told Abby's parents of the need to meet privately on the first day of family week, but had not elaborated as to the meeting's content. She regretted they would miss the art therapy experiential, but this session was more important. The simple truth was that no significant strides could be made, no real communication could be effective, no true healing could begin, until the long-kept secret was revealed. Initially, Abby had resisted taking this step, claiming the truth would kill her mother. Eventually Kyla convinced her it must be done. So, now they waited, three pairs of anxious eyes fixed on Abby, who huddled on the couch, forearms clamped around her waist. Kyla reached a hand over and lightly touched her on the shoulder, not surprised in the least to feel her trembling beneath the lightweight pink sweater. "Remember what we talked about. I'm right here," Kyla murmured. "Go ahead when you're ready."

Abby's head remained bowed. Her wavy brown hair, draping like a curtain on either side of her face, also began to quiver. She spoke in an anguished, halting whisper. "When I was a little girl…" Her voice choked. In unison, both parents craned forward in their seats, expressions grim, yet expectant. Abby inhaled a deep breath, then exhaled a sigh saturated with pain. "When I was little," she repeated, paused, then launched in. "When I was even younger than Sara is now, Granddaddy would take me into his room and…" She told it all, not leaving out a single brutal detail.

Kyla, palm still resting lightly on Abby's shoulder, regarded Jim and Mary intently. Abby's words were slowly redefining their world, creating a whole new reality about the past, and more specifically, a stunning new truth about a person both thought they knew. At the outset, both faces were suffused with shock; eyes dilated, skin leached of all color, as though an alien force had drained their bodies of blood. Yet what registered next in their expressions bore no relationship to one another. As Abby told her story of victimization and sexual abuse, Jim's expression gradually transformed from stupefaction to horror to infinite sorrow to absolute fury. Color burst back into his face, painting his cheeks, scalp, even the tips of his ears, a dark crimson. A twitch convulsed at the corner of one eye. His jaw was set, his lips pressed together in a thin bloodless line, his hands curled into fists. If a man could look fully prepared to kill another human being without giving it a second thought, he did. Conversely, Mary's shock was reconfiguring into something else altogether. She grew still as a photograph; she did not even blink. Try as she might, Kyla couldn't quite determine in what direction the woman's emotions were taking her. But if the tendril of dread and intense foreboding currently wrapping around the base of Kyla's spine was any indication, it wasn't good.

Abby sniffed, dabbed a tissue against her nose. "When Sara started getting older, I got so scared. I was so afraid he would hurt her, too. That's why I never let her go over to his house alone. Then he had that stroke…" Abby's right leg started jiggling. Though the worst of it had already been voiced, Kyla knew this part was also difficult for Abby to confess, due to her profound, and terribly misplaced, guilt. "I was so happy he was sick. I wanted him to die. Every day, I asked God to make him die. I knew I was such a bad person for asking that, but I just wanted Sara to be safe and I didn't want to worry anymore."

Soon, Abby's voice trailed off; her recitation was over. A hush descended on the room, except for the impossibly loud ticking of the clock on Kyla's desk. For a brief moment, everyone remained motionless, gazing in different directions. Abby stared at the floor, Jim looked at his daughter, Kyla focused on the parents, and Mary was consumed with some point far off in the distance. Perhaps, she was peering deep into the past. Suddenly, the silent spell broke. Mary bolted up out of her seat, startling everyone. The chair teetered a bit, threatened to tip over completely. Mary's features were distorted by pure rage. Abby's head jerked up just in time to watch her mother completely unravel. "Those are lies. Every one is a dirty, filthy lie from the pit of Hell. My father is a good man, a wonderful man. He was a judge. He never did those nasty, nasty things."

Jim's head whipped around. "Mary, get a hold of yourself."

She didn't even glance his way. Instead, eyes narrowed, Mary pointed a rigid finger at the woman sitting alongside her daughter. Screeching, she spewed her considerable wrath directly at Kyla, "You. You call yourself a therapist?

Just what have you done with my daughter? Fed her full of lies. I've read about how you people can get your patients to believe almost anything. What did you use? Dreams? Hypnosis? You filled her full of horrible disgusting memories of things that never, ever took place." Her accusing finger quivered as if electrically charged. "Is that what you did with my Abby?"

"No, Mama, what I told you is true." The girl lifted a hand to her mouth and bit down hard on the skin of one knuckle. "All of it really happened, it really did," she insisted, her pleas muffled by her clenched fist.

"Lies." Mary spat the word savagely as if it were a curse. Then she spun around and headed for the door, calling behind her, "Come on Jim, we're leaving. We're getting Abby out of here and taking her home." Jim remained in his seat, eyes locked on his daughter.

"Daddy?" Abby's face crumpled as she shot him an imploring look. "Do you believe me?"

Tears spilled over Jim's eyelids and slid down his face. "Oh sweetheart…of course I believe you."

Kyla stood and edged away from the couch. Jim immediately claimed the vacated space. He enveloped Abby in his arms, drew her to his chest and cradled her protectively. In a matter of minutes, Jim had aged a dozen years. "I'm sorry, baby. I'm so sorry he hurt you. Dearest God, if I had only known…I'm so sorry," he crooned the same words again and again as tears trickled down his face and splashed onto Abby's hair.

Wanting to give the two some time alone and needing to locate Mary, Kyla walked out into the hall. From where she stood, she could see the Cardozas' rental car was still in the parking space. Abby's mother couldn't have gone far. She went to the end of the hall and looked out the window. Mary was just outside the door on the landing, hands pressed against her face. Breathing deeply, Kyla took a minute to compose herself. Though she knew absolutely that Mary's venomous accusations were defensive in nature, they had rattled her all the same. She had expected Abby's mother to have a difficult time accepting the truth, but hadn't anticipated her reaction to be this severe. Early on in the therapy as Abby and Kyla had discussed family relationships and dynamics, it was easy for Kyla to imagine how Mary felt about her father.

Throughout her entire life, Mary had been deeply enmeshed with the judge, a man she thought was tantamount to a saint on earth. Abby, though unable to assign the right words to this dependant relationship, had known it too. Mary's idolatry of her father had proven a key factor in why Abby had never disclosed her secret.

Mary noticed Kyla just as the therapist stepped through the door. "Get away from me. I have nothing to say to you." She turned her back on the other woman.

Normally, Kyla would have reached out, established physical contact in order to bridge the deep chasm between them. Not today. "I know you want me to leave you alone, but I can't. Abby is my patient and I have to do what is best for her. And what is best for Abby right now is trying to convince you that everything she just said in there is the truth. I'm sorry it hurt you, but Abby had to tell you. She has been living with incredible guilt and shame for years; it's what led to her eating disorder. As her therapist, I had to help her get out from under the weight of that terrible burden. This was the only way."

Kyla was still speaking to Mary's back, which seemed to grow stiffer with each passing minute. "I know you don't want to talk about it now and I understand that, but please think about this. Is Abby the type of girl who lies? Is she the kind of adolescent that makes up stories, especially if they might hurt someone she loves, someone like you? Though I have only known your daughter for a short time, I don't think she is. If you agree, then ask yourself if there is any way that what Abby just told you could be true." Mary's spine could not possibly become any more rigid. Now her shoulders were growing hunched. Kyla had to make her final point quickly or risk revisiting the explosive scene in her office. "Mary, talk to Jim. Better, ask someone else, another family member if it could be true. You have a sister, don't you? Ask her. Do it for Abby."

Kyla pivoted and pulled the door open. "I'll let Jim know you're out here."

—⊸∅∅∅⊶—

Rebecca introduced herself to the group, then requested introductions in return. Once everyone was identified, she proceeded to explain the role of art therapy at the treatment center. "We say that art gives our patients a voice. In other words, what they are thinking or feeling, but can't express verbally, can often come out in clay, in drawings or paintings. Hopefully, it will do the same for you today. Lexy…" She shifted her attention to the young woman sitting alongside her husband at a nearby table. "Tell the group one of our guidelines."

"There are no mistakes in art. It never lies."

"Very good. Now Robin…" She looked over at the other patient. "Can you name another?"

As with Lexy, Robin didn't miss a beat. "There is no right or wrong."

She gave Robin an approving smile. "Excellent, again. Someone did a fine job of teaching both of you. What's more, we never talk about talent or skill; as far as we are concerned, everyone is an artist."

Eager to get on with the activity, the art therapist rubbed her palms together briskly, then gave the group assignment. "For the next forty-five minutes I want you to show through your artwork what it is like for you to live with an eating disorder. You can use anything in this room to express your feelings." She made a wide sweeping gesture with one hand to indicate the art supplies in their entirety. "I will put on some soft music, which is guaranteed to inspire you. And finally, one more important guideline we haven't yet mentioned: there is absolutely no talking during this time. I want you to concentrate exclusively on placing your feelings and thoughts into your work. Any questions?" The room remained silent; only blank stares were directed at Rebecca. She smiled back at the assorted family members, concerned not in the least by their nonplused expressions. It followed the same pattern every single week. At the outset, confusion was always the name of the game...until the activity began. Then gradually, each person got out of him or herself and into the art. During her tenure at the ranch, Rebecca had conducted this activity with people from all walks of life; she had seen politicians working alongside plumbers; housewives next to heads of multi-million-dollar corporations. Regardless of group makeup, the end result was always the same. Because art knew no bias, it was the great leveler. With the diversity of today's group, she eagerly anticipated the outcome.

Rebecca flipped on the music, then returned to the table and reclaimed her chair. Rebecca taking her seat, officially heralded the beginning of the activity. She sat, they stood. Most were overtly uneasy, still confused. Yet they embarked on the assignment, drifting around the room to stacks of colored paper, tubs of paint, drawers filled with assorted items. No one spoke. Only two members of the group moved with confidence, Lexy and Robin; each was familiar with the drill.

In time, all had returned to their respective tables with their chosen supplies. The room was awash in afternoon sunlight with the occasional light breeze scampering through. The industrious sound of people working was eclipsed by the soothing strains of stringed instruments, augmented by the trill of a flute. This traditional Native American music, tranquil and calm, was the ideal adjunct to the art.

The two patients set to the task, as did Natalie and Grayson, and interestingly, Josh. In opposition, Pamela and Stanton continued to look put off, as if they would rather be anywhere but here. She studied her professionally manicured fingernails while he simply stared at the table. Lexy's husband and sister fell somewhere in the middle, somewhat willing, somewhat reluctant. With both, willingness eventually won out, and Scott and Loren got busy.

Soon, all were involved. Rebecca's job was to monitor the time and remain available if anything was needed. Fortunately, all needs seemed to be met, so she merely observed. Everyone, with the exception of Pamela, eventually became engrossed in their projects. The only real surprise came when, only a few minutes into it, Stanton put down his pencil and sat back in his chair, wordlessly proclaiming the completion of his work. Rebecca figured he would just have to sit and watch as she was doing. Who knew? Perhaps sitting alone with nothing to do would open his mind to something he needed to learn. Stranger things had happened during art therapy.

Time passed. Consulting her watch, Rebecca gave the group a five-minute warning. Many appeared startled, their expressions clearly saying: where did the time go? The art therapist stood, switched off the music and moved to the center of the room. "Okay, time's up. Now we get to show and tell. Each of you will stand and explain to the group what you did and what it meant. Comments from the group are encouraged. If you need elaboration, or pick up on something I missed, speak up. Sounds easy enough, doesn't it? Who wants to go first? Any volunteers?"

"I'll go," Natalie said and rose from her chair. She held her sheet of white construction paper up for all to see. "This is me." She pointed to the figure in the center of the paper. "There's a dark cloud over my head because that's how it feels when an eating disorder is in your life. The cloud never goes away. And you can see I'm crying because I am always sad. The heart next to me is my love for my daughter."

"What are those squiggly lines next to your head?" Lexy, seated nearby, asked.

Natalie looked down. "Confusion."

"And is that Robin on the other side of the page with the dark mist around her?" Rebecca inquired.

"Yes. The darkness is the eating disorder. She is trapped inside it. And the dotted line connecting us is my desire to reach out to her, but not knowing how."

"Natalie, you have no hands."

Surprised, she examined the picture. "Guess I forgot."

"You remembered everything else, even to put shoes on your feet. What do you think it means to have no hands?"

Robin's mother thought about it. "That I'm helpless. I can do nothing to help my daughter," she said in a small voice.

"I agree. Any comments?" When no one spoke, Rebecca said, "Next. What about you, Josh? Want to share your work with us?"

All eyes were now on Josh. A faint blush stained the boy's cheeks, but he dutifully got up and held his paper aloft. It had been divided vertically down the middle, yet contained only one face. One half was created in shades of blue and had tears streaming from the eye; the other half of the face was cast in vivid reds and was frowning, the corner of the mouth turned down.

"You're sad and you're mad," Rebecca observed.

Josh nodded. "Tell us about that," she instructed. "Better yet, tell Robin. Have you ever told her how you feel about her eating disorder?" As expected, the boy shook his head. "Tell her now."

Josh swung his gaze over to where Robin sat. He swallowed audibly. "I hate your eating disorder. I don't understand it and I hate it. It's trying to kill you and our family is all screwed up because of it. I wish you had never gotten it. I want it to go away and have you be normal again. I want you to come home. Lute misses you. He goes into your bedroom looking for you, but you aren't there. Do you know what it's like to watch him? I hate it."

"Josh, do you hate your sister?"

He fastened his gaze on the therapist, every line and contour of his young face registering wholesale shock at the question. "Robin? Do I hate her? No, I love Robin. I could never hate her. She's my sister." Realizing what he had just divulged with such heartfelt honesty, Josh sucked in his breath, then clamped his mouth shut. Obviously mortified, he sank back into his seat. Conversely, Robin's face softened in a way most of them had never seen before.

"Okay, now that we've heard from a brother, let's hear from a sister," Rebecca said, moving on. "Loren?"

Loren, idly twirling a strand of hair round an index finger, took her time getting up from her chair. She slouched against the table. She held up her picture, which was dominated by a large pair of very red glittery lips. The lips were outlined in black with vivid hues of orange and yellow radiating out to the edges of the previously white paper. She had used oil pastels to create the look. Rebecca could see a tremendous amount of pressure had been applied to the paper. This girl wasn't just angry, she was enraged. The minute the thought entered Rebecca's mind, she received immediate confirmation. Loren turned the paper over. On the back was an enormous lightening bolt drawn in the same intense shades of orange, yellow, red and black.

"Loren, on the front you drew a mouth; what do you think that means?"

She sighed, ever bored. "It means I like lips. I like to draw them. That's all."

"The mouth appears closed. What does that signify?" Rebecca allowed her gaze to canvas the group. "Anyone?"

Natalie jumped in and Rebecca gave her an approving smile. "You can't speak. Loren do you feel you're not allowed to talk or express your feelings in your family?" On the heels of her mother's question, Robin added, "Or do you feel like you won't be heard even if you do speak?"

Loren, obviously geared up to oppose the therapist, was taken aback when questions started coming in from other camps. She stood a little straighter and her brittle demeanor cracked a bit. "Talk to my family?" She proffered the idea as someone might propose drinking bleach. "Are you kidding; is that some kind of a joke?" She released a dry humorless chuckle. "No, I never do."

"How does that make you feel?" Rebecca interjected.

Loren shrugged. "I don't know."

The therapist had anticipated that answer. But Rebecca's mind remained consumed with that lighting bolt. "In fact, how does this whole situation of your sister and her eating disorder impact you?" Loren was trying to regroup, get her defenses back up. She shrugged a second time. Rebecca wasn't going to let her retreat that easily, not when her angst was so dramatically expressed on the paper. "What does lightning signify to you?"

Loren now held her paper in both hands, staring down at the brightly colored bolt as if wondering how it had gotten there. She thought about it before replying. "It's violent, destructive, electrically charged."

"Good. Now, if you had to attribute an emotion to lightning, what would it be?"

She hesitated. "Anger?"

"Yes, I think so," Rebecca responded in a subdued voice. "Do you think just maybe you are a little bit angry about this entire situation? Perhaps you are mad about other things in your life as well?"

In art therapy, Rebecca frequently utilized the expression, "A picture is worth a thousand words." An equally true, yet less-used saying was, "The eyes are the mirror of the soul." Today, with Loren, both applied. Her artwork reflected the repression under which she had lived; and now, her eyes betrayed her by providing a glimpse into her emotions. Rebecca could clearly see the hurt, the pain, the rejection; it was exactly what she'd seen when looking at Lexy. Yet, just like the mouth on the paper, Loren's mouth remained firmly closed, lips pressed tightly together. After all, this girl knew the family rules; she knew how the game was played and she wasn't going to say a word. Loren looked over at her sister, then back to the therapist, then gradually lowered herself into the seat.

"Thank you for sharing with us, Loren." Before she could even beg the standard question, Robin, perhaps identifying with the discomfort Loren was experiencing, offered to go next. Her picture showed a girl all curled up, surrounded by a black box in the middle of the page. Each corner was painted yellow, but these corners, too, were encased in black boxes. She pointed to the center of the paper. "This is me, I'm trapped. This red smudgy color around me is anger. I am boxed in by my eating disorder and don't know how to get out."

"What are the corners all about?" Grayson, his first time to speak, tossed out the question.

Robin grimaced. "It's sort of like sunlight. The yellow is hope. I know it's out there, but it, too, is boxed in and I can't get to it."

Natalie inquired, "Robin, why are you in a fetal position?"

In response, Robin averted her gaze. Eventually she whispered the words no one in the room thought they would ever hear from this headstrong, often obstreperous, girl. "Because I'm scared."

Robin sat. No one spoke. Rebecca made eye contact with Grayson and gave him a look. He understood and complied. He pushed back his chair and stood. "My turn. This is Alexa. I drew her as a heart because I love her so much." He gestured to the center of the page where he'd drawn a deep red heart imprisoned behind black bars. "As you can see, she is locked inside a cage. These are the other family members." He pointed to a cluster of stick figures off toward one corner.

"Is that some sort of a drill pointed at the cage?" Natalie asked, peering closer.

"Yes, it is supposed to be a drill. Guess it doesn't look too realistic," Grayson admitted sheepishly and gave the group an embarrassed, self-deprecating grin. "That's me wanting to fix Alexa."

Rebecca gave it some thought. "I wonder about the rest of the family? Do they need fixing, too?"

"Oh God yes," he burst out with forthright honesty. Sitting next to her husband, Pamela flinched. Everyone saw it. Evidently, his wife didn't appreciate his candor one little bit.

"What do you do for a living?"

"I'm a doctor, a plastic surgeon."

"Oh," Rebecca said, the drill now taking on even greater significance. "So you're in the business of fixing things, fixing people."

"I guess you could say that."

"But you can't fix Lexy or your family. How do you feel about that?"

A dark shadow fell across his face. "Terrible. Frustrated. Impotent. Furious."

"I imagine you do," she acknowledged as he reclaimed his chair. From his seat on Grayson's other side, Scott stood up. "I might as well go." As he displayed his drawing, someone gasped. Rebecca vaguely recalled Scott was in some facet of insurance or banking. But from what she saw on the paper, this young man could easily have been a successful artist. The picture was expertly rendered, intricate with detail. It depicted Lexy seated comfortably in an electric chair; Scott, fully in view, yet unable to touch her, shackled to a wall, wrists and ankles bound by chains. His face was contorted by torment. The drawing was emotionally charged, painfully graphic, heartbreaking.

Holding the picture in one hand, Scott looked like a man incapable of speech. Rebecca opened it up to the group. "What does this artwork say?"

Grayson peered up at his son-in-law. "Alexa is committing suicide and you can do nothing to help her or stop her. Is that right?"

Scott nodded and dropped back into his chair. Lexy, stunned, continued to look back and forth between the drawing and her husband. Wanting to give Lexy the time she needed to absorb what she saw, Rebecca called out, "Pamela, let's see what you have there."

The woman who so strongly resembled her daughter, stood, held out her picture. "This background is where Alexa is, this shape here is the eating disorder and this hand is trying to push it away." She pointed, spoke rapidly and started to sit down again. "Wait," Rebecca said, her voice calm, yet insistent. "You say that green and orange arcing shape is the eating disorder?" When Pamela nodded, the therapist requested, "Will you please hold that up again? Now, will all of you look at it; I want to know what you see?"

Everyone studied the picture, then exchanged inquiring glances with one another. Rebecca believed they saw exactly what she saw. And why not? It was blatantly obvious. The shape of the head, even the flicking tongue. "Okay group, what do you think it is?"

"A snake," they answered in unison.

"It is not a snake," Pamela shot back vehemently. "It is just a shape."

From her seat at an adjoining table, Robin leaned closer. "Hey, it's a snake. Can't you see that?"

Scowling, an angry flush spread across Pamela's face. "I've already told you, it is not a snake," she reiterated, eyes flashing, and plunked herself down into the seat. Her umbrage was out of proportion for the situation. If the snake had sprung from the page and bitten her on the forearm, Pamela would have continued to repudiate its existence. Clearly, she did not want to participate in this activity, which was certainly her prerogative.

Though it would have proved intriguing to explore the idea of the snake, the therapist recognized there was no percentage in it. She proceeded. "Lexy?"

She got to her feet and explained her work, which resembled a bull's-eye. "On this outer ring, I put yellow. It is the hope that is out there. But you see I have all this blue between me and the hope. That is sadness. In the very middle, I am underneath all these colors."

Lexy remained distracted, still overwhelmed by Scott's drawing. Rebecca said, "And the colors are..." she prompted.

"All these emotions I have: pain, anger, shame, loneliness. The eating disorder held them down inside of me and kept them trapped for so long. I was never able to express my feelings. I still believe I am in bondage to my emotions." Lexy dropped her picture back on the table, then sank back into her chair.

All eyes turned to Stanton, the only one left. He slowly got to his feet. Before showing his work, he gazed down at it. Rebecca had a sudden flash of insight. This man, though surrounded by his family, was without connection. He was totally alone, isolated in his own world. Stanton was probably the type of individual who was very comfortable at work, where he was in control and in charge. How difficult it must have been for him to sit there alone in the art room doing nothing while the others worked around him. With nothing to occupy him and completely out of his comfort zone, he might have been forced to think, to go places he didn't want to go—his family, Robin's illness, maybe even his role as a father. Who knew? Rebecca figured it would all come out at some point during family week.

Robin's father displayed his work. The white sheet was completely blank, except for a little face drawn in the lower left corner. It had two eyes, a dot of a nose, and a straight line for a mouth. He licked his lips before identifying himself in a soft monotone. "That's me."

"So living with Robin's eating disorder has made you feel…"

"All alone."

Everyone stared. The three members of his family appeared astounded by what they saw and heard. Stanton Hamilton feeling alone, perhaps even…lonely? Though Scott's artwork had certainly proved the most riveting, somehow, this stark picture was by far the most pathetic and sad. Rebecca pointed to the face. "I wonder…how does it feel to be that little person in the corner surrounded by all that empty space?"

"Really, really lonely." Saying no more, Robin's father lowered himself into the chair.

Recognizing the power of silence, Rebecca also said nothing. Allowing the experience of the past hour and a half to fully sink in, she took a surreptitious glance at her watch. Only a few minutes remained to wrap up. After a while, she said, "Being mindful of the time, we need to end, but in general, I'd like to know how you feel about what we just did. Not everyone has to answer. In a few words, can anyone describe this experience?"

Grayson surveyed the room, the occupants, the artwork. "It's amazing. I can't believe what I've seen and learned." Several nodded and uttered affirming sounds. Then Stanton spoke up, surprising everyone. "I can't believe how incredible this type of therapy is. Art...who would have guessed?" He shook his head slowly, underscoring his bafflement.

Pleased by the input, Rebecca continued, "Artists often title their work. If we put all your work together, what would you call it?"

Natalie frowned in thought. "Revelation?" she offered, her tone questioning.

"Or something about truth," Josh suggested, shrugging.

"I got it," Loren blurted out, appearing to shock herself with her outburst. "The power of pictures."

Chapter Ten

It was the third morning of family week. The previous day had been spent in eating disorder classes and sessions on after care. Now the entire group was assembled in a large room reserved for family counseling. Conspicuously absent was Abby's mother, who had failed to return after the first day. The others knew a private session had occurred Monday afternoon, but only Jim and Abby knew of the horrible fallout. Today, as with yesterday, Jim had elected to join Abby, while Mary had remained in the hotel room. Locked in private misery where no one, certainly not her husband, could reach her.

This morning would be the group's first Truth in Love session, the name culled from a scripture in the Bible, specifically Ephesians 4:15. Considered the most important aspect of family week, it was also the most dreaded by patients and family members alike. This was because at its very core was truth; and for these families, honesty was rarely the coin of the realm. Not anymore. Today, truth was not only the coin, it was the only currency allowed.

Much preparation had gone into this day. Both patients and families were required to thoughtfully consider many issues in advance including their individual role in the family and the part they may have played in the evolution of the eating disorder. In essence, each person was forced to look at their own stuff, something people rarely wanted to do, then place their thoughts on paper for reference purposes. Each Truth in Love was observed by the rest of the group. This often proved beneficial for all involved. Whereas spectators were required to remain silent during the session, they frequently provided valuable insight and support once the therapy time had concluded.

The Hamiltons were on the docket to go first. Robin, with Tom at her side, sat facing her family in a makeshift circle. Though five participants were expected, another unseen party was also present. It was fear. Indeed fear and its sidekick, anxiety, hung over the room like an invisible fog. Everyone felt it, even those seated outside the circle.

Tom addressed the assembled group. "Before we get started, I always ask if the family wants prayer." As expected, Robin shook her head in the negative. Yet, in a move Tom never could have anticipated, Natalie said, "Yes, prayer would be nice." Robin's eyebrows ratcheted up several notches, but Josh and Stanton didn't seem too terribly surprised. In Tom's rule book, one taker was certainly sufficient, so he bowed his head and prayed aloud for the group, asking for God's peace, direction and favor on this session. Concluding, he told the family, "Our goal today is to help you see the world the way Robin sees it, in essence, to get inside her skin. We aren't here to judge the intent of your past behavior toward Robin, we are here to examine and understand the effect it had on her. Before we start, I want to do a quick check in. Robin, how are you feeling right now?"

"Scared," she responded without hesitation. "I'm afraid of their reaction and I'm afraid they won't believe me."

Tom nodded his understanding. "And what is your goal for this session?"

Robin, expression somber, voice serious, said, "I want my family to hear me. I want them to really listen and understand."

"Okay, good." He shifted his attention to Stanton, Natalie and Josh. "We will start with the themes of Robin's life. These are the reoccurring patterns or circumstances that led to, or resulted in, her eating disorder." He flicked a glance back at his patient. "Go ahead when you're ready."

Clearly agitated, Robin tucked her hair behind one ear, then referred to her sheaf of papers. "My first theme is abandonment. I have never felt loved at anytime in my life, yet the feeling of real abandonment began when Josh was born. Even though I was little, I remember that time so clearly, how excited everyone was to have him. Like having me was never good enough, and everyone had just been biding their time, waiting for this great kid to come along. From then on out, no one saw me anymore…"

Initially, Robin spoke slowly with great apprehension, as if keenly aware of every listening ear in the hushed room. Yet with each word, each new thought, she gained in confidence. She, unlike her family, was comfortable with this topic. This was well-trodden ground between her and Tom. As Robin elaborated on this theme throughout her childhood and into the teenage years, Natalie appeared stricken, Josh guilty. Tom, observing, perceived these reactions as confirmation that much of what Robin had felt was the result of what had truly occurred. Interestingly, Stanton's face registered nothing at all.

As Robin completed that theme and prepared to move on, Natalie interjected in a timid voice, "May I say something, please? Is it okay?" After receiving encouragement from Tom to interrupt at any time, she spoke directly to her daughter. "Robin, since you've been gone, I've done a lot of soul-searching. I have spent time reflecting on the past, thinking about our family, trying to understand how your eating disorder came about. So much of what you just said is true and I am so terribly sorry." She turned to Tom. "I know there is a lot we need to get through in this morning session, but will we have more time this week to discuss this further?" He gave her a reassuring nod. "Good. Robin, I just need for you to know right now how sorry I am and how much I hope you will be able to forgive me for my mistakes."

Dumbfounded, rendered speechless by the admission, Robin sat motionless. She and her mother stared at each other for a long time. Then Natalie reached out and clasped a hand around Robin's wrist and gave it a tender squeeze. "I *do* love you," she whispered before releasing her grip and settling back in her chair.

Robin, still at a loss, looked over at Tom. He gestured to her papers, silently giving the girl permission to continue. She cleared her throat. "My second theme is peer pressure. From the time I got my first subscription to a teen magazine, I have felt the need to be skinny…" As Robin explained how this necessity to be thin played into her eating disorder, Natalie's expression turned to sympathetic understanding, Josh's face grew neutral, and Stanton remained blank. Tom couldn't help but wonder if anything ever truly touched this father.

"My third and final theme is perfectionism." Robin darted a quick glance up at her father, then returned to her paper. "I have always felt the need to be perfect—the best at sports, academics; well…everything. Second was never good enough, I had to be the first in everything. The best or nothing."

Knowing how critical it was for Robin to get this out on the table and be fully understood, Tom interjected a question, "Why did you have to be the best?"

Robin said to her therapist, "So my father would love me."

"Don't tell me, tell him," Tom directed, pointing at Stanton.

Eyes glistening, Robin gazed at her father, her face defined by naked pain. She dropped the paper to her lap. "So you would love me. I just wanted you to love me, to be proud of me, to be happy I was your daughter. But it was never enough; no matter what I did, there was always something else that I hadn't done quite right. I tried and tried. Then a couple of times at the beginning of high school, you walked by and told me I was getting a little chunky."

At last, Stanton's face showed something, a look of genuine astonishment. Clearly, he did not recall making any such comments. But Robin had, and now, she plowed on. "It was true. I was a fat cow, really disgusting. I wasn't just chunky, I was gross. No wonder Paul broke up with me and went after that skinny cheerleader; who could blame him?" Tom wasn't the only one who winced as she made these claims. "So I started to diet. I lost weight and you noticed. After all those years of trying, I had finally found something I could do really well. I was a perfect anorexic. So I kept getting skinnier and skinnier. In time, I became pretty good at bulimia, too. When you got mad and yelled at me, I told myself it was because you loved me." Robin's voice broke, tears streamed down her face. "All I wanted was for you to love me. Was that really asking too much? All I wanted…was love."

Stanton had gone white. Everyone was staring at him, including Natalie and Josh, their expressions vaguely accusatory. "But Robin, I…"

"You what?" Tom asked him. "Talk to your daughter."

"I…I always loved you. I was always proud of you." The affirmations did not come easy. Tom could almost see the invisible pry bar Stanton was using to get the words out.

"And how did you show her?" Tom inquired.

"I, I…" His voice faltered. Robin's father looked around wildly, like a drowning man in search of a life raft, only to find himself surrounded by empty seas. "I worked hard, I provided a good home, I paid for things."

Tom didn't need to ask if this was what Stanton's father had done for him; he could guess the answer. So often, every father was only as good as his own father. The same held true with mothers. Stanton simply did what he knew. Tom pressed, needing more from this man, "But how did you show her that you loved her?"

Distraught, Stanton sounded as desperate as he appeared. "I guess, I guess, I didn't," he eventually acknowledged. Needing reassurance, seeking an ally, he turned to his wife, his son. They both grimaced and shook their heads. "Josh, don't you know I love you?"

"No." The single word was immediate and riveting in its simplicity.

Stunned silence.

"Both of you?" Agonized, he looked from Josh to Robin and back. "You never knew?" he asked, voice hollow. Both children shook their heads in the negative.

Desperation rapidly transformed into defeat. Tom, watching, could see it coming...Robin's father was going to break. Suddenly, it was as though all the pent-up emotion of recent years, to say nothing of the stress of the past few days, coalesced into one huge release. Stanton dropped his face into his hands and emotion surged out of him. It came first in the form of a prolonged, heart-wrenching wail, then converted to tears. Stanton didn't simply weep, he sobbed, great racking sobs that tore through the room. His shoulders quaked, his entire body heaved.

Stupefaction became the order of the day; obviously, no one had ever seen Stanton cry before, much less totally break down. Though in their individual expressions Tom could tell they wanted to act, the entire family was literally stunned into immobility. They simply gaped at him. Eventually, they redirected their attention to Tom, wordlessly beseeching him to do something about this situation and do it right away. Each was now feeling a high level of discomfort. They saw it as bad. Tom saw it as good. They wanted to shut it down, but Tom wanted them to stay with the emotion and work through it. So he did nothing but wait.

Stanton's catharsis eventually ran its course and the crying soon abated. He remained hunched over, forearms flattened on thighs, face held in cupped hands. Tom allowed silence to reign for a few minutes; only the occasional sniffle penetrated the hush. Finally, Tom asked, "Stanton, what are those tears about? What are you feeling right now?"

Robin's father sat up. Natalie handed him a box of tissues. He took several and blotted his cheeks as he considered his answer. "I feel so bad. I wanted to be a good father. I feel such regret." His breath came in hitches. "I never knew; I never knew any of this."

Tom turned to Josh and Natalie. "How are you two feeling?"

Josh hesitated, then said in typical teenage fashion, "Blown away."

Natalie, less forthcoming than her son, finally said, "Touched, hopeful? Maybe this could be a start for our family. At least, I hope so."

"We have a lot more to talk about. But right now, I think we need to take a break. Is that all right with you?" He addressed the question to Robin who nodded her agreement. "After the break, Robin will tell you more about the eating disorder and you can explain at length how it impacted each of you as well as the family as a whole. We will also explore what Robin is willing to do toward recovery and discuss your expectations regarding the same. But before we do that, is there anything more you want to share with your daughter, Stanton? Any kind of gesture?" Though Tom knew touchy-feely wasn't this man's comfort zone, Tom wanted to open the door all the same.

Stanton, eyes puffy, skin blotchy, tentatively stretched out a hand to his daughter. "Robin," he murmured in a choked voice. She grabbed his hand and squeezed it. In an equally emotion-riddled voice, Robin said, "Daddy, can I have a hug, please?" They both stood and embraced, a little awkwardly at first, but as Natalie had said...it was a start.

⸻ ❧❧❧ ⸻

Mary, cheeks stained with dried tears, sat still in the hotel's overstuffed armchair. Her face registered nothing, no expression, no emotion. This seemingly blank slate was illustrative of what was currently transpiring in her mind. Nothing. Since that horrible meeting on Monday in Kyla's office, she had screamed, raged, wept for hours on end. And now there was simply nothing left. They had all betrayed her. The people she had trusted at the ranch, Abby's therapist, Abby herself, and Jim. While her daughter's betrayal could be forgiven, due to her impressionable youth, Jim's could not. He, her husband, believing all those lies, trying to force her to also believe. It was a nightmare. And today, as on Tuesday, he had returned to the center, leaving her alone to suffer. It was unforgivable.

Mary ran her fingers through her stringy, unwashed hair, licked her dry lips. Though she wanted to focus, wanted to make concrete plans to remove Abby from this environment as soon as possible, she found she couldn't conjure one beneficial thought. She was simply too drained, too weighed down by depression. So she remained in that chair, staring blankly at a thin column of light sneaking in through a small opening in the drawn bedroom curtains. Dust moats danced and spun in the radiant beam, providing momentary distraction. Without intending to do so, Mary allowed her gaze to follow the shaft of light to where it came to rest.

It fell directly on the white telephone propped on the bedside table. She flinched, as though jabbed by a pointed dart, then frowned. She looked around the room. The chest of drawers, the artwork on the walls, the king-sized bed were cast in grayish shadows. But that phone, it was lit...as though for a reason. Shaking her head, Mary cursed, something she never did, not even at the worst of times. The phone was not summoning her, not beckoning her to traverse the room, pick up the receiver and place a call. What a ridiculous notion; clearly, she was overtired. It was a benign instrument, nothing more. By waiting only a few minutes, the angle of the sun would shift and that single corridor of light would illumine something else in the room...perhaps the bedside lamp, or the ornately scrolled walnut headboard. She simply had to wait patiently.

She looked back at the phone, seemingly unable to resist its gleaming white surface. Mary got up, walked over, sat on the edge of the bed. No longer was the phone lit up, for now the sunbeam was right in the middle of her back, boring through her cotton housecoat, directly between her shoulder blades. Disconcerted, Mary eased off the side of the firm mattress and slid onto the floor. Reaching up, she pulled the phone set off the table. It bleated a staccato ding as it thumped onto the Berber carpet. She suddenly felt better, as though she and the phone were now on an even playing field. She idly fingered the key pad. At once the thought came to her: Why not just pick up the receiver and call her sister. Why was she acting so silly and scared? She would call Ruth and get this thing settled once and for all. In fact, it was exactly what she needed. Ruth's input would surely galvanize Mary into action, giving her the strength she needed to get dressed, call the airlines, get Abby and go. Without another thought, she yanked the receiver off its cradle and punched in the familiar number. Three rings later, her sister picked up.

"Ruth, it's Mary," she said, deeply gratified to hear her voice sounding strong and in control.

Startled, her sister asked, "Hey, what are you doing calling me? Aren't you in Arizona?"

"Sure, we're here, but I needed to discuss something with you."

"Okay. I was just washing some dishes and there are no kids in the house, so this is a good time. Shoot."

In her haste, Mary had failed to consider how she would go about this conversation. Several moments passed.

"Mar? You still there?"

Mary tried to clarify her jumbled thoughts. "Yeah, I, I needed to talk to you about Daddy."

"Swell, my favorite topic."

"Ruth, why have you always hated him so much?" Mary entwined her fingers into the white phone cord, a nervous habit of hers since childhood. Observing the action, she released the coiled cord and it twanged back and forth crazily in the air.

"Why are you asking that now?"

"I want to know."

"I've told you a hundred times before, it's all in the past; there is absolutely no reason to get into that now," Ruth responded, repeating the same tired words she always said whenever Mary requested a reason for her sister's prolonged hatred of their father. "What's done is done. It will only cause…"

Mary cut her off, her voice moving swiftly out of the realm of strong and into the realm of insistent. "It's about Abby. I need to know right now."

Ruth drew in a sharp breath. "Did he do something to her? Mother of God, did he hurt Abby? I never thought…"

"Never thought what?" Mary swallowed hard, then barely able to get the question out asked, "Did he do something to you?"

"Mary, you always needed him so much, especially after Mom died," she reasoned, sounding on the verge of crying. "You were so young and he was everything to you. It served no purpose to tell you, he was all you had."

"He was all you had, too."

"Me?" Ruth gave a harsh, derisive snort, obliterating all vestiges of potential tears. "No baby sister, that's where you're wrong. I never had him like you did, not like a father, at least. I only knew him one way—the way he was when he would come to my room at night. And believe me, that had nothing to do with being a father. It only had to do with being a sick, weak, perverted man who put his own needs above all else, even the welfare of his five-year-old daughter."

God in heaven, it was all true. As this realization slammed home, a whimper of infinite pain ripped from Mary's throat. She dropped the receiver as though it were on fire; it bounced once on the carpet, then clunked into the phone. Yet, she could still hear her sister's voice coming to her in random snatches. "Hurt me…had to protect you…couldn't tell mother…hate him…years of therapy…" Like a snowball placed on a hot radiator, Mary melted down into a puddle on the floor. She curled into a fetal position. Now in a near catatonic state, she stared into space, saw nothing, and blessedly, felt nothing.

⸺◈◈◈⸺

This afternoon, a new circle had been formed in the counseling room. Lexy and Dan now sat across from the four members of her family. He asked if prayer was wanted and she responded in the affirmative. Not unlike Robin, Lexy expressed trepidation regarding how everyone would receive what was to follow. She stated her goal was to achieve honesty, understanding and improved communication.

For the next twenty-five minutes, she addressed two of her themes: societal pressure and rejection. She described her upbringing with the necessity to always be socially perfect. Whereas Robin had felt the pressure of academic and athletic perfection, Lexy felt required to be visually and behaviorally perfect. In her family, academic or athletic achievement was not valued, therefore, no pressure was applied in these areas. Quite the reverse, if Lexy brought home a good grade of which she was proud, little notice was taken. But make one minor social faux pas and she would be severely taken to task, often chastised for days. The underlying concept was that if she just grew up correctly and married the right man, the rest would take care of itself.

This pressure to be perfect was relentless and ultimately fostered a sense of wholesale rejection. After all, no one wanted the real Alexa, the daughter with thoughts and feelings of her own, who might have desires and aspirations for the future that were contrary to the plan. This Alexa was anathema. And whenever she tried to assert herself, she was firmly squelched. And Lexy had certainly tried to do so in those early years, to no avail. Eventually she succumbed and became the ideal. Only when Lexy escaped to college did she have an opportunity to explore who she really was. By then, it seemed too late, for the real her had been lost, buried under layers and layers of plastic. Only during the previous few weeks at the ranch had she been able to rediscover fragile tidbits of her original self.

As Lexy revealed these themes, speaking clearly and precisely, Dan scrutinized the family. He concentrated on how Lexy's insights were being received. Grayson and Scott appeared attentive and sympathetic, a willingness to understand showed in their expressions and gestures. Occasionally, one or the other would pose a clarifying question, or offer a heartfelt apology for something he had done, or failed to do. Especially Grayson; Dan could easily tell his regret went as deep as his love.

Loren had grown subdued during the past few days. Adolescents often underwent change while at the ranch. When a family member was in treatment, siblings such as Loren only heard talk of ranches and horses and perhaps even saw the odd piece of artwork sent home to family. Understandably, they began to view treatment as fun. But once they spent time here, they discovered it was a real inpatient facility, with rigid rules and regulations, omnipresent monitoring and severely restricted freedom. In other words, this was a place they would not want to be. Now, seated next to Lexy, Loren listened, actively listened to her sister. What's more, she no longer regarded Lexy with undisguised loathing. What Dan saw in Loren, though not quite love, was something very close. Dan suspected Loren could relate to what Lexy said about her life because much of the same probably applied to Loren's own upbringing. Often he would catch her nodding her head in comprehension and commiseration.

Of course, it appeared as if Pamela would remain Pamela until the bitter end. This woman was not going to give an inch. Elegant as ever, she had sat in stony silence, mask firmly in place, throughout Lexy's delineation of her life themes. Maintaining perfect posture, she never moved, her expression never varied; she could easily be a highly polished marble statue. Dan wondered if Pamela had any idea of what was pending. He doubted it. Otherwise, surely, a look of discomfort or anxiety would cross that beautiful countenance. Or would it—could it?

"My final and most important theme is trauma," Lexy said. "More than anything in my life, it was trauma that led to the eating disorder, the self hatred and abuse, my inability to be a good mother...everything." Emotion flooded into Lexy's face; conversely the exact opposite occurred in the expressions of Grayson, Scott and Loren. All the sincere compassion and sorrow disappeared as though a switch had been thrown. One by one, their faces went blank. If cartoon balloons had appeared above their heads, each would say: "Did I miss something? Did I hear her right? Did she say trauma? What trauma?"

Lexy saw their bafflement as did everyone in the room. She inhaled deeply before plunging on. "When I was in my first year of college, long before I met you, Scott, I got pregnant."

The fictitious thought balloons vanished, eclipsed by a collective gasp.

"At first, I told myself I was wrong. I couldn't possibly be pregnant. But after a while, I was forced to face it. I didn't know what to do. Good girls didn't get pregnant. I was terrified."

Tears trickled down Lexy's face. "I went home one weekend." She looked over at Dan. "My mother took one look at me and knew right away that I was pregnant."

"Tell them," Dan murmured and gestured with one hand toward her family.

All eyes were fixed on Pamela as Lexy recalled the past. "She said only one thing could be done. I must have an abortion. She made an appointment and took me."

Lexy looked straight at her mother and spoke directly to her. "But you just dropped me off at the doctor's office. You never came in. You never knew. Before I had the procedure, the medical staff insisted that I have an ultrasound. It was office policy. They wanted to make sure I knew exactly what I was doing." Lexy, teeth chattering, began to breathe raggedly, experiencing the pain anew. Voice growing shrill, she was edging toward hysteria. Dan knew she needed support and wanted it to be provided by someone other than him. He established eye contact with her sister, who was seated closest to Lexy. "Help her," he mouthed to the girl.

Without hesitation, Loren scooted her chair a little closer and placed an arm around her sister's back. Though no acknowledgement was forthcoming, Dan was certain that on some level, Lexy felt the consoling gesture. "They said they wouldn't terminate the pregnancy unless I agreed to the ultrasound. So I had it. I lay there on my back, all alone, and saw my baby. Suddenly, it wasn't just an idea any-more, a problem that needed to be taken care of, it was a baby; a real baby inside my body with arms and legs, hands and feet. I saw it move. I saw its little heart beating. Then, then I went right ahead…and ended its life." Lexy collapsed into Loren's arms, overcome by a tempest of emotion.

The shock that swept through the room was nearly palpable.

Grayson clamped his hands over his face. "Oh for the love of God," he whispered in a hoarse, choked voice.

Pamela, a shade paler, stood abruptly, eyes strafing the room as if searching for a way out. She glared down at the group. "There was no other option. I did what I thought was best for everyone. I will not be the guilty party here. It's in the past, over. I refuse to listen to any more of this." She whirled and stalked in the direction of the exit. Dan glanced across the room at an aide and jerked his head toward the door. The woman gave a curt nod of under-standing and went after her.

Dan waited quite a long time for Lexy's private storm to pass, before beginning to process what had just hap-pened with the family. "I'm sorry Pamela left," he said in earnest. "She really needed to be here for this." At that pre-cise moment, the door swung open. Pamela, looking decidedly displeased, came into the room, the aide trailing behind. "Good, you're back. We were just starting. Have a seat. First, we need a feelings check. Scott, tell me what's going on."

"I'm stunned," Scott offered. "I never knew any of this. I feel terrible that Alexa had to go through anything so hideous. I am angry and sad for her." He thought hard for several moments as tears welled in his eyes and spilled down his cheeks. Dan pointed to Lexy; Scott directed his words to her. "I am hurt that you never told me. Alexa, you're my wife, I love you more than I can say. If I knew, if you had told me about this, I think I could have helped you." He paused again. "And also…I actually feel…somewhat relieved. I hope that doesn't sound awful. Please understand. I feel a sense of relief because now maybe I can begin to grasp how you must have felt when you were pregnant with Logan. Is this—all this guilt and pain—what's kept you from being close to our son?"

Lexy, now extricated from Loren's embrace, responded to her husband in a frail voice. "I wanted so much to love Logan, but I couldn't forget what I'd done. I thought I didn't deserve to have him. I felt so much shame. I wanted to punish myself…I literally wanted to die. I thought if I died, you could marry someone else, someone better than me, and Logan could have the kind of mother he deserved."

"Oh God." Overwhelmed by this revelation, Scott placed a hand over his eyes and slumped in his chair.

Loren, crying unabashedly, regarded her sister as if Lexy were an intricate puzzle that had just received the final few pieces and was now a complete picture. "So that's why you changed so much back then. I thought I had done something wrong and you didn't love me anymore. But it wasn't me at all, it was the abortion." She also sounded relieved.

"Loren, I never stopped loving you," Lexy said. "I just hated myself so much. Self-loathing was the only thing I knew."

"Well, I'm mad, mad as hell if anyone wants to know," Grayson burst out. "Alexa was pregnant? Pam made her have an abortion and I never even knew? She's my daughter, too."

Dan jumped in. "Let's start there. You're angry and you blame Pamela." Grayson grunted his agreement. Then Dan turned to Lexy. "Do you blame your mother?"

"No. I was the one who got pregnant. I can't blame her for that. And she reacted to it in the only way she knew how. My mother is who she is. A pregnant daughter would have been an embarrassment."

Dan looked back at the family. "Just in case you haven't already heard enough axioms, let me toss out another one. In therapy, we don't blame, we explain. We are not here to make family members pay for past action—that gets us nowhere. We don't blame, judge or excuse previous behavior. What we want to do is explain how certain actions impacted our patients. Lexy's right. Pamela did what she knew to do. In her world, an unmarried pregnant daughter would be an embarrassment, a negative reflection on the family as a whole. Right or wrong is not the issue; the effect is what matters. Does that make sense?"

Grayson, facial muscles tight as cold steel, folded his arms across his chest. "I understand what you're saying, but…" His voice trailed off, he sat back in his chair, fuming.

Dan looked at a still-weeping Scott. "I don't know," he replied and shook his head slowly as if dazed. "It may take a while to get past the blame, the anger. She hurt Alexa. In turn, my son was hurt. So was our marriage. I know that wasn't the intent, but that was the result. What was it all about anyway? Image. Society. How things look. I recognize that is who Pamela is, but it's all so wrong, so empty, so…nothing." Frustrated, Scott raked a hand through his hair. "If Alexa can forgive and in time, move past this, I probably can, too. But, now all I care about right now is helping my wife get better."

"Good," Dan said, then shifted his attention to Lexy's mother. "Pamela, I need you to check in, too."

Pamela's expression reconfigured into a caustic smirk. "Feelings, you and your feelings. You know what I feel like? I feel like I'm on a Barbara Walters special. Is crying some sort of requisite for everyone who walks through those doors? Well I'm sorry, but I am going to have to let you down. I simply will not blubber and carry on like the rest of you—that's not the way I was raised. Right or wrong, I was brought up to be a lady at all times. And a lady does not air her dirty laundry in public. Now with that said, am I sorry my daughter was hurt? Yes, I am very sorry. That was never my intention. I saw a problem and I did what I had to do to fix it. Are you happy now? That's it. I had no idea it would turn out this way. I have only tried to do what's right for both my daughters throughout their lives." And with that, Pamela settled back in her seat and folded her arms across her chest, lips compressed, wordlessly declaring she was done.

"Thank you," Dan said, then moved on. "As Scott so aptly put it, we are here to help Lexy get better, so let's return to that goal right now. Just as we don't want to blame family members for previous actions, we also don't want to blame Lexy. We want to understand the whys behind her past behaviors. Lexy, I think it's important for your family to get an idea of what was going on in your life back in college when you got pregnant. Can you clarify for us where you were at that time?"

A shadow of a smile crossed Lexy's face as she considered the question. "This sounds a little clichéd, but when I went to college, I went searching for love. More than anything in my life, I just wanted someone to love me, you know, for me. She paused, threaded her fingers through her hair and frowned. "The problem was I was still caught up in that 'good girls don't sleep around' mindset, so I never took precautions. You see, by going to a doctor, or buying birth control, I would have been forced to admit I was a 'bad girl.' Naturally, all that ultimately proved was that I was a 'stupid girl,' since I ended up pregnant."

"Which then led to the abortion. Which then led to the eating disorder," Dan supplied.

"Yes."

And ultimately led to…?"

Lexy canted her head to one side. "The self harm?"

"Yes. Lexy why did you start cutting yourself? Your family needs to know."

"Because I hated myself for the abortion. It was all my fault. I hated my stomach because that's where the baby had been. I needed to punish myself for being bad. Somehow, I had to pay for what I had done."

"But you could never have cut deep enough or bled enough to pay that price, could you?"

Lexy shook her head. "Never. I know now that nothing I did would have ever been enough. And as time went by, my shame and guilt only became greater, not less."

Dan looked back at the family. "Can you understand how this happened, how one thing led to another? Can you see that all of these behaviors were strategies Lexy had designed to cope with her life? Often they weren't healthy or successful, but she was coping the best way she knew how. Can you make sense of that?" Dan could tell Lexy's family, for the most part, was honestly trying to comprehend. Soon, he received a couple of affirming nods. Dan allowed his gaze to travel from one family member to the next to the next. Then he posed a question he deemed critically important. "As members of Lexy's family, you were often on the receiving end of her choices, many of which had fairly negative repercussions. Now, can each of you forgive her for the decisions and mistakes she's made?"

This time, he didn't have to wait, the response was immediate. Grayson shot forward in his seat. "Forgive Alexa? Of course I forgive her." Without prompting from Dan, Grayson turned to his daughter. "Alexa, since the moment you were born, I have loved you without condition. I love you simply because you exist. There is nothing in the world you could do to change that. You have never been bad. I would forgive you for anything, everything. Right now, I just feel relieved. I never understood what was at the root of the bulimia, and much worse, the self-destructive behavior. Now I do. There is no blame involved; I finally understand what happened." His voice choked. He turned away to collect himself, then turned back. "I just want you to get better. I want you to stop hurting your body."

"I feel like your father does," Scott told his wife. "More than anything, I just never understood. I never stopped loving you, but I was confused and hurt by your actions. Now I see how it all happened. I don't blame you for the decisions you made. We've all made bad decisions. Of course I forgive you."

Fresh tears glistened in Loren's eyes. "I'll forgive you if you'll forgive me. For years I've been holding everything I could think of against you. I've been trying to hate you."

"You were young and I hurt you," Lexy said. "It was my fault."

"But it wasn't your fault," Loren insisted. "It was just a bunch of things that went wrong. I would have done the same thing you did. Remember, I'm part of the same family. But instead of trying to understand you, I tried to hate you." She sniffed and reached for a tissue. "Can you forgive me?"

Lexy nodded. "You're my sister; nothing else matters."

Dan glanced over at Pamela. She remained locked in her rigid shut-down position. But he thought he detected something flickering in her eyes. Everyone waited. Eventually she said, "I have nothing to forgive you for."

"I wasn't always the daughter you wanted."

Pamela stared at Lexy for a long time. "That was more about me and my expectations than you and your desires. I might have been wrong."

Dan spoke to the family as a whole. "Okay, good. This is very important. Lexy wants recovery, but she can't do it alone. She will need your support. It looks to me as if all of you are going to be in a position to help her and provide what she needs." Pausing a moment to let that sink in, Dan regarded Lexy. His heart lifted in his chest as he saw in her what he had seen so many times with previous patients. Hearing words of forgiveness, words of acceptance and love, had an immediate and profound effect on her. She sat a little straighter, her shoulders no longer sagged. She actually appeared lighter, as though an enormous burden, a tremendous weight, had truly been lifted off her. The lessening of shame and guilt also showed in her face, yet it was impossible to define just how. Once again, Dan was struck by the amazing life-altering power found in forgiveness.

The session thus far had been productive, yet intense. Dan decided they needed a break before going on. As patients and family members milled around chatting with one another, getting cold drinks or smoking cigarettes outside, Scott and Lexy stood and joined hands. For several minutes they regarded one another as if they were the only two people on earth. Two people who hadn't seen each other for a very long time.

Chapter Eleven

Abby and Kyla sat perched on their favorite rocks, surveying the pasture. Subtle, yet detectable changes had occurred to the surroundings since their initial conversation on these very boulders so many weeks ago. Much of the late-summer foliage had withered and died; the air had grown markedly chillier; the slate-blue sky was dotted with heavy-bottomed dark clouds. Abby and Kyla had also undergone transformation, for both had put on weight; one to create new life; the other to sustain existing life. Yet, Kyla's newborn would be many months old before Abby had sufficient time to reach a healthy weight. Though their relationship would always be one of therapist and patient, they had grown closer.

Kyla pulled her bulky sweater around her a little tighter and looked over at Abby. "I know family week didn't go exactly the way you had hoped. But that doesn't make it bad. As far as I'm concerned, the most important thing we needed to get done, got done. I know you don't understand as well as I do how critical it was for you to tell your parents about the abuse."

"No, I still don't really get it," Abby agreed, mood somber.

The therapist grimaced as she sought the right words. "Dark secrets eat away at the soul of the person who holds them inside. What your grandfather did to you was shameful. As long as you kept it a secret, you carried his shame for him. By exposing it, you gave it back; it was no longer yours. It's like carrying a huge backpack full of rocks. We needed to take that pack off your back and return it to the person who should have been carrying it all these years. You had that burden long enough."

Abby's shoulders sagged. "But it hurt my mother so much." A touch of anguish lingered in her voice, although many days had passed since that grisly scene in Kyla's office.

"I know it did and I'm sorry about that, but it couldn't be helped." Kyla shoved her balled-up fists beneath her arms for additional warmth. "And now she will have to figure out how to deal with it. She will have to make some choices regarding her father, their future relationship, and your family. But that is her business, not yours. You know what, Abby? You have enough of your own business to attend to and we are going to continue dealing with that for as long as you're here. Okay?"

The girl hunched forward on her granite seat to get a better view of the horses sedately cropping grass in the field. "Sure."

Tracking Abby's gaze, Kyla also appreciated the tranquility provided by the grazing horses. "Tell me the truth, don't you feel just a little better now that you aren't the only one carrying those rocks?"

Abby pursed her lips, thinking it over. "Kind of. It felt good for my dad to know what happened to me. I really don't feel worried anymore, especially about Sara." Her expression turned quizzical. "Which is weird because I shouldn't have felt worried anyway since my grandfather was stuck in the hospital; but I did."

"See, that was just the past, still hanging around hurting you. I'm glad you feel a little better. That sense of relief will only grow over time." Kyla swung her gaze back to the girl. "And even though your mother went home early, you spent a lot of good time with your dad, both here and over the weekend, right?"

Abby brightened, remembering. "Yes. It was wonderful just being together. He learned a lot while he was here and he liked getting to know the other parents. Robin's mother was especially nice to him. I think she felt bad that my mom left early and went home. When he and I would talk about what had happened to me, he would cry a lot, but somehow…"

"You were able to comfort each other?"

Abby nodded her head vigorously. "That's right, we were. How did you know that?"

"Ab, I've been at this therapy thing for a long time. I figured that would happen with the two of you. I bet it felt good."

"It did. And for the first time since I've been here, I felt like everything was going to be okay; like all the stuff you and I have talked about and the things I've learned are going to come together. Now when I picture going home in a few weeks, I think it will be all right. I think I'm going to get better."

"Great. That is so good to hear." Kyla smiled at her patient. "And speaking of good, we have a date with someone." Kyla heaved herself off the rock and onto her feet. Abby jumped down.

"A date? With who?"

"You'll see. Come with me." After smoothing her sweater down, Kyla took off in the direction of the barn. She walked several paces, then halted. Turning around, she glanced back at Abby, who stood still, hand over her mouth, giggling.

"And what is so funny, young lady?"

Abby burst into full-fledged laughter. Kyla had a growing suspicion that this joke was destined to be at her expense. That was fine with her. She would willingly be the butt of any joke, if only to see this child laugh. "I'm waiting."

"I can't believe it. You're waddling. Really, no kidding, you look like a duck."

Kyla threw her hands out, palms up, fingers splayed. "Oh sure, make fun of the pregnant lady," she said. "Now will you cut that out and come with me?"

Abby stuck her hands in her back pockets and caught up with Kyla. The two headed in the direction of the barn. Within moments, Abby saw the surprise.

"I asked them to bring her out for you. I think it's time for you to take your first ride," Kyla said. Belle was secured to the hitching post, all saddled up and ready to go. Abby ran over and threw her arms around the mare's neck.

Kyla came up and stroked the horse between the eyes. "You know, Marla never lets anyone ride Belle, but she made an exception for you today. I told her it would be your very first time on a horse and that it would be particularly special if you could go on Belle."

"Really? It's okay to ride her so soon after her baby?"

"You bet." A member of the equestrian staff, sitting high atop an enormous black gelding, loped up to where they stood. Kyla gestured to the woman. "Suzanne is going to take you out, as another special favor to me." The therapist planted her fists on her hips. "Boy, you better darn well appreciate this for as many favors as I am racking up on your behalf."

Suzanne dismounted and handed the reins to Kyla and prepared to give the girl a leg-up into the saddle. An expression of dread swiftly flashed across Abby's face. "What if I'm still a little scared?"

"That's okay. Remember what we've talked about. Feelings are never bad; it's what you do with the feeling that matters. Are you going to let that fear keep you from riding today, or maybe even forever?"

"No." Abby shook her head in an emphatic negative.

Kyla thought about the situation for a moment, then suddenly asked, "Hey, what's your favorite worship song?"

Perplexed, the girl responded, "Rejoice."

"When I was young and afraid of something, I would sing to myself. That always made me feel less scared. How about trying that?"

"Okay, I will," Abby agreed, striving to sound very confident.

Suzanne stood alongside Belle. Crouching a bit, she cupped her gloved hands, fingers entwined. Abby lifted her foot. Presently, the girl was firmly ensconced in the old leather saddle with stirrups properly adjusted and reins in hand. She looked astonished, as if wondering how it had all happened. "I'm up so high," she declared, the sense of awe reflected in her words.

Kyla backed up a few paces. "Pretty cool, isn't it?"

Gripping the saddle horn, an anxious smile trying to establish residence on her face, Abby peered down at her therapist. "I would say you look small down there on the ground…but you don't." Abby threw her head back and laughed expansively at her own joke.

"Enough with the pregnancy jokes," Kyla retorted and flung a hand in the direction of the corral. "Now will you please go ride that horse."

For the next fifteen minutes, Kyla watched as Abby rode, first on a lead rope, then on her own. She could tell by the girl's expression that she was living exclusively in the moment without a single thought given to the past and the abuse it had contained. Right now her focus was on Belle and the utter joy of riding. Abby's smile, still a shade anxious, never faded; nor did the worship song, which Abby continued to sing, long after its comfort was no longer needed.

———⟨∅/∅/∅⟩———

"Buzz, buzz, buzz," Robin spouted off in a sing-song voice. "That bee is driving me nuts. Can't you get it out of here?"

Tom rolled his eyes at her, mimicking her as she had mimicked the winged creature. Then he sighed theatrically and rose from behind his desk. "If you insist." He paced the length of the room. Fortunately, one of the windows had never possessed a screen. Even more fortunate, it was the window closest to the irritating intruder in question. He yanked the pane of glass open, then with the aid of a single sheet of paper, encouraged the insect toward the opening. With one swift motion he swept the black and yellow bee outside and on its way. "Better?" He slammed the window shut.

"Yes," she confirmed, running one index finger around the lip of the iced tea glass she had brought into the office. "Thanks."

He returned to his chair and propped his feet on the trash can. This was their first session together since family week. Robin had spent the weekend with her family away from the ranch. While in Phoenix, she had gotten her hair cut fashionably short. It looked good on her. She had also gone to the local mall and bought new clothes. Shopping, the first time out, was never easy for patients. As advised, she had avoided looking in the dressing room mirrors. From what Tom understood, these mirrors could even cause a woman with a healthy body image to feel insecure. "Now that you can finally concentrate, you were saying…Hey, you got new shoes, too."

Robin held one foot up in the air, showing off. It was one of those high-tech running shoes from the designer who always used red, white and blue in everything he created. Tom scratched his head, confounded. He could never remember the guy's name. "Very flashy," he commented as she swiveled the shoe this way and that, inspecting the look before plunking her foot back on the floor.

"Yeah. The shoes were the only thing I got to buy in the old size. Dude, do you know how I felt having to buy those big sizes?"

"First of all Robin, they were not big sizes. Sure, they were sizes new to you, but they were still pretty small. We have to work more on how you perceive and label such things. And yes, I really do know how you felt." He dropped his feet to the floor, anchored both elbows on his knees, and leaned forward. "I imagine it was incredibly difficult."

"It was." Glowering at the recollection, she took a swallow of raspberry iced tea. "All I could think was how much I wanted to go running. Just go out and run and run and run until I burned off all this gross fat."

Tom frowned slightly at her phraseology, but chose not to admonish her again for her choice of such emotionally charged words. "Gross" and "fat" were not inextricably linked. They were definitely going to have to work on that. "But Robin, just look...you felt anxious, you wanted to go running, but you didn't have to. Somehow you got through it okay. I am really proud of you."

She gave him a "no big deal" shrug, but he could tell she was pleased by the praise. Suddenly, she popped up in her seat, barely managing to keep the tea from sloshing out of the glass. "Did I tell you I had to get a new bra, too? Whoops, I probably wasn't supposed to say that." To Tom's complete astonishment, she actually blushed. But in Robin's inimitable style, she recovered quickly. "But I did tell you—so tough. Mine had gotten a little snug, not that I had anything there to really brag about, but you catch the drift." She glanced down at her chest, which remained out of view behind a new navy blue sweater. "No kidding, my boobs are actually growing; I never thought I would see the day. It's sort of...interesting."

Tom was at a loss for what to say, so he fell back on the standard, "Uh-huh."

"Really, that part, the boob thing, isn't all bad. I just wish I didn't have to grow other places, too. Why can't women have good breasts and still be thin?"

"They can, and do," he told her truthfully. "What you, or other women shouldn't have is an emaciated bony body and huge breasts. That look can only be achieved through an eating disorder and breast augmentation. Then you just end up looking fake, distorted and freakish."

"I guess…"

"Well, I know. I've seen enough pictures of that very thing on the cover of Hollywood tabloids to know it's true."

She sank back in her chair, tapped the edge of the glass against her bottom teeth. Tom could tell she was about to shift conversational directions. Eventually, she shook her head slowly from side to side. "I am still blown away about my dad. Did that really happen or was I temporarily existing in an alternate universe? Do you think he really got it? Can he really change, be different?"

"I promise, it really did happen in our Truth in Love; and according to what we discussed in subsequent sessions, I think your father truly did get it." He shrugged. "Now whether that will translate into genuine change remains to be seen. The fact that he and your mother have committed to long-term family therapy together is an excellent sign.

"Your dad's situation is a lot like yours in the sense that if he wants to change, he has to replace certain old behaviors with new ones. That's why we've spent so much time teaching you new coping skills. If our goal was simply to eliminate your eating disorder, it would never work because we would have created a vacuum. A vacuum will only exist for a short time before it will fill up with something. In your case, the obvious solution would be to fill back up with an eating disorder. With your father, it would be to return to the old, established behaviors."

After placing the glass on a nearby table, Robin canted her head to one side. "I wouldn't have thought it would work the same with him."

"Yeah, it's real similar. And as with you, it won't be easy for your father. Practicing new behaviors, trying to change is never easy. Whether it's an eating disorder or a set of personality traits, it's difficult."

Robin grunted contemplatively and sifted her fingers through her hair. Throughout their conversation, Tom had watched her closely. Though she often fiddled with her hair, she never came close to yanking or pulling. Definite progress on the trichotillomania front. From out of nowhere, she said, "Josh is still a little geek."

Tom, chuckling, thought her tone belied her words. He strongly suspected she said those things more out of habit than real conviction. "Growing up, my older sister always thought I was a geek, too. Then, she ended up naming her first child after me. I'm guessing there might be hope for you and Josh as well."

A brief silence ensued. Then Tom cleared his throat and said, "Robin, though I was certainly pleased with the progress made during family week, I want you to know two things. First, it is only a start; one Truth in Love does not a functional family make. It will take time and a huge amount of effort for your family to change and grow. Each of you has years of bad habits under your belts. It may take months, or even years to change. Like everything else, it's a process."

She studied the cracks on the ceiling, considering his words. "You're saying there's no presto-chango about this, right?"

"Exactly." He pinched the bridge of his nose between thumb and forefinger. "You need to be patient with them, the same way they must be patient with you."

"Check." She flung an arm over the back of the chair. "What's the second thing?"

He paused briefly to ensure her full attention. "You must understand that your recovery is completely separate from your family. Your dad has his work cut out for him, which he may or may not do. Your mother and Josh will have theirs." He steepled his hands together, fingertips touching. "But you have your own work, your own recovery to attend to and it cannot be linked to anyone else. If your dad messes up, it doesn't mean you have permission to do so as well. You are responsible for you; whatever anyone else does or does not do is not relevant. Get what I'm saying?"

Robin nodded. "I think so."

He collapsed his hands together, fingers now interlaced. "Robin, I have never heard you say that you truly want recovery." When she opened her mouth to reply, he shook his head and quickly interjected, "No, please don't even respond to that now. We still have a couple more weeks to work together. I just want you to know that my hope is that by the time you go home, you really will want recovery as much as I, and everyone else, want it for you. That's all I wanted to say about that."

Robin scrunched up her face, her expression registering a constellation of dichotomous emotions. It was obvious she remained torn about the whole idea of recovering. She wanted it, she didn't want it, she did, didn't...Tom understood. Many patients remained ambivalent throughout their entire inpatient stay. If he, or any therapist, could merely start a patient on the road to recovery, then they had done their job. What Tom didn't mention, and wouldn't, was how desperately he wanted Robin to become a believer in Jesus Christ before returning home. If only she could embrace the Lord, it would make the entire effort of recovery so much easier. But, in the final analysis, both areas were her decision. Either Robin would choose recovery, choose the Lord, or she wouldn't. Tom's job was to continue working with her during the time he had left and most important, pray. The rest was up to her.

⟞⟋⟋⟋⟞

The wooden cross was plain, without a glimmer of gold, nor sheen of silver to capture and disperse the sun's light. Indeed, it was as beautiful in its simplicity as the Son of God, who had hung on a similar cross more than two thousand years ago.

Surrounded by a shelter of willowy trees, the simple structure stood alone in an open clearing behind a corral. No one knew how long it had graced the field or who had originally placed it there. It mattered little, if at all. Though the cross itself possessed no adornment, the ground beneath was liberally decorated with many objects of various sizes and shapes, textures and hues. A small hand mirror here, a picture of a bone-thin model torn from a fashion magazine there. Propped against its base was a smooth stone painted a vibrant blue. Across the rock's flat surface, "shame" was written in bold blood-red letters. Whereas a casual observer might perceive this odd assortment of items as nothing more than mere litter, those associated with the center knew otherwise. For patients often visited this cross to lay down their individual burdens and bondages; to place before the Lord their eating disorder, or perhaps their broken heart or wounded spirit. Each patient would place her pain in the shadow of the cross, then ask the Lord to heal the deep hurt.

In the twilight of this day, Dan and Lexy slowly approached the weather-beaten cross. They stood before it, silent. Lexy had come in a pair of dove gray sweats with no makeup and her hair hanging loose. Dan understood without having to be told. Lexy was coming to God exactly how he had created her, without adornment, without artifice. She wanted Him to see only her heart. Lexy carried two items with her. She handed one of them to Dan, then removed the letter she had written from the envelope. She unfolded the single sheet of lavender-scented paper. He could easily make out the lovely scrolled words written in a royal purple ink on the flimsy stationery. Lexy looked down at the paper, up at the cross, over at Dan. Her eyes displayed a depth of emotion rarely seen anywhere, in anyone. "You can do this Lexy; I know you can," he encouraged in a soft voice.

"I know," she agreed, striving to sound strong as she raised the single sheet of pastel-colored paper. Gripping it in both trembling hands, it caught the waning light of dusk. She took in a shuddering breath, to calm and steady herself. Before embarking on the short journey to the cross, Lexy had told Dan that she wanted to do this without breaking down. Such was her commitment, that she wanted only to honor her child and honor the Lord, without the distraction of tears.

The wind whipped her hair into her face and fluttered the paper. Never releasing the letter, she pushed her hair over one shoulder with the back of a hand. Lexy began to read in the strongest voice she could muster: "My precious child…I had you in my life for such a very short time. I never got to know you, never got to see your face or give you a name. I never got to read you a bedtime story or teach you the colors of the rainbow. I ended your life before it began. Will you ever know how desperately sorry I am, how much I want to hold you in my arms and watch you grow? No, you can never know. Today, I am asking you to forgive me for my selfishness and sin. I pray for your forgiveness. I pray that the very moment your life ended on earth, you were delivered straight into the arms of God. Perhaps someday I will see you in heaven. I will never forget you. I will always be your mother. I will always love you."

With great care, Lexy refolded the letter and returned it to the envelope, tucked in the flap. Dan placed the other small object into her outstretched hand. She knelt; he joined her on the ground. At the very foot of the cross, Lexy placed first the envelope, then on top of it, the tiny clay infant she had created with such loving care. She clasped her hands together in prayer, turned her face up to heaven. "Father God, please forgive me. I have been wrong about so many things. The way I've lived my life, the way I've abused my body, the way I have always denied you. Most of all, Lord, I am so sorry for the abortion. I need your forgiveness. I need you to stay with me through the weeks and months ahead or I will never make it through recovery. I need you to be my God and guide my steps. Thank you Jesus."

She dropped her forehead onto her interlaced fingers. Several moments passed. Eventually, Dan spoke. "Lexy, do you trust me?"

She looked up. "Yes, absolutely."

"Okay, good." He gave a fractional nod. "Now I want you to listen to me. I have known the Lord since I was a young man. I know his character; I know who He is. Lexy, He does forgive you. Do you believe that?"

She grimaced. "I want to so much."

"Then do. He is trustworthy, He never lies. The Lord is immutable, meaning He never changes. The God that King David cried out to in the Psalms is the exact same God who is with us right now. He says in His word that if you ask for forgiveness with a repentant heart, He is faithful and just to forgive you. Say 'I am forgiven.'" She repeated the words. "Now, you must also forgive yourself, because Lexy, if you won't, then you make a mockery of His beautiful gift of forgiveness. If God, the savior of the entire world, can release you from bondage, then you can do the same. Say 'I forgive myself.'"

She took only a moment to digest what he had said, before stating, "God forgives me; I forgive myself."

Dan smiled. "Good."

The two stood, turned and retraced their steps of minutes earlier. The letter, the clay infant remained. Unseen, was the guilt and shame. It, too, was left behind, destined to remain forever…in the shadow of the cross.

Epilogue

The blue plastic raft meandered around the swimming pool. It gently spun this way and that, propelled along on its travels by forceful jets strategically placed just beneath the surface of the water. Reclining on top of the undulating air mattress was a slender girl with long limbs, bronzed skin and sun-bleached hair. Eyes closed, she appeared as tranquil and calm as the water upon which she floated.

Reveling in the hot afternoon sun and cool water, Robin was calm. Since returning home, she had learned to look for and find peace in small things like the trill of a desert dove, the beauty of a summer sunset, or the purr of a kitten. Elation sparked through Robin at the thought of her kitten. The little boy had been a surprise welcome-home gift from her mother six months ago. Robin named him Tom Cat in honor of her therapist at the ranch. Only over time did she come to realize how apt a name it was, for every day without fail, he offered his own brand of therapy. He constantly delighted her and made her laugh with new methods of mischief. And if she was out of sorts, he was always available to lend comfort. Robin needed only to nestle the sleek kitten against her neck, close her eyes and focus on his rumbling purr, and she would feel soothed.

Robin had cherished all moments spent with Tom Cat for they were good; in opposition to many other aspects of her recent life that were far less positive. The truth was, recovery from any addiction, whether drugs, alcohol, anorexia, or bulimia, was incredibly difficult. Often, she thought breaking free from an eating disorder was almost harder than other addictive behaviors because people had to eat to live. Robin would have to confront and deal with food every day, every single day for the rest of her life.

Up until the moment Robin walked out of the ranch and made the journey to the center's transitional facility, she had not fully committed to personal recovery. She had only agreed to give it a try, mostly for her parent's sake. Spending additional time at the step-down treatment center had certainly been the correct decision for her. If she had gone straight home, she wouldn't have lasted a day.

Transferring from such a rigid environment to one of complete freedom would have been too overwhelming. She needed a few extra weeks of care, supervision and support in an atmosphere not quite as stringent as the inpatient facility itself, but one still managed by professionals.

Returning home had presented new challenges with family and friends. The entire experience was made more arduous because the holiday season had officially shifted into high gear. To Robin, it seemed as if Christmas translated into one thing and one thing only: food. It was everywhere. No wonder so many former patients relapsed during the holidays. Robin had to utilize every skill taught to her while in treatment just to make it through that stressful season. But she had done it and her parents had been overtly proud of her. Amazingly, Robin had been proud of herself.

Of course, she recognized she could never have done it on her own. The aftercare people at the ranch had recommended a therapist and dietitian for her to work with in Tucson. On the few occasions Robin had succumbed to the seductive voice of the eating disorder, her therapist had proved invaluable. Together, they had examined what was transpiring in Robin's life to cause her to rely on the old aberrant coping method instead of a healthy strategy. He helped Robin see that the few times she returned to the behavior were only slips, not falls. A couple of binge/purge episodes did not make her a full-fledged bulimic.

The ranch encouraged all former patients to get involved with some aspect of volunteer work. Initially

Robin resisted, claiming she was far too busy, but eventually she was persuaded to give it a try. With her mother's assistance, Robin became active in a local literacy program. She found she liked helping others learn a basic skill that had come so easily to her. What's more, she discovered what the professionals already knew: when you were helping someone else, you couldn't concentrate on yourself. Somehow after spending time with a fifty-year-old man who couldn't manage to read a simple sentence, the size of her denim jeans just didn't seem all that important. Though on some level, Robin knew how isolated and self-centered she had become through her eating disorder, volunteering brought it into an even sharper focus.

Dipping a hand into the pool, Robin splashed water on her legs. She could almost hear a sizzling sound as the chilly water encountered baking flesh. The simple motion caused the raft to execute a few more radical twirls. She laid her palm flat on her stomach. Briefly, she thought her abdomen wasn't as concave as she would like, then quickly jettisoned that thought. She was getting pretty expert at identifying an unhealthy thought, then cutting it off before it had time to take root. Like it or not, Robin had embraced recovery. What's more, she discovered she was as good at practicing positive healthy behaviors as she had been at practicing her eating disorder.

Despite the various struggles, she was satisfied with how life had unfolded in recent months. Her mother and father were in marriage counseling and the four of them still did family therapy. They were learning a lot about certain roles they had fallen into over the years, some positive, others not. The entire family was working on improved communication. Her Dad occasionally acted like a jerk, but that was okay because so did she. Josh was such a nerdy teenage kid, no therapy on the planet could possibly help him.

Robin and her mother had come a long way since the week spent together at the ranch. Though they still experienced the occasional disagreement or clash of wills, currently that was the exception, not the rule. In fact, the two had interacted more in the past six months than throughout the previous seventeen years. Whereas they remained mother and daughter, they spoke like two women, often like two women friends. Robin realized her mother was not only smart, but interesting; she actually liked being with her. Who would have thought? Certainly not Robin.

The sliding glass door at the back of the Hamilton house opened and shut with a thud. Crooking her neck, Robin peered over, shading her eyes with a hand. It was Amber, all suited up for sunbathing, dark glasses perched on her nose, clutching a towel and tanning lotion.

"Hey babe, I came to join you; got to catch some rays before tonight." She strolled over to the edge of the pool and dropped her gear on the cool decking. "Rob, you have got to do something about that brother of yours. I mean he was so checking me out in my bikini as I walked through your house. Like he's never seen a girl before." She spread out her blue and red University of Arizona towel, uncapped the lotion and began applying it. The air was instantly redolent with the pungent aroma of coconut. "Little freak," she muttered under her breath as she slathered lotion onto a forearm.

"Just watch, your little brother will be doing the exact same thing to girls in a couple of years," Robin remarked.

"Yikes. That is one frightening concept." Amber flopped down on her stomach and anchored her chin on her balled-up fists. "At least I won't be around to watch it."

"Let me know when you get too hot and you can have the raft," Robin mentioned as she floated by.

"Check." Amber mused aloud, "I still can't believe we're actually graduating tonight. After all these years, we're finally done with high school. Done—wow. It doesn't seem possible."

"For me, it almost wasn't possible. I hated having to do all that schoolwork while I was in treatment, but I guess now I'm glad they made me."

"Yeah, so am I. If I had to graduate without you, it would have been such a drag. And now we're able to do what we had always planned—be college roommates. Too cool. In just a few months we'll be freshmen, again. "

"Yeah. The only bummer is that I can't take Tom with me."

Amber laughed. "What is up with that crazy cat? Just when I got to your back door, he sprang out at me from behind the couch, whacked my leg, then ran away, like a million miles an hour."

"He wanted you to chase him. It's one of his favorite games."

"I know you will miss him, Rob, but it's not like we're going out of state or anything. We'll be right here in town. Maybe we can sneak him into the dorm one night," Amber suggested.

Robin flipped over on the raft to get some sun on her back. "Yeah, maybe."

With much to talk about, the two friends chattered on. They sounded like what they were: two eighteen-year-old girls; yet with one notable difference. Conspicuously absent from their conversation was any talk of dieting, weight, or clothing sizes. Those topics were permanently off limits. Besides, Robin and Amber, friends to the end, had far more interesting things to discuss, such as vacations, jobs, boys; important things...such as life.

Throughout the night and well into the day, the dark pewter clouds hovered close to the ground...and wept. Tears fell from the sky and pooled in vast puddles of sorrow.

The lone man trudged along on the sodden lawn, his pace measured, his destination clear. Footfalls hushed, he moved without hurry. In one hand he carried an enormous bouquet of yellow daisies, the only bright splash of color in this drab green and gray landscape. Arriving at the intended location, the man halted. For long moments, he remained as still as the polished granite stone he stood before. The rain pattered on his black cap and trickled down his exposed neck. Water droplets beaded on the flowers' delicate petals.

Jim Cardoza spoke. "I brought you these for your birthday. Daisies were always your favorite." He held the plastic vase of flowers out in front of him, as if the pristine gray stone actually possessed vision and could appreciate the gesture. But the slab had no eyes with which to see. It had only one name and brief inscription to distinguish it from all the rest: Mary Abigail Cardoza…Beloved daughter of Mary and Jim.

Jim placed the flowers on the ground in front of the newly chiseled gravestone, then sat down next to it, inured to the drenched soil, the frigid water soaking through his trousers to his skin. He rested one palm on the stone and talked to it. "Fourteen years ago today, you came into this world. And now you're gone. Abby, you left too soon. There was so much more we were supposed to do together." He cocked his head to one side and nearly smiled. "Remember the lavender paint we bought together? We were going to redo your bedroom this summer. I still have it in the garage. I got new paint brushes…they're all ready to go…"

He breathed deeply, then released a heavy sigh. "Remember how much you loved Belle? Today, your mother and I were going to give you a horse for your birthday. Your very own horse. We thought you and Sara could ride her together, but now…" After a moment, he added,

"And I wanted you to know, Kyla called from the ranch. It was good to talk with her. She was sorry about you. The new baby is doing fine."

Jim, spirit shattered, laid his cheek on his hand. He pictured his daughter, lying down there in a white casket, beneath the earth, eyes closed, Teddy tucked in the crook of one arm. Sara had insisted Abby take the bear with her, not wanting her sister to be lonely.

Abby, dead. All these weeks later, he still couldn't quite take it in. She had been doing so well in her recovery, gaining weight, regaining health. Then one day, Abby's heart simply stopped. The anorexia had exacted too high a price. The prolonged state of starvation had caused the heart muscle to deteriorate and weaken dramatically. If Abby's heart had been healthy and strong like that of a normal thirteen-year-old, it could have fought back and rebuilt. But it wasn't healthy or strong. Who could have known Abby had inherited the cardiac malady from which her grandmother had suffered and eventually died? No one could have known, least of all Mary and Jim. Least of all Abby. A genetic abnormality and a prolonged eating disorder had proved a lethal combination.

So now, Abby was gone, their family destroyed. The Cardoza home was now locked in a miasma of despair, perhaps forever. Mary was devastated beyond reason. Sara was no longer Sara. Though she met regularly with a therapist, a specialist in childhood trauma, she rarely did anything these days but sit alone in a huddled ball and suck her thumb, clutching a new stuffed bear, who to date, remained nameless.

All this, the result of an eating disorder. Could those two words possibly sound more benign? Jim had always perceived a disorder as something you fixed, then went on with life. But this disorder had the power to kill, even once-healthy individuals with no history of medical problems. Only after Abby's death did he discover how many women and girls died every year from such illnesses. But of course, it was too late.

Jim glanced over to the next gravestone, weather worn and blanketed by mossy growth. So similar to Abby's, the inscription read: Abigail Grace Shwimmer...Beloved Wife of Earl. Abby's grandmother. Mary and Ruth always assumed their father would rest for eternity alongside their mother. Not anymore. Abby's revelation of childhood abuse and subsequent death put an end to that idea for-ever. The judge, still in the nursing home, would now live the remainder of his life and face his eventual demise alone. Where his eternal resting place would be was Earl's business. Where he would spend eternity was God's.

How Jim wished he could lie down and die too, be buried right here alongside his Abby. Life held nothing for him except pain on top of more pain. Unfortunately, death was not a luxury available to him. He must remain alive for Sara. His only prayer was that he might be a better father to his second daughter than he had been to his first. He had let Abby down. On the day of her birth he had promised to protect her from danger and harm. Ultimately, he hadn't protected her from anything, neither sexual violation nor an eating disorder. He had failed miserably. No matter how long he remained on this earth, he would never forgive himself. Never.

He ran a hand along the damp stone. "I love you Abby…I will always love you." Then he heaved himself to his feet, looked down at Abby's grave, looked up at the sky. He shook his head in defeat, in resignation; then turned and walked away, alone.

⟞⟋⟋⟞

"These are the yummiest toes in the whole world. I must have a big bite." Lexy, gripping one tiny foot in each hand, made chomping sounds with her mouth and zeroed in on the captive toes. Lying on the hand-painted changing table in his bedroom, fresh from his evening bubble bath, Logan squealed with exuberance at the familiar game. At the point of contact, Lexy dispensed with the chomping and converted to kissing. She covered every available toe with rapid-fire kisses.

"I love you, I love you." Lexy lifted Logan from the table and swung him into her arms. Chest to chest, he in a clean diaper, she in a silk slip, he clamped his little legs around her waist. He draped one arm around her neck and rested a cheek on her shoulder. They hugged. She buried her face in the soft hollow of his neck and ran a palm up and down his bare back. His warm skin was as smooth as butter. Inhaling deeply, she breathed in the sweet smell of him. For minutes, she held him tight, swaying gently from side to side. Lexy felt nearly overwhelmed by love for this child. It was as if she couldn't hug or touch or squeeze him enough.

Her heart was so full of gratitude, it could very possibly burst. "Thank you Lord, thank you so much," she said aloud. Seven months after leaving treatment, she was profoundly appreciative for so many things: her precious son, her husband, her life. Never before had she known what true joy was, but now she did. Joy was a pure gift from God.

Downstairs, the front door opened. "Hello. I'm here," came a voice from the first floor.

"Get ready. Logan's on his way," Lexy called back. Planting one more kiss on his earlobe, she plopped him back on the table and grabbed the shirt she had pulled from the drawer earlier. "Your Auntie gave you this. She'll be so excited to see you in it," she told her son. The black and teal shirt went over his head and she wrestled his arms into the short sleeves. Once again, she lifted him from the table and onto the floor. He was off like an arrow shot from a bow—chubby legs pumping, plastic diaper crunching— to greet their guest. Lexy went into the hall bathroom, where she'd placed her things prior to the bath. She removed the new cocktail dress from a plastic hanger, zipped herself into it and stepped into high heels. She quickly applied lipstick, fluffed her hair with her fingertips, then followed her son downstairs.

"Wow, you look amazing," Loren declared when Lexy entered the family room.

Logan, seated on the floor across from Loren, a pile of brightly colored LEGOs between them, regarded his mother. "Mama pretty," he commented, then returned to his building project.

"That dress, those shoes. How did you do it? They're a perfect match," Loren went on. "Turn around so I can see the back."

Lexy complied. "Isn't it great? I wanted to get something special for tonight, but this was even better than I had hoped. I had this idea that I would buy black, but when I saw this dress on the rack, I was sold. Then to think, I found the shoes the same day."

"And are they ever sexy. How high are those heels? Four inches?"

Lexy giggled. "If not five. I've never had anything like them. I think Scott will really like both the dress and the shoes."

"If he doesn't adore them, he's totally out of his mind," Loren said in no uncertain terms. "And look—your copper lipstick matches. Girlfriend…you have got it going on tonight. Hey, Logan's wearing his Panthers shirt."

"First time, just for you." Lexy ambled across the room and took a seat on the couch. "Go ahead and do it; you know he's dying to show you."

Loren laughed and turned to the little boy. "Logan," she said to garner his attention, then with great enthusiasm, called out, "Touchdown." Immediately, he threw his arms straight in the air looking for all the world like an NFL referee. As he had done on the changing table, he screamed in jubilation and then pitched over on his back, kicking his feet in the air.

Lexy shook her head, flummoxed. "I have no conceivable idea why he gets such a kick out of that. Ever since Scott taught him that trick, he just can't get enough. I can hardly wait for football season to start again so there can be a legitimate reason for these antics. I declare, if he doesn't grow up to be a Carolina Panther, it will surely be a shock to my system."

"Could you even imagine? Scott would lose it."

"He would be thrilled." Lexy smiled at the thought. "Like a pig in mud."

"So where is the main man?"

"Upstairs in the shower. He played golf with Dad today. He said he thinks Dad is really doing great."

"I agree. Honestly, I don't know if I've ever seen him this way before. Sure, he's happy, but even more than that, he seems…" She wrinkled her brow in concentration. Watching, Lexy thought what a conniption their mother would have if she saw Loren doing that. How many times had Lexy been admonished never to frown, since it created unsightly lines in the forehead? "Relaxed…calm, like he's free. He can just be himself. He says he wants to get a puppy. A Labrador. I don't think he was allowed to have a dog in the house before. And Lex, you won't believe this…" Eyes sparkling, Loren placed a hand over her mouth and started to giggle, just as Lexy had done earlier. She barely managed to get out, "He says he's going to name the dog Bugger. Can you imagine? Our father? Mom would positively freak."

"Bugger? Oh that's too much." Lexy threw back her head and laughed out loud at the outlandish name. "I can't believe it. He *has* changed."

Several months earlier, Grayson and Pamela had separated. Since he never had an emotional attachment to their home, he left and moved into a rented condominium. Loren, nobody's fool, went with him, claiming there was no way on God's green earth she would remain there alone with her mother. It seemed to be working out for all involved. Recently, Grayson had even been in touch with Jackson and reconciliation appeared to be in the works. Talk of divorce had not yet surfaced. Only time would tell how all of it would work out.

Still chuckling, Lexy watched as Loren selected a fire-engine red block and added it to Logan's oddly shaped building. "Thanks so much for coming over, especially on a Saturday night."

"No big," Loren replied. "Since finals were over yesterday, there was a lot of partying going on last night. Tonight, I'm thrilled to stay here with my very favorite date."

Lexy stretched out her legs and crossed her feet at the ankle. She admired the glittery copper shoes. "Speaking of school, I'm all registered for next year."

"Awesome. And Jennifer can stay with Logan?"

"Yep, since the teaching job she got is only part-time, she'll be able to be with him in the afternoon while I'm in class. He is usually napping during that time anyway. The extra money will help her make ends meet."

"And you told her she could call me anytime, right? My senior schedule is going to be almost embarrassingly easy."

"I did. She's glad you'll be on hand if anything comes up."

Logan, now recovered from touchdown mania, tried to affix a blue piece on an already-precarious area of his building. Three pairs of eyes remained riveted on the structure as it tilted drastically to one side. The building paused in its journey, as though contemplating which course of action to take, then made the decision. It collapsed. Unfazed, Logan began again. "How long will it take you to get your degree?" Loren asked, retrieving a rogue block that had skiddled across the carpet away from the construction site.

"I don't know. First, I need to make sure Logan is all right with the change. Then, you never know…if Scott and I decided to have another baby, that would influence the time frame as well."

"Are you trying for that now?

"No, not at all. But we will be considering it at some point in the future. Both of us want at least one more child.

But right now, Scott and I believe the only thing that really matters is my continued recovery."

"How is that going? You know, I always want to ask, but then I don't want to butt in too much, but I want you to know I care." She hunched her shoulders. "It's hard to know what's right."

"I understand." Lexy gave her a sympathetic nod. "I'm sorry it's so tough for you. I think it's going very well. I meet regularly with my therapist. She keeps me accountable. I joined a support group at my new church. All the group members are in some type of recovery, so we are able to talk and share our struggles. It's good. I try to stay focused on all the blessings in my life; there are so many of them. I never, ever want to forget and go back to where I was before." She shuddered a bit at the thought. "With that said, I still have my difficult days. But for the most part, I think I'm on the right track and will stay there."

"When you have a hard time, is it usually associated with Mom?"

Surprised and impressed by the perceptiveness of the question, Lexy responded, "You know what? You are one smart kid."

Loren shrugged. "I spent a lot of years watching."

"And obviously learning, because you're right. When I have a stressful day, it often has to do with her. When I see her, even talk with her on the phone, a lot of those old perfection tapes start playing in my head. I was engrained in her world for such a long time and she knows exactly which buttons to push. It's hard to resist the lure of old habits. The thing is, I don't want to lose her, but at least for right now, I have to maintain some distance, just to protect myself. It will take time to achieve the right balance. I know I can do it; it's just not that easy."

"I bet."

"Hello ladies and gentleman," Scott greeted the three as he came into the room.

Logan gave his daddy a gap-toothed grin as his second construction project toppled to the floor. "Well, don't you look handsome," Loren said. "Happy anniversary."

"Thank you on both counts." Lexy stood and Scott gave her a hug.

Loren observed the two for a few moments. Then, still clutching a white Lego, she threw her hands up in a gesture of exasperation and said, "Scott, for God's sake, tell her."

"Tell her what?"

She rolled her eyes in vexation, as only a teenage girl could do. "Tell her how fabulous she looks. You know it really is okay. I don't think one tiny compliment on her appearance will screw up her therapy or send her into an immediate relapse."

Scott swung his gaze back to Lexy, abashed. "Have I been doing that? Not complimenting you when I should?"

"Yes, I've definitely noticed it," Loren cut in, before her sister could reply. "Maybe that was a good approach in the beginning but Lex is obviously doing so well, I think you can ease up a little. Especially tonight. She looks totally hot and should be told."

Scott grinned at his wife. "Your sister sure does have a mouth on her. But right now, she happens to be right. Alexa, you are always beautiful to me, but tonight you are especially so." He stepped back and gave her a serious once-over. "Totally hot? Absolutely. That's an incredible dress."

"And check out the shoes," Loren chimed in.

Lexy angled a shoe on the carpet for his inspection. "Wow," Scott exclaimed.

Lexy beamed. "Thank you. Your approval is very much appreciated." She tossed a look over at Loren. "And amazingly, I think my mental health is still intact." The sisters laughed.

"I'm definitely outnumbered here," Scott grumbled. His words had little impact. Everyone knew he was delighted by the deepening friendship between the two.

The three conversed for a while before Loren peered up at the wall clock. "You better hit the road or you'll miss your dinner reservation."

Agreeing, Scott and Lexy kissed Logan, hugged Loren and left. After a while, Logan grew tired of the construction business and began rubbing his eyes, a sure sign of toddler fatigue. Loren figured it was time to go upstairs, sit together in the rocking chair and read books until bedtime. Making a mental note to put the LEGOs away later, she hoisted Logan onto one hip and headed for the hall.

But for some uncanny reason, before leaving the room, she felt drawn to the photograph of Alexa and Scott on the mantel above the fireplace. She strode over and retrieved it with her free hand. She showed it to her nephew. "That's your mommy and daddy. See, she's in her pretty white dress and he is in a black suit. That's called a tuxedo. This was taken the day they got married, long before Logan was born." The two examined the picture. One by one, he placed a little index finger on his parents and identified them aloud. "That's right: mommy and daddy," Loren confirmed. She replaced the photo and moved toward the stairs, still bewildered by her own action. Why had she stopped to study that picture? After all, she had already looked at it about a million times. It had always been there; ever since the day they had purchased the house and moved in.

Some time later, as they cuddled together on the rocker, it finally came to her. She knew why she had wanted to take a closer look at the picture. "Son of a gun," she said to herself. It wasn't because today was their anniversary. It was because tonight, perhaps for the first time since they were married, she had directly associated her sister and brother-in-law with the couple in the photograph. Obviously, it had nothing to do with where they were or what they were wearing because all those factors were different. But it had everything to do with what she had seen this evening between Scott and Alexa. Mostly, it was the expressions on their faces. As they stood together earlier,

Behind the Broken Image
Order Form

Postal orders: The Remuda Cornerstone Bookstore
48 N. Tegner Street
Wickenbrug, AZ 85390

Telephone orders: 1-800-445-1900 ext. 4242

E-mail orders: cornerstone@remudaranch.com

Please send *Behiind the Broken Image* to:

Name: _____

Address: _____

City: _____ State: _____

Zip: _____ Telephone: (_____) _____

Book Price: $16.99 + shipping/handling

Or order from:
ACW Press
1200 HWY 231 South #273
Ozark, AL 36360

(800) 931-BOOK

or contact your local bookstore

Author's Note

Though this book is a work of fiction, it is based on fact. Every year, untold numbers of women and girls throughout the United States die from eating disorders. More than one-third of all Americans struggle with anorexia, bulimia, binge-eating disorder or obesity. Eating disorders are now epidemic because just as with Alexa, Robin and Abby, millions use food to help them cope with painful emotions such as grief, shame, anger, loneliness, or guilt. Whether compulsive overeating or under eating, the strategy is at best, temporary; there is simply no substitute for true emotional healing.

If you, or someone you know, struggle with an eating disorder, please get help. Outpatient programs or qualified therapists are available in all parts of the country. For information regarding referrals in your area or inpatient treatment, call Remuda Ranch Programs for Eating Disorders at 800 445-1900.

both of them were brimming over with adoration for one another; they looked exactly as they had in the picture.

Loren sighed in contentment, pleased by how things were turning out in all of their lives. She smiled, snuggled Logan a little closer, and picked up the first book on tonight's reading agenda. *Good Night Moon.* It was a personal favorite of both Loren and Logan. She propped the book on one knee, bestowed one final kiss on her nephew's head, then opened to the first page and began to read.

THE END